A MONSTER'S TALE

A
MONSTER'S
TALE

KELSO SIMON

The Book Guild Ltd

First published in Great Britain in 2018 by
The Book Guild Ltd
9 Priory Business Park
Wistow Road, Kibworth
Leicestershire, LE8 0RX
Freephone: 0800 999 2982
www.bookguild.co.uk
Email: info@bookguild.co.uk
Twitter: @bookguild

This work is entirely fictitious and bears no resemblance to any persons living or dead.

Typeset in Adobe Garamond Pro

Printed and bound in Great Britain by CPI Group (UK) Ltd, Croydon, CR0 4YY

ISBN 978 1912362 905

British Library Cataloguing in Publication Data.
A catalogue record for this book is available from the British Library.

MIX
Paper from
responsible sources
FSC® C013604

This book is dedicated to my girls,
Melissa, Kelsey, Millie and Izabella.
Your love makes me believe I can move mountains.

1

THIS CHARMING MAN

The sun beat down on a fatigued thirty-two-year-old Brett Kelso as he made his way to the bus stop on his way home from a hard day's work. The frown cast upon his face expressed sheer frustration as he cursed under his breath at the three teenage lads who were listening to grime music from a mobile phone as the three of them brazenly stood at the bus stop glancing at the broad-shouldered Brett walking towards them.

Brett Kelso would usually be met with an infectious, warm smile and he was well known for his brash sense of humour and energy; even though he was big and broad in stature any menace that may have come with his size was usually quickly replaced with laddish charm. He was very engaging, always ready to greet you with a compliment, a sincere handshake and a reassuring pat on the shoulder. People liked to be around him. He could be a loveable prankster and would find great pleasure in making others laugh.

Like the time he strolled into his local pub when he knew one of the lads was in there taking a girl out for a drink for the first time, thus making his way over to greet the girl and his mate in just a pair of underpants and a curly wig, offering them a drink straight-faced as if nothing was out of place. Or the time he swiped the keys to his best mate Steve's dad's brand new camper van to the absolute horror of Steve, before driving off down the road in it, stopping to randomly pick up two old ladies who were waiting at the bus stop in the rain and dropping them off into town.

If anybody was feeling down, Brett would be the first person to go out of his way to cheer them up and make them feel better, but there was something happening to Brett Kelso. Recently, sadness had begun to fill his dark-brown eyes. His infectious smile was starting to fade. His caramel-coloured skin was not carrying the same glow and his heart ached with the pain of unfulfilled ambition.

Some years ago people used to say he was one of the best hip hop MCs they had ever heard grace a microphone. He was a very talented lyricist and was once a big personality on the stages of the local clubs. He'd once had big dreams of becoming a star and having something profound to say to the world and making a change, but like a lot of things, these dreams had come to nothing.

The crowded rooms of venues and bars, and people cheering his verses and patting him on the shoulder and telling him how talented he was, were now faint memories. His life had become what seemed like endless days working hard yet having nothing to show for it. The breaks hadn't come his way and he felt trapped inside the same routine day in, day out, with the constant struggle of financial strain weighing down on his shoulders. His frustration was even more evident as he finally reached his flat, tired after the long bus journey. He threw his keys on the settee before slumping down next to them with a deep sigh as he held his shaven head in his hands.

"This wasn't the way things were meant to turn out," he said to himself under his breath.

Brett worked as a mental health support worker in the supported accommodation service and had done so for the past three years. He enjoyed the role but it could be very challenging. His job was about making a difference to the lives of people who had a history of mental health issues, supporting them to maintain independence within their living accommodation after long hospital admissions. It was a very demanding job and things were beginning to take their toll. The night shifts, the work on bank holidays, the weekend work, the endless paperwork and the challenging behaviour were beginning to suck the enthusiasm out of him, not to mention having to work over the holidays like Christmas.

He'd got into the job for all the right reasons and he genuinely wanted to make a difference but he wasn't prepared for the lack of empathy towards staff in such a job.

The system seemed to hold the needs of staff at the very bottom of the priority list.

The money he was being paid was just about getting him by and the strain of struggling month to month was a constant source of frustration. He felt he had nothing to show for the hard work he was putting in and was struggling to earn a decent living. Every month he was just making it to the next payday. He went to work every day and worked hard to help and support others yet he seemed to be the one struggling.

He had a small two-bedroomed flat and he was just managing to cover the rent. He couldn't afford to run a car, and a nice holiday abroad with the lads wasn't even worth thinking about. He hadn't had a steady girlfriend for over a year and he was lonely, particularly as most of his friends were in relationships. He'd never really struggled for women in his life before but he seemed to be going through a phase where nothing was coming together for him and he felt like he'd made all the wrong moves in life and was now at an uncompromising dead end. Even if he met a nice girl he'd probably struggle to pay to take her out for a meal. Life was a grind with not a lot to look forward to. He was now fast approaching thirty-three years of age and feeling like he'd failed. To add to his frustration there were many people around him who seemed to be having the opposite kind of fortune.

A lot of people he knew or knew of around his home city of Leicester seemed to be living well. There appeared to be more and more wannabe gangsters emerging these days, lads fuelled on bravado and pumped on steroids living like high-rollers inspired by today's celebration of status and celebrity lifestyle culture. Some of these folk had made some good money in the drug game and with wads of cash came inflated egos.

The women were becoming a lot more unapproachable in recent times too, heavily influenced by TV programmes like *Made in Chelsea* and *The Only Way is Essex* and controlled by glamour and hedonistic self-indulgence. These were tough times to be a single man earning just enough money to get you through the month. Status was what women seemed to be drawn to, and to Brett it seemed like everyone was trying to live by the standards of celebrities or playing toy gangsters. Brett Kelso felt stifled by it all, surrounded by plastic people with plastic minds and plastic hearts.

The wannabe gangsters were ten-a-penny, jumped-up party boys that had watched too many 'Brit flick' gangster films. But they had the flash cars and the designer label clothes and they weren't grafting hard all day for them. They walked with an arrogant swagger and glowed with the confidence that a pocket full of cash can bring. They were the ones enjoying the finer things in life. Brett took them for what they were, wannabes that had made some quick cash and thought they were the top boys. None the less, they had the good-looking girls on their arms, they had the flash motors and the luxury holidays, they didn't stand queuing to get into the clubs. They always seemed to have people around them, they were given attention and shown respect, they were the ones that would pull the wads of cash out of their pockets when they were standing at the bar. They were on top whilst Brett was struggling.

One of the people that particularly caused Brett immense frustration was a guy called Kristian Bell. Kristian was well known around Leicester and people seemed to respect and fear him; by all accounts he was an arrogant bastard and totally full of himself, but he had the cash and the good looks. He was light-skinned for a mixed-race guy and he had these hazel-green eyes that were his most striking feature. He was always well groomed with a neat, short beard and he always looked sharp. He'd been heavily involved in the cocaine game in the past and had made some good money, but within the past couple of years he had allegedly stopped any business to do with drugs and now he owned a restaurant and a tanning shop. He was never short of cash and was always driving a flash car and was well known for being a lady's man. Life seemed good for Kristian Bell.

Brett hated Kristian from his head to his toes. The reason why he held such hatred for Kristian was because Kristian had fathered a child with Brett's older sister, Maria. Kristian didn't treat Maria with any real respect. He'd cheated on her countless times and Brett was certain that he'd slapped her about on occasions. They were no longer together in a relationship but Kristian just seemed to breeze in and out of Maria's life when he felt like it.

Maria and Kristian's son, Damian, was three years old now but Kristian had never been a proper dad to his son. He'd sometimes not see Damian for months on end but then just turn up out of the blue and expect to take his son out for the day or the weekend, or take him off for days on end. He didn't give Maria money either; he'd always say he didn't have it or he'd expect not to have to because he would buy Damian expensive clothes and toys and stuff but he had more than enough money to be able to maintain his son. But he was nothing but a selfish and abusive man-child, and he didn't think he had to explain any of his actions to anyone.

He would usually turn up at the door unannounced and could be very disruptive to Maria's life. He hated it if Maria became involved with any other man even though they were not officially together. If Maria had a new boyfriend or began seeing someone, Kristian would start enough trouble to make sure it didn't last. He was possessive and controlling. He could also be a very nasty bastard and this was something he was also well known for. He had a lot of people and muscle around him that had come with the money and status he'd acquired in the drug game and this made him a dangerous man to cross. Maria still seemed to be a bit smitten with him and still maybe a little bit under his spell, or why else would she let him get away with treating her the way he did?

Brett knew that Maria was still sleeping with Kristian, and this hurt him because he hated to think of his sister allowing herself to be used. He had told Maria countless times that she should get Kristian out of her life and he'd offered her support to do this, but Maria always seemed to let Kristian back in.

Brett would just love to give Kristian what he deserved, a good beating, and tell him to get out of his sister's life for good as he saw Kristian for what he was, a selfish, abusive bully. The man was a pain, a hindrance and he never did Maria any good. Damian was just a trophy to Kristian along with his several other kids that he had scattered across town by numerous other women. Brett knew Maria would never be happy with Kristian lurking in the shadows, but Brett also knew that if he was to give Kristian the beating he deserved, he would have to be prepared for the repercussions, and with a person like Kristian Bell it would just go on and on until one of them was dead or in prison. That's how it is with people like Kristian Bell. Brett couldn't afford that to happen as he had the person closest to his heart relying on him and he couldn't ever let that person down no matter what the reasons, which brings us to the most important thing in Brett's life.

Brett was father to a four-year-old girl called Macy, and she was the purest thing in Brett's existence. No matter what was going on in his life, Macy was his absolute priority without question. She didn't live with him as Brett had separated from her mother, Lisa, his ex-girlfriend.

Brett and Lisa had split up when Macy was still just a baby after six years together. It was a bad relationship really and could be quite volatile, mainly because the two personalities massively clashed. Lisa could be very emotionally demanding and every day was just a series of heated arguments, so one day Brett decided enough was enough and he left the council house they shared. He'd had enough of all the bitterness and the spite so he had to call time on the relationship. Brett had care of Macy on an overnight visit every weekend on either a Friday or Saturday depending on his work shift pattern. Sometimes he would have her on a Sunday and drop her off to school on a Monday morning.

Things were very tense between Brett and Lisa these days, mainly because Brett didn't agree with the way Lisa was bringing up Macy. Lisa had let herself slip, too, over the past couple of years and Brett would be concerned about Macy a lot. Lisa was out partying most weekends and Brett had heard she would have folks on the estate where she lived around the house drinking and partying, particularly at the weekends, and he was also concerned about the kind of people who were caring for Macy when Lisa was out partying as she'd often leave Macy with local teenage girls from the estate. Brett wasn't happy about this at all.

Lisa's priorities seemed to have slipped and this was a constant source of stress for Brett. He would confront Lisa about having people off the estate drinking and smoking weed whilst Macy was there and there was also an occasion when the police were called to the house because of the loud noise and disturbance.

A lot of the time when he went to pick Macy up, she would look untidy as if Lisa hadn't made much of an effort with her. Lisa hadn't always been like this, and she wasn't dirty or unclean, but her standards just seemed to have dropped over the past couple of years and she didn't seem bothered by anything Brett tried to say to her. Brett would usually end up bickering with Lisa and just leave before it turned into a big row but he wasn't at all happy about the way Lisa was raising Macy, but he was between a rock and a hard place as he couldn't tell Lisa how to live her life. He knew how difficult Lisa could be if someone was giving her a hard time and she could also be very selfish.

There had been an occasion when Lisa had stopped all

contact between Brett and Macy for a couple of months after a series of arguments over what was best for Macy. This was a living hell for Brett, and this kept him on edge as he knew that if he rocked Lisa's boat too much she wouldn't think twice before stopping all contact again.

Brett knew of friends that had ex-partners who had stopped them from seeing their kids altogether and this scared him, so he was careful. He just played the game; as long as he was close to Macy and had a strong influence and presence in her life he would just do all he could to make sure she was OK.

2

CAST NO SHADOW

It was Friday afternoon around four o'clock and Brett was just finishing an early shift at work. He was happy to be finishing for the weekend as he'd worked most of last weekend and the rota at work was driving him crazy. The shifts were all over the place and he was finding it hard to make any plans outside of work. Brett jumped on the bus from work and made his way to pick up Macy.

Brett got to Lisa's house and knocked on the door. The St Andrew's estate where Macy lived had seen better days and Brett was concerned about Macy growing up on what was a very run-down estate that was well known for some of its troublesome residents. Lisa opened the door. She was still in her nightgown with her blonde hair tied back in a ponytail and it was obvious to Brett that she had not made the effort to get herself dressed that day. Lisa just opened the door and gestured Brett to come in with a backward nod of her head as she walked back into the house. She didn't look particularly pleased to see him and didn't really acknowledge him. Brett could smell the cigarette smoke as he walked in the house and noticed a few empty beer cans and full ashtrays, which indicated that Lisa had had company the night before.

Lisa was a good-looking girl really and could look really tidy when she made the effort. She'd always had a good figure. She had quite striking blue eyes and nice thick, natural blonde hair and she could turn more than a few heads on a night out. Brett was more than aware that she would still get the male attention, but he was more concerned that the kind of lads she was attracted to weren't the type he would want in Macy's life. This played on his mind, although Lisa was still single as far as he knew. The crowd that Lisa chose to associate herself with was a hindrance for Brett, particularly her best friend, Tara. Tara was not exactly the quietest of girls and would be out in town partying every single weekend without fail. Tara was a notch on many a lad's bedpost and she didn't try to hide it.

Macy had heard the sound of her dad's voice in the house and came out of the living room and into the hallway to see him. She was a beautiful little kid. She had a thick head of chocolate-brown hair that came to her shoulders in loose ringlets and a tint of golden brown in her skin tone. As she saw her dad she smiled and ran towards him. He picked her up and gave her a big hug.

12

"Hey you, cheeky, give your dad a big squeeze," said Brett. Macy was in a fit of giggles and happy to see her dad.

Lisa went upstairs to get Macy's overnight bag as Brett and Macy waited in the hallway. After around five minutes Lisa returned with Macy's things. Brett bid Lisa farewell after a bit of chit-chat about how Macy had been and then made his way home with Macy.

Later on that night Brett and Macy were back at Brett's flat watching a film together and chilling on the settee. It was getting late and Macy was falling asleep.

"Do you want to go to bed?" said Brett to Macy. Macy nodded her head tiredly with her eyes half open. He cradled Macy in his arms and carried her to her bedroom that was really a small storage room that Brett had made into a cosy little room for her and tucked her in her bed.

"Love you lots," he said to her as he kissed her on the head. He made his way out of the room leaving the door ajar around six inches.

Brett made his way into the kitchen to get himself a beer and began to settle for the evening and see what was on the telly. It was getting on for ten o'clock and as usual there was nothing on. He went through his DVD collection but couldn't find anything he fancied watching so he was sat there with himself and his beer switching from channel to channel on the telly.

After a while Brett was beginning to nod off to sleep out of a mixture of boredom and tiredness when he noticed that the young couple in the flat beneath his were playing music again. Brett didn't mind that they were playing music, it was just that they would blast the volume, especially at the weekends. They never seemed to care how late it was or the fact that Brett had a child trying to sleep.

They were a young couple in around their mid-twenties and they wouldn't look out of place on an episode of *Jeremy Kyle*. They didn't work but regularly seemed to walking back from the shop with carrier bags full of beer and vodka or having takeaways delivered. They were constantly arguing and shouting or banging around. They had a pet dog, a Staffordshire bull terrier, and their backyard was covered in dog shit that never got cleaned up. They also seemed to have people there a lot and they would sometimes make a lot of noise outside at the front of the flat. They were far from the ideal neighbours.

Brett had gone down to the flat in the past and had asked them politely if they would turn their music down and keep the noise to a minimum. He had manners, he wasn't the sort of person to go and kick off without giving the opportunity for things to be sorted calmly, but it was an ongoing situation and it was beginning to piss him off. They would initially turn the music down but it would seem to go back up again after a while.

He'd explained to them that he had his daughter most weekends, and asked them to consider this when they played their music, but this hadn't resolved the problem. Brett wanted to kick off big time, he'd had enough of being polite, but what would kicking off result in?

Brett was a reasonable guy but somebody's inconsiderate ways were affecting his daughter and he felt well within his rights to stop being reasonable, but in all of these kinds of situations, Macy was always the first thing on his mind. Any situation that could get him into trouble he had to try and manage, because the last thing he needed was an arrest for anything related to violence. He had Macy to consider and with the way Lisa was these days, he wasn't taking any risks.

He also had his job to consider; any arrests for violence could have a big impact on not only his present job but any job in the future that involved working with vulnerable people or kids. He'd thought about working with teenagers and the youth sector for some time and decided that's what he wanted to do so he had to do his best to stay on the right side of the law.

He managed to settle and get his head down for the night without the music bothering him too much but this was mainly because he was tired and just couldn't be bothered with going down there again. It would just piss him off.

***

The next morning Brett was getting ready for the day. Macy was sitting at the kitchen table eating her cereal and Brett was getting dressed.

Later that morning Brett took Macy into the town centre. He would usually take her out somewhere like the cinema or swimming and for something to eat then he would treat her to a new toy or some new clothes.

They spent their afternoon together in the town centre shopping for a new doll for Macy and finished the day feeding the ducks as they walked along the canal on the way home. It was getting on for six o'clock and time for

Brett to drop Macy off home. He would always become a bit sad when the time came for him to drop Macy off. He'd usually get used to her energy and cheeky ways and having her around and then have to take her back to her mum but he would usually fight the gloom and not ruin his day, so he made his way to take Macy back home.

He got to Lisa's door and gave it a knock. To Brett's surprise the door was answered by a young girl, say no older than sixteen or seventeen, a ponytailed, brown-haired white girl whom he had never seen before. Before he had a chance to say anything to her, she leaned down to Macy.

"Hello, you!" she said to Macy as she leaned down to her.

Macy seemed to know who she was as she gave her a smile.

"Where's Mummy?" asked Macy as she looked up to the girl looking somewhat disappointed.

"Oh Mummy's gone out tonight," the girl replied, "but I'll be babysitting you so we'll have some fun!"

Macy began to look a little sad as she was looking forward to seeing her mum.

Brett sensed that Macy was getting upset so he picked her up; he wasn't happy about the situation as he'd never seen this girl before but he didn't want Macy getting upset before he left so he reassured her.

"Hey!" said Brett reassuringly. "Everything will be all right, you've got your new doll to play with and you can ring Mummy anytime, I'm sure she won't be long, here you can ring Mummy now and speak to her on my phone like a big girl!"

Brett called Lisa's number on his phone and when Lisa answered he gave the phone to Macy who snatched the phone keenly to speak to her mum. Macy started to speak to her asking her where she was. As Macy spoke to her mum on the phone, Brett took the opportunity to speak to this girl who was babysitting Macy for the night. As he looked over the girl's shoulder and into the house he noticed a young baseball cap-clad white lad no older than seventeen sitting in the living room; he also noticed a packet of cigarettes on the side of the chair and some rolling papers. Brett wasn't at all sure of this lad so now was the time for some questions.

"So who are you, then?" Brett asked the girl, expressionless, looking her straight in the eye.

"Oh, I'm Chantelle, I'm just a friend of Lisa's, I come here a lot, I live across the road, Macy knows me, I've babysat loads before," replied the girl reassuringly but a little nervously.

Brett sensed that the girl was nervous so tried to reassure her.

"Look, I'm not being funny with you but I just like to know who is looking after my daughter as I don't know you and Lisa didn't tell me I'd be dropping Macy off with a babysitter."

"Oh, that's fine, I understand, I'd be the same if it was my little girl," she replied.

Brett then moved his head to the side looking in at the young lad that was sitting in the house.

"And who are you, lad?" Brett asked the lad.

The lad turned his head "Aaron," he replied sheepishly.

"Well, I'm Macy's dad, mate, and if you're having a smoke later don't be doing it around my daughter, is that clear enough?" asked Brett in a snappy tone looking directly at the lad.

The lad nodded reassuringly. "Yeah, of course, mate," he mumbled nervously.

Brett took the phone from Macy as she was saying goodbye to her mum as he wanted reassurance from Lisa about who this girl and this lad were. He put the phone to his ear but as he said hello he noticed that Lisa had already hung up. He immediately tried to ring Lisa back but now the phone was on answerphone. Perhaps Lisa had purposefully switched off her phone because she knew Brett would want to talk to her. Brett just gave up and said goodbye to Macy and gave her a big hug and reassured her. He then made his way home.

He was angry about the fact that Lisa had left his daughter in the care of two teenagers that he didn't know anything about and also that Lisa seemed to spend most of her spare time out drinking, or at the local pub, so he decided to ring her again to reassure himself. He knew deep down that this would probably result in an argument but if he didn't speak to Lisa the situation would just nag away at him. Lisa's phone rang for a while but finally she answered. "Yeah," she answered flatly.

"Lisa, who are these youngsters looking after Macy? I'm only asking," he said as he knew Lisa would become defensive.

"They're all right," replied Lisa, "do you think I'd leave her with someone I don't know and trust?"

"Well, where do you know them from and how do you know they are responsible enough?" replied Brett.

"Look, I don't have to explain myself to you all the time, I'm her mum and I know how to look after my daughter. If you must know I have known her and her mum for years and she has looked after Macy a lot of times before, she is fine!" said Lisa sternly.

"Well, there's no need to get so snappy," replied Brett, "I was just making sure. I needed to reassure myself."

"Well, you should know I wouldn't have just anyone babysitting for her!" snapped Lisa and then she just hung up the phone to Brett's frustration.

That usual, unsettled feeling was still with Brett even after the phone call. He wished he could trust Lisa but she just didn't seem anywhere near as responsible as she once was and her priority at the weekend just seemed to be going out and getting smashed, but what more could he do?

3

WOMEN SEEM WICKED WHEN YOU'RE UNWANTED

It was Saturday night and Brett had planned a night out with his two best mates and possibly a few lads from down his local pub, the Empire. He was looking forward to getting out with the lads and leaving his stresses behind for the night, he really felt like having a good night. A bit of new clobber would have been nice for the night but as usual he didn't have the cash flow for a night on the piss and new clothes.

There was a new nightclub opening in the city centre called Aquis House and a lot of people he knew were going there tonight. He got himself freshened up and ready and decided to head off down to the pub.

He was meeting two of his best mates, Bez and Steve. They were a couple of lads he'd known since he was a kid and the three of them always had a good laugh when they were out together.

***

He arrived at the Empire at 8:30pm, which was half an hour late and was not unusual for him. As he walked in the pub the atmosphere was good, it was a Saturday night, the weather was good and there were more than a few good-looking ladies dotted around the pub. He noticed Bez and Steve at the rear of the pub playing pool so he made his way over.

"Easy lads," he said, greeting them as he reached them. They both greeted Brett with a handshake a pat on the shoulder and took the piss out of him for being late.

Bez was a big lad, he'd been a podgy lad throughout growing up and this was always the main line of banter for the lads when it came to Bez. He still carried that bit of chub and was fair-haired from the short bristles of his shaved head to his eyebrows. He was a proper lad though, always game for a laugh and laid back but was known for a bit of a temper and had a short fuse at times. The lads would always take the piss out of the fact that when he became agitated and frustrated his face would turn red.

Steve was a proper lad's lad, Bez and Brett used to call him Stavros as a joke with regards to him resembling someone Italian or Mediterranean. He had olive skin and thick black hair and was usually trendily unshaven. He always looked sharp and couldn't walk past a mirror or shop window without checking himself in it. He also couldn't walk past a girl without trying his luck even though he'd been in a relationship for the past ten years. Brett and Bez would call him 'the lady boy' as it would take him as long as any woman they knew to get spruced up for a night out. Steve was a top lad though and he'd been a great friend to Brett over the years. He was a cocky lad at times and could come across as a bit sure of himself but was always there for Brett when the chips were down. He was usually the first to start ordering the doubles and the shots and if you were out with him you knew it was massive hangover time the next day.

As the minutes passed, the three of them were knocking the drinks back, the banter was flowing and the pub was packed; they were all in good spirits enjoying the atmosphere and each other's company. It was warming up to be a good night and even more so when a bunch of good-looking young ladies made their way into the pub. One of them particularly caught Brett's eye straight away. She was a dark-brown, almost black-haired girl and she had lovely tanned skin that was glowing as she walked into the pub. She had a petite figure and Brett couldn't keep his eyes off her. She was very chic, stylish and definitely knew how to put herself together for a night out. Brett knew from looking at her that he would have to try his luck before she left.

Immediately the lad's topic of conversation was the group of girls. They were like three dogs with their ears pointing up and their tails wagging. The girls looked in good spirits and looked as if they were ready for a good night on the town.

Brett was having a good time with the lads but he kept looking over at the girl to see if he could make eye contact. She turned her head to look around the pub and she looked straight at him. He looked back at her and she gave him a little smile and then turned away. Steve had noticed this exchange and wasted no time in Brett's ear.

"You're in there, mate, I seen the little look she just gave you, but have you got the balls to go up there and put it on her?" said Steve with a smug grin.

This was now a little challenge and Brett knew that should he approach the girl, his every move would be scrutinised by Steve and Bez. But it didn't matter; the challenge was now on whether Brett wanted it or not.

"Give me time, lad, there's no rush," said Brett trying to act calm and collected.

But he was far from collected; he wanted to get over there and make sure he took his chances before she left. He was determined to at least get her number and lay some foundations for the near future.

Brett kept looking over at the girl and she was looking back and every now and again giving him a little smile. Brett had now got the signals he needed and decided he was going to go over and talk to her, but he didn't want to do it whilst she was sitting with her pals and in full view of Steve and Bez, who were bound to be monitoring him ready to take the piss should he fail to get a result, or make a complete twat of himself, so he just had to pick the right time.

A little while later, Bez had taken a work call on his

phone and had moved from the busy area in the pub lounge into a quieter space near the entrance of the pub. Steve had just made his way to the toilet and the girl had made her way over to the bar. Brett took this as a signal and an invite for him to go over to her. It was as if she was making herself available for him to approach her as she gave him a little smile as she walked over. This was now his chance. On the way to the toilet Steve happened to look back and gave Brett a grin letting him know that he knew what was happening. Brett grinned back at Steve as a gesture of confidence but making a move on a girl was always a daunting experience.

He could hear the little voice in his head, you know that voice that fills you with doubt whenever you try to do something that takes bottle, and he could hear it trying to talk him out of it.

Forget it, you're gonna make a twat of yourself here! said Brett's voice in his mind, but he chose to ignore it and carry on.

Brett made his way over to the bar where the girl was standing. What few nerves he had now didn't matter, he was there and had to carry this through. As he got to where she was standing he gave her a smile.

"Hiya, you all right?" said Brett with a flirty smile.

"Yeah, you?" replied the girl warmly smiling back.

Up close she looked even more gorgeous, she really was a stunner. Striking brown eyes with a hint of mischief in them and Brett really liked the way she nervously bit her bottom lip as she stood at the bar. She had nice full lips that looked as if they were made to be kissed and she was quite dainty and petite, which Brett liked. He could smell her perfume and she smelt delicious. She looked fresh, tidy and brand new.

"So where you off to tonight?" asked Brett directly with a raise of his eyebrows.

"Oh, we're going to town and we may go to that new club that's opening, what about you?" she replied.

"Yep," said Brett, "looks like we're going there as well, by the way, what's your name?" he asked swiftly at the end of his sentence.

"Abbey," replied the girl with a welcoming smile, "what's yours?"

"I'm Brett, can I buy you a drink?" said Brett whilst moving a little closer. He held his hand out and gently offered her a handshake.

Abbey held her hand out and gave a nervous chuckle as she softly shook his hand.

"Oh no, that's OK," she said graciously refusing the offer of a drink. Brett could see she felt a bit cheeky accepting a drink and that she was being polite refusing one.

"Oh come on, let me buy you a drink!" insisted Brett with a reassuring smile.

She paused for a few seconds. She obviously liked the look of Brett and knew that by accepting the drink it would lead to more conversation.

"Oh, OK then, thank you," she replied.

"So, what you drinking then?" asked Brett. By now he was feeling a bit more relaxed and getting into the flow of things.

"Could I have a white wine spritzer please?" she replied.

"Yeah, course you can," said Brett.

Brett got the attention of the barmaid and ordered the drinks making small talk as he waited. When the drinks arrived the conversation began to move on a phase. The conversation started well with little discomfort and as they talked Abbey noticed her friends were eagerly looking on every now and then.

Steve and Bez were also by now back at the pool table and were looking on too. Steve was trying to get the attention of the other girls by glancing over at them but he was more concerned about trying his best to put Brett off his stride by pulling stupid faces whilst Abbey was of course unaware of it. Brett nearly laughed on a couple of occasions but managed to keep his composure.

As the conversation progressed the both of them were getting more and more relaxed. They'd gone through all the usual chit-chat like asking each other where they were from and stuff. Abbey seemed keen and was becoming more talkative. The two of them seem to click and the conversation was almost effortless and the awkward silences were few and brief. Brett would usually find something he didn't like about a girl after five minutes of conversation but on this occasion all of his boxes were ticked.

It had been a while since Brett had met a nice girl. Brett tried not to get his hopes up so early on but he hoped that maybe this could lead to something. He was tired of being alone.

The conversation continued for what seemed like a few minutes but was actually over forty and Brett was beginning to feel like he'd abandoned the lads a bit so he took the chance to make his excuses and touch base with them.

"I'm just gonna go and see what the lads are up to, before they start giving me a bit of stick," said Brett jokingly.

"Yeah, I better do the same, before my lot start having a whinge at me," replied Abbey with a grin.

"Do you fancy meeting up later? Seeing as we're going to the same place," asked Brett.

"That sounds good to me!" said Abbe. "Tell you what, let me give you my number, you can ring me later and we can meet up, can't we?" said Abbey with a reassuring hint of promise in her voice.

That was exactly what Brett wanted to hear, the foundations had been laid, the small talk and all the chit-chat was not done in vain.

Brett took his phone out of his pocket and Abbey began to give him the first few digits of her number but before she could finish she noticed her phone vibrating in her clutch bag, she fiddled with her bag hastily to get to her phone.

"Can I just answer this? I'll be with you in a minute," said Abbey as she finally got into her bag and grabbed her phone looking down at the screen.

"Tell you what, I've got to pop to the loo, I'll get your number when I get back," said Brett with a nod as he gulped the last drop of his pint. Brett had needed a piss for a while but was more interested in laying the foundations with Abbey. Abbey smiled and nodded quickly before answering her phone.

Brett made his way to the toilet and was pleased with himself, whistling as he pissed in the urinal. Abbey was a very tidy-looking lass, he was well into her and she seemed like a nice girl; this was a good start to the night and he felt relaxed and was looking forward to what the rest of the night would bring.

Brett soon made his way back from the toilet and went to make his way back to Abbey to get her number. As he was on his way, Steve called him over.

"What's the crack? Are we hitting town or are you gonna spend all night with that bird?" said Steve with a smirk.

"Just give me two minutes, mate, and we'll head into town no problem. I'm just getting the digits," replied Brett smugly.

Brett was seconds away from making his way back to Abbey to get her number when a group of lads marched into the pub. There were about eight of them altogether, big lumps, and you could see from the second they walked in that this lot fancied themselves as big-time Charlies, they just carried that aura. They looked a flash mob though and judging by the size of a few of them they were no strangers to the Gym… and the steroids. They almost bounced into the pub being loud and brash as they made their way to the bar. Brett recognised one or two of them as they were local lads and he knew a few of them were involved in the coke game on a big scale. One of the guys was a black lad called Levi Small and he was well known for running security for most of the bars and clubs in town.

Oh here we go, plastic gangsters night! Brett thought to himself as they made their entrance into the pub. But this lot had the money, you could see that, and they had the flash motors in the pub car park to go with their brash swagger.

One of these chaps was a lad called Aiden Glover, but most folk referred to him by his second name, Glover. Brett,

Steve and Bez did not like him one bit, neither did a lot of people, he really fancied himself as the big man, not to mention a lady's man, and really thought he was one of the top boys around town. He was arrogant and cocky and looked down on people. He treated anybody outside of his circle with disdain. The money he made from selling coke and selling used cars had gone to his head, and here he was as usual pulling a massive wad of notes out of his pocket as he approached the bar. Glover had some cash all right and did well for himself but the main reason Brett didn't like him was because he was a bully. Brett had seen him bully people on a few different occasions.

Glover was a big guy, stood about 6ft 6in with big square shoulders, and his sheer frame would make him stand out even in a packed pub. He had a stubble beard and cropped black hair, almost a skinhead. He'd always be dressed in the designer labels, and you could usually see an array of sleeve tattoos on both of his bulky forearms as they poked out of the sleeves of his shirt. He wasn't a particularly good-looking lad, he had quite a flat nose like that of a seasoned boxer and was brutish in appearance, but he always seemed to do well with the ladies and often had a sexy girl on his arm – this certainly wasn't down to any boyish good looks. He was a sight to see really because of his size and the fact most of his front teeth were capped in white gold.

Glover's arrogance and persona didn't just come from the fact that he had money. You see, he was also big pals with a bloke called Mitchell Webb. Now Mitchell Webb was the real deal, a proper old-school hard nut who had earned his reputation through sheer notoriety and the fact that he'd go toe to toe with anyone and come out on top. But he wasn't a bully like Glover. He was approaching his fifties but could still walk in any pub in Leicester and get massive respect. He had his hand in a lot of pies and was as ruthless as they come if you were stupid enough to cross him. It was Mitchell who first put Glover in business with his car dealership. If you fucked with Mitchell Webb, you had your hands full and having someone like Mitchell on his side just made Glover feel like he was invincible.

People began approaching Glover and his mob as they made their way into the pub and shaking their hands, greeting them as if they were celebrities. Brett was trying his best not to take any notice of them but he did notice one of them approach Abbey and her pals and begin talking to them, and it didn't take long for most of them to follow suit. Soon almost the whole lot of them were over there like vultures baiting for scraps.

Brett was looking over as he still hadn't got Abbey's number and he could sense what was happening. This lot had seen a group of fit-looking girls, they weren't wasting any time going in for the kill and they had the cash and the bravado to make Brett feel like the 'Abbey ship' was sinking. Glover was looking over at the girls from the bar and decided he wanted a piece of the action and soon made his way over.

The girls seemed to be enjoying the attention of this lot and now the drinks had started being ordered and the crisp banknotes were being brandished like bait. This definitely made the girls tick, not that any of them would admit it.

Glover was now speaking to Abbey and for a split second Brett's stomach started to sink. He looked over at

Abbey to see if she would notice him and gesture to him the green light to carry on where they left off but her eyes never turned back in Brett's direction; she now seemed totally preoccupied with Glover. In the blink of an eye the mood had changed for Brett. Abbey had seemed like a nice girl and the foundations had been laid but now the presence of Glover and his cronies had seemed to change all that. Abbey's eyes seemed to light up as she was talking to Glover. He was flashing a bit of cash, and now a guy like him obviously had more appeal to her than a lad like Brett, and it now seemed like the conversation Brett had had with her may as well have not even taken place. He had now just been totally ignored.

Steve and Bez noticed the situation and they felt a bit bad for Brett, it was a bit of an ego-bruising for Brett really.

"Oh fuck this and fuck that bird, let's fuck off into town and get on it, leave her to it, Brett, let her get used and abused by a twat like him," said Bez before he swiftly necked what was left of his pint.

"Listen, mate, I couldn't give a fuck, he's welcome to her," replied Brett with a forced half smile and a shrug of his shoulders.

Brett made out to the lads like he didn't care but the situation did get to him, it made him feel like a nobody. He had hit it off nicely with a good-looking girl for her to toss him aside at the arrival of someone like Glover.

Is that what it's all about? Is that what girls want these days, people like Glover? Plastic, wannabe, shallow cunts! Brett thought to himself.

The lads soon finished their pints and left the pub leaving

Glover and the rest of them to it and made the short journey to the city centre on foot. It was a warm summer's night and the atmosphere was good. There had been a chance of some showers on the forecast earlier but there was no sign of any rain so the three of them headed out into the night.

They hit the bars, drank some beers, chatted to a few girls and were generally having a good time. Town was absolutely packed and they were all well on their way to being pissed. They'd had a good couple of hours in town and time was ticking on and Brett reminded the lads that maybe they should get down to this new club Aquis House as it was getting on for twelve o'clock and there would certainly be a queue. The three of them made their way to the club, each of them stopping to piss up a wall along the way. As they turned the corner to reach the club they couldn't believe their eyes at the size of the queue to get in; it was huge, stretching right to the corner of the street.

"Fuck me, I'm not queuing to get in there!" said Steve with a massive sigh

Brett and Bez were looking somewhat deflated.

"So what do you want to do?" asked Brett holding his hands out not knowing what to do for the best.

"Well, fuck it, we are here now let's just get in the queue we might as well, this is where everyone is gonna be!" said Bez.

Brett sighed. The one thing everybody hated doing was queuing, especially in a queue this long, but there wasn't much in the way of choice, this is where everyone was going to be tonight, the promotion for the place had been massive. The three of them agreed to just go and queue in line, what else could they do? They made their way over to the club somewhat deflated.

They were stood in line with the minutes slowly creeping by. They were having a chat but eager to get themselves in this club and start drinking more alcohol. It was getting cloudy and they had been in the queue for over half an hour. It finally came to the point when they were near the entrance of the club and feet away from the door. There were around five people in front of them that had also spent the best part of the last hour waiting in line. Now the queue seemed to cease moving and the bouncers didn't seem in any rush to carry on letting people in. The three of them began to get a bit agitated.

"This is taking the piss," they mumbled to themselves, and then as if it couldn't get any worse, it started to drizzle. Now the three of them were really pissed off; here they were standing outside the club after spending close to an hour lining up and now it begins to rain.

"What the fuck are these bouncers doing?" snapped Steve shaking his head in frustration.

"Fuck knows," replied Bez, "but I'm fuckin' off in a minute, I'm not standing here to get soaked!"

But they did stand there, what choice did they have? This new club was the place to be tonight and besides, they had waited for nearly an hour to get in.

Brett was standing in the queue with the other two, wet, pissed off and looking miserable. The night had started with so much promise and now he was pissed off; he just wanted to get into the club now and carry on drinking.

A taxi then pulled up right outside the club where they

were all standing, and who steps out but none other than Glover with two of his pals by his side and Abbey, the girl who Brett had been talking to earlier.

As they stepped out of the taxi Abbey turned to the side and noticed Brett standing in line, wet and waiting to be let in. Brett felt embarrassed to be seen standing waiting to get into this club having been gradually soaked by the drizzle. Abbey just looked away pretending not to see him and walked forward with Glover, who also noticed Brett. Glover just gave him a smug grin as if he knew that Brett had tried his luck with Abbey before him, and to make matters worse there was no queuing or waiting in the rain for Glover and his party, they walked right up to the entrance where the bouncers greeted Glover, shaking his hand and patting his shoulder and exchanging pleasantries. The bouncers just lifted the red rope and gestured them into the club; the perks of being a plastic gangster. Brett felt shit. It was a shit one, and they were still not being let into the club.

Steve just shook his head, grinned and began to submit to the situation with ironic laughter.

"What a wanker!" he said, referring to Glover.

The three of them stood, still waiting to get into the club, not much conversation was going on between them. The wind was out of their sails because of the rain, the long wait to get into the club and, on Brett's part, an arsehole like Glover.

Finally, the bouncers let the queue flow and the three of them were let into the club; they walked into the club muttering obscenities under their breaths. They walked the club in expectation and they weren't disappointed; this really was a stylish place, no expense had been spared, it really did look the part. There was a huge bar area, chill-out rooms and a main dance-floor section, which was like a mini arena, it was absolutely jam-packed and the place was buzzing.

The lads were liking what they could see so it was time to get back in the mood, but Brett couldn't seem to get back in the mood, he'd paid twenty quid on the door and after examining the money he had left on him he realised it was going to be tight and he had to save some cash for the taxi home. He wanted to let go and have a good time with the lads but here he was in this brand new club after waiting an hour to get in standing in the rain and now he knew he would be scrimping and scraping.

Bez and Steve were back in good spirits though and determined to have a good time. As the night rolled on Brett was having a good mooch around the place looking out for any nice-looking girls that may take his fancy; he had settled in by now and the alcohol was flowing again.

The lads were putting themselves about a bit trying it on with a few of the party girls. They bumped into a few lads that were also locals in the Empire, so now the three of them had become eight, the more the merrier!

The night rolled on and Brett had begun to enjoy himself and by now the wet wait in the queue was at the back of everyone's mind. The time was now approaching 3am and on his way back from the toilet Brett checked to see how much cash he had left on him; to his disappointment he realised he had £26 left on him and that was his limit and a tenner of that would be for the cab home. Limited funds meant he would soon have to be going home.

As he was walking back from the toilet, Brett spotted Glover again, as if twice wasn't enough for one night. Glover was acting the big boy as usual in the VIP lounge surrounded by people and a few women, including Abbey, stood next to a table with a few ice buckets of champagne and bottles of Grey Goose vodka perched on them. All this just felt like a kick in the teeth to Brett, it was always the same. People like Glover shouldn't really have got to Brett, he was better than that, but recent times seemed such a struggle. The world seemed such a cruel place to an honest man.

Here's me working my bollocks off, making a difference to people's lives, and I'm skint and struggling, and there are wankers like Glover and Kristian Bell living large. I must be doing something wrong! he thought to himself.

He made his way back to the lads; he was more than a bit drunk by now so he decided he'd get a last beer and call it a night. The night was coming to a close, everyone was pissed and getting home was next on the cards. Steve was absolutely wasted and struggling to put two sentences together, this was time to hit the streets and get a taxi.

Brett, Steve and Bez headed out into the street with the rest of the revellers pouring out with them. *It was bound to be a pain in the arse to get a taxi*, Brett was thinking to himself.

Bez and Brett were drunk but Steve was by far in the worst state and needed to get a taxi home as quickly as possible. They walked the city centre streets, the pavements still damp from the drizzle. The three of them managed to get a taxi eventually and they all ended up crashing at Brett's flat.

***

Brett woke up the next morning and found himself on his settee with Steve and Bez already awake talking. Neither of them were very animated. Bez was flicking through the channels on the TV remote and Steve was just sitting at the end of the settee looking the worse for wear. Bez looked over to Brett with a blank and lazy expression.

"You got anything to eat, mate? We're starving," asked Bez

"I've not got much in, mate, I've not had a chance to do any shopping yet this week!" replied Brett feeling rough and just managing to force the words out.

"Oh come on, mate, you must have some bacon or something?" asked Bez.

"I haven't got anything, mate, got to get a few bits later," replied Brett.

"Tell you what, mate," said Steve rustling around in his right jean pocket, "if I give you some money, Brett, will you pop to the shop and get some bacon and eggs? I feel rough as fuck, mate."

Brett paused for a second.

"I can't be arsed, lads, I feel rough myself," Brett replied in slightly strained frustration.

Steve and Bez then both encouraged Brett to go as they were all feeling rough.

"Come on, mate," said Bez, "the quicker you go the

quicker you'll get back then we can all eat. We'll knock it up for you, mate."

Brett looked at both of them and after a few seconds and a roll of his eyes he reluctantly agreed.

"OK. Fuck it, I'll go, but you two will be doing the cooking!" he said with a mumble. Brett snatched a crumpled-up ten-pound note from Steve's lazily outstretched hand.

Brett swiftly shoved a jacket on and made his way out of the front door. Brett was feeling the effects of his hangover as he began to walk from his estate over to the shops. He was still a bit drunk as well and also decided he was going to get himself a beer or two for the hair of the dog. A swift beer with a hangover usually made him feel a bit better.

Brett stood at the traffic lights waiting for the lights to change when he noticed an old man wearing a flat cap walking his dog just grinning at him. The old man was grinning then looking away shaking his head gallantly to himself. Brett didn't know what to make of it, was he still visibly that drunk that he was drawing baffled looks from an old man out on a Sunday stroll? The traffic lights changed and brought the cars to a halt and Brett made his way over the crossing.

Brett made his way to the Lucky Supermarket, which was his local shop. He walked in and began to mooch around and look for bacon and eggs for a fry-up. As he walked down the aisle of the supermarket he noticed two girls looking at him. They were young, pretty girls, no older than their early twenties. He didn't take much notice but they kept looking. One of them gave him a big smile with a bit of a cheeky giggle. He gave a small grin back and looked away. He looked back a couple of seconds later and the girl was still smiling at him. *She seems a bit keen*, he thought to himself. It looked like she was then going to say something but her friend quickly pulled her away and they made their way out of the shop.

Maybe she was gonna ask for my number or something but her friend didn't want her to make a twat out of herself. I don't know, he thought. He carried on with his business and picked up the bacon, eggs and bread. He went to the counter and placed the items down for the shop attendant to register. The shop attendant was a young Asian lad about seventeen years of age. He looked at Brett.

"Good night, was it?" asked the lad.

"Yeah, not bad," replied Brett, slightly puzzled.

Was it that obvious he'd been out on the piss?

Brett had now become paranoid. The old boy in the street had gave him funny looks, the two girls seemed overly eager, and now the teenage shop attendant seemed to know he'd been out on a bender. As he left the shop he looked down at his torso and his jeans to check that everything was in order. *Were there any big holes in his clothes or anything?* he thought to himself, he also took his jacket off and had a look at it to see if Steve or Bez had put any stickers on it for a joke or something but there was nothing.

He swiftly made his way back over the traffic lights and began the walk back to his flat. He noticed a flash motor parked up in the side street near the traffic lights. It was a brand new BMW 5-series, pure white, and it was just the kind of car Brett liked. He loved BMWs. He went over and gave it a good browse. As he got closer and saw his refection in the driver's window, he could see black lines on his face. He looked closer and to his embarrassment he could see somebody had drawn a beard, a moustache and glasses on his face with a black marker pen, he looked hideously stupid. Obviously Steve and Bez had got a bit happy with a marker whilst he was asleep.

That pair of absolute cunts! he thought to himself, and now he knew why he'd drawn looks from people on his way to the shops. He couldn't believe it. He was pissed off but could also see the funny side. Boys will be boys, and he would have done the same to one of them given the chance, but he had truly been had by Steve and Bez and they were going to have a field day with this one. He made his way back to the flat knowing what would happen as soon as he walked through the door, and he was right. As soon as he walked through the door and made his way to the living room he heard the complete fits of laughter coming from Bez and Steve, they were in hysterics the both of them. Brett just stood there grinning and nodding.

"All right, you got me, fair cop, but realise this is coming back, you pair of cunts!" he said to them both whilst making his way into the kitchen. He wasn't even sure if they could hear him over their fits of laughter.

***

That night Brett was sitting in his flat by himself. Steve and Bez had long gone and the laughs were over for another week or two. Brett was on his iPhone browsing on Facebook. He couldn't help but become frustrated when he came across pictures and posts of people enjoying what looked like a lavish lifestyle, the nice cars, the luxury holidays, the expensive clothes, the endless partying. People that didn't seem to work or do anything meaningful yet they appeared to be living it up and doing well for themselves.

Most of them weren't even friends, just people he would say hello to in the street and a typical example of how everybody seems so obligated to add everybody they've ever spoken to on Facebook these days. It made him feel like he was missing out and all the fun was happening somewhere else.

He noticed a couple of posts from an ex-girlfriend of his from around two years ago, a girl called Lydia. He had been seeing Lydia for around four months when she seemed to just lose interest. She was quite insensitive and ignorant in the way she ended it, through a text message, and she seemed to change and become more shallow and self-centred over the last few weeks of their short relationship.

He noticed the pictures with her boyfriend who was apparently some sort of big-shot events planner. It looked as though they were living a good life, enjoying good times and having fun. There were photos of them in Las Vegas and one of her in a brand new convertible Audi A4, eager to tell the world of Facebook that her man had just bought her a car. The words of the post read: 'Feel so spoilt look what my baby bought for me mwah Xxx!' This made Brett again feel somewhat of a failure. He barely had the money to take Lydia out for a meal when they were together. Brett hated the fact that he was frustrated and had feelings of bitterness but he felt like everyone was getting by in life except for him.

Pictures of a shallow ex-girlfriend that had found herself a wealthy boyfriend to spoil and pamper her reinforced these feelings of failure.

He was sat in his flat alone and he was bored. He had a week of hard graft to look forward to and he was about skint. This is when the real loneliness kicked in. There was nothing on the telly and he was still a bit hung-over. He looked through his phone to see if there was anyone he could ring but most people were usually tucked away on a Sunday night and he didn't have the money for another night on the beer so he just sat on his own flicking through the channels.

After another hour or so he couldn't take it so he swiftly leaned up out of his seat and decided to go and get himself some alcohol. It was getting late and his local shop would be closed by now but he remembered the local Chinese takeaway had an alcohol license so he could get a few beers from there. He flung his jacket on and made his way out of the front door.

It was a typical Sunday night, there wasn't much life on the streets as he glumly walked with his hands in his pockets. It was very quiet, the buzz of the weekend had faded into almost stillness of Sunday night and he felt alone as it seemed he was the only living soul around. He was fed up but knew the world would seem like a better place once he had more alcohol inside him.

He finally arrived at the Chinese takeaway and made his way in, looking somewhat sullen and downbeat. The scent of oriental cuisine and the clanging of pans from the kitchen immediately hit his senses as he walked forward. He stood waiting for service, leaning down with his elbows on the counter. As he waited he glanced around at the people waiting for their takeaway. He noticed a couple sitting facing him. They were a young couple, a young lad and a pretty blonde girl. They were holding hands and giggling with one another and whispering sweet nothings in each other's ears, they looked so in love and engrossed in one another. Brett had forgotten what that feeling was like. He'd had plenty of girlfriends but hadn't found anyone special. The casual Friday night shags were nothing compared to that feeling of being totally in love. Here were two people totally besotted with one another blissfully lost in each other and he was all alone on a Sunday night waiting in a Chinese takeaway to buy alcohol.

A small expressionless Chinese lady made her way out of the kitchen to serve Brett. Brett smiled at her as she grabbed a small pen from behind her ear in readiness to write down his order with the words "Can I take order please?", her broken English missing the word 'your'.

He promptly asked for six cans of Strongbow Super. The Chinese lady, looking bemused, swiftly placed the pen back behind her ear and sharply repeated his order back to him. Brett nodded and the lady went back into the kitchen to fetch the ciders. Brett heard the roar of the fire that was cooking and caught a glimpse of a wok being shaken over the flames as the lady walked back through the kitchen door. This reminded him that he was hungry as he felt a little rumble in his stomach but this Sunday night mission was for alcohol, not food. After a couple of minutes, the Chinese lady brought out the ciders already placed in a blue carrier bag and struggled a little whilst reaching up to place the bag in Brett's hands. He paid for the ciders with the change out of his pocket that he'd rustled around to find. He then left the restaurant taking a last glimpse of the two lovebirds that were sat waiting.

Brett was barely out of the takeaway before he reached down into the blue carrier bag and grabbed a can. He cracked one open and gulped it down as if for dear life. He strolled onwards to get home, crushing the empty can with his fist and tossing it to the floor whilst letting out a loud burp. As he looked up he noticed a woman walking his way. She was a good-looking, dark-haired woman walking with her arms tightly folded, trying her best to snuggle herself out from the slight chill in the air. He wondered what she was doing, out all alone on a Sunday night looking as spruced up as she was. He gave her a friendly smile as she passed him, which was returned with a look of complete disdain from her as she swiftly went on her way. Brett took little notice of this and just shook his head with a grin of irony whilst hearing the clunking of her high-heeled shoes get fainter and fainter as she disappeared into the night. As he continued to walk the almost-empty streets back to his flat he strolled past the houses imagining the couples and families behind the doors sat together cosily watching the television, whilst he had the remaining five cans of Strongbow Super to keep him company.

4

PLEASE – PART ONE

Brett had finished work and he made his way to pick up Macy for her weekly visit and then back to his flat for a typical Friday night with Macy. He had Saturday off, but would have to work a late shift on Sunday, which was pissing him off the more he thought about it.

That evening Brett was relaxing on the settee with Macy watching a film and again, Brett began to hear the pumping bass-line and the noise from the flat downstairs.

Oh for fuck's sake, not again, he thought to himself. He decided to try to forget about it as he had Macy sitting comfortably with him on the sofa, but it was beginning to piss him off.

An hour or so later he was tucking Macy into bed and giving her a bedtime kiss and the music was still playing. It had got louder so he decided he was once again going to go down to the couple in the downstairs flat and have a word, so after he had given Macy half an hour to get to sleep he reluctantly locked the door and made his way down to the flat. As he was walking down the stairs the music and the voices were getting even louder. He turned the last flight of stairs and saw a couple of young lads with baseball caps standing outside the front door of the flat smoking spliffs. The potent smell of skunk weed filled the air. He was more than a bit pissed off. He made his way slowly over. He didn't see the lad who lived in the flat.

"Could you pop in and tell the guy who lives here to pop out for a minute please?" Brett asked the lads directly.

One of the lads seemed reluctant in his response but after a few seconds sheepishly made his way inside the flat. The other lad didn't acknowledge Brett at all, he just walked slowly into the flat. Brett was calm but inside his anger was beginning to boil.

The tenant of the flat came to the door looking somewhat bemused. He was a skinny-looking white lad around mid to late twenties with a somewhat unkempt moustache and dark-brown little beard sprouting from his chin. He looked at Brett with a slight frown.

Brett began to speak in a calm but clear and direct manner.

"Look mate, I have asked you before and I have explained

46

to you that I have my daughter on weekend nights trying to sleep, now could you please turn your music down?"

The lad looked at Brett still looking somewhat bemused.

"Yeah, but people are entitled to play their music sometimes, mate, it's not like I've got it blasting every day!" replied the lad with a half shrug of his shoulders.

Brett paused looking the lad straight in the face, he imagined himself just smashing his fist into that skinny pale face. He knew he was more than capable, but would that solve anything? Violence would lead to more bullshit and Brett had to think about Macy, who was asleep just above them.

"Look, we are all entitled to play our music or whatever, but I have asked you politely to turn it down, I can hear it thumping and thumping upstairs and it's waking up my daughter!" said Brett raising his voice in sheer frustration.

The lad just swiftly turned around and mumbled, "Yeah whatever!" and slammed the door in Brett's face, leaving him standing there.

Again Brett imagined himself losing it and just kicking the door off and going mental, but once again he was thinking of the possible dire consequences.

Brett angrily walked back up to his flat grimacing in frustration. He'd tried his best to be polite and was more than reasonable with his request for the volume to be turned down, he'd explained the reasons why and still he gets treated like a mug. He was absolutely sick of his kindness being taken for weakness.

5

LAST NIGHT I DREAMT THAT SOMEBODY LOVED ME

The following Saturday night, Brett was once again in his local with Bez. Steve wasn't out and had actually stayed in to earn a few brownie points with the missus so it was just the two of them. They were having a laugh, supping a few pints and chatting. They decided they weren't going to go out on a mad bender or go clubbing but fancied making a few stops to a few haunts and they decided to head down to the city's west end on the canal front.

There were a good few boozers down there and it was usually busy. They'd bumped into a few other lads as well that they knew well as regulars from the Empire who had decided to join them on the trip to the west end. They were a bunch of local likely lads who were usually in the same trio: Ryan, 'Irish' Dave and Rob. Brett was thinking how easy it would be for it to turn into a messy night.

The group of them arranged a cab and made their way to the west end. The atmosphere was good and Brett was feeling good again in the haze of laughter and the flow of alcohol. They were in a pub called the Soar Point, located on a stretch of the canal that ran through the city and spirits were high.

An hour or so passed and Brett found himself standing at the bar getting a round in for the lads. Once again he was carefully watching his money as he wasn't exactly flush. He was waiting to be served and was glimpsing around the pub when he noticed an ex-girlfriend of his, a girl by the name of Kimberly Edwards. He knew it was her as soon as he saw her. She was sitting at a table with a group of people.

Brett and Kimberly had been teenage sweethearts. They had been together when they were both sixteen and then again on and off for around a year when they were eighteen. Brett had never forgotten Kimberly. Kimberly had this tough exterior, but on the inside she was a real sweetheart. She was also very sincere and determined and one of the most genuine people he had ever known. She was quite striking, her dark hair was always long as she rarely cut it, and she had these high cheekbones, and her hazel-green eyes stood out against her olive skin.

They had always carried a fondness for each other and always spent time talking if they ever bumped into each other. Their relationship fizzled out because they were both so young and when Kimberly became busy with her A-levels they drifted apart. Brett was a little too immature for a girl like Kimberly at that time, and also the fact that, back then, he had wanted to be Jack the Lad and to try his luck with every girl that came his way. He broke Kimberly's heart with his immaturity but that was something she had never told him, and being the sweetheart she was, she never held it against him.

Brett regretted ever losing touch because he had never found anyone as genuine as Kimberly. They had lost touch over the past few years but she would always pop into his mind from time to time.

He immediately started to make his way over to her, hastily sliding his way through the people in the busy pub. The lads were all waiting for their beers but he didn't care at that moment, he hadn't bumped into her for around three years or so and he wanted to see that sincere smile of hers. She wasn't the kind of girl that dressed as though she was asking for attention but there was a sexy confidence and determination about her. When she was at school all of the school bad-boys that everybody thought were cool tried the charm on her, but she never gave any of them the time of day, she could never be bought with prestige or popularity and Brett loved that about her.

As Brett reached the table he could see she was in the middle of conversation. He leaned down slowly and gently put his hand on her shoulder. She looked up to see who it was and a smile immediately beamed across her face when she saw it was Brett.

"Hello!" she said a little nervously but pleasantly surprised.

You could tell she was pleased to see him. Brett always seemed to have this ability to make Kimberly go a little bit shy.

"Well, it's been a while," said Brett with a smile.

"Yeah, you all right?" she replied.

"You know me, I'm OK," said Brett.

Kimberly paused for a while as she didn't know quite what to say, she then swiftly began to introduce Brett to the group of friends she was with. Brett was polite and shook hands and greeted Kimberly's pals but he just wanted to have a good catch-up with her and for it to be just the two of them. It had been so long and he knew she was bound to be the same sweet lass she had always been.

"Kimberly, it's been so long," said Brett enthusiastically, "why don't you come to the bar with me and I'll buy you a drink?"

Kimberly looked around at the table of people she was with as she felt a bit guilty for straying off with Brett but it didn't take her long to make her excuses and rise from her seat to make her way with him. She made her apologies and made her way with Brett to the bar.

Brett was so pleased to see her, for a minute he had forgotten that he was supposed to be getting a round in. They both got to the bar and Brett asked Kimberly what she would like to drink. She had a small white wine and politely insisted she pay for it but Brett wouldn't have it. He ordered a pint for himself and a round of pints for the lads. He looked over for Bez and the rest of them and saw Bez on one of the fruit machines with the other lads nearby standing talking. Brett excused himself and hastily carried two pints over to the lads, asking Rob to pop back to the bar to grab the other two.

"About fuckin' time, mate, we thought you'd done a runner!" said Bez as Brett made his way over with the beers whilst still intently focused on the fruit machine.

"I've bumped into Kimberly, I'm gonna have a chat with her, I'll be back in a minute!" said Brett to Bez as he and Rob swiftly handed the pints to the rest of the lads. He then swiftly made his way back to Kimberly. Bez knew Kimberly from when she and Brett were together as teenagers and it was no surprise to him that Brett was making time for her.

"So," said Brett with a burst of enthusiasm as he reached Kimberly, "tell me what you've been up to since I last saw you then."

"Oh God, it's been so long," said Kimberly eagerly, "I'm a probation officer now, I work with youth offenders, that's what I always wanted to do, it's hard work but I love it."

"I always knew you'd be brilliant in that kind of thing," replied Brett with a smile.

"I did some travelling as well a few years ago, I went to Australia and south-east Asia, it was fantastic, I'm so glad I went, it was a brilliant experience, I just had to get the travelling thing out of my system," said Kimberly.

"Sounds brilliant, I bet you didn't want to come back, so did you go out there with a group of friends then or what?" asked Brett.

Kimberly paused for a second. "No, I went out there with Daniel, my boyfriend, it was something we always planned to do."

Kimberly looked as if she felt awkward mentioning that she had a boyfriend, she didn't keep eye contact with Brett when she mentioned him and she was eager to move on with the conversation. But Brett's heart had sunk a bit, he was hoping Kimberly was single, he was thinking in such a short space of time that he would like to get to know her again, but he also felt a bit sad, sad that he hadn't met anyone to share an experience like travelling with, the last ten or so years of his life felt like a bit of a waste.

By now Bez had finished with the fruit machine so he decided to make his way over to see Kimberly. He'd always got on with her.

"You all right, Kimberly?" said Bez whilst brashly giving her what can only be described as a bit of a man-hug, along with a kiss on the cheek.

Kimberly had always liked Bez and knew he was a good lad and one of Brett's closest mates.

The three of them spoke about some of their teenage years gone by and it felt nice them all meeting up again. After half an hour or so Bez made his way back over to the rest of the lads giving Kimberly another kiss on the cheek and Brett a pat on the back as he left.

Brett and Kimberly talked and talked, they had so much to say to each other after so long. Brett began to talk about his daughter Macy and of course the subject moved on to Lisa and the problems associated with her, he also mentioned how he was sick of his job and how he thought he'd have done more with his life. His frustration was beginning to show and Kimberly began to see the sadness and frustration in his eyes. It was a bit of an unintentional outpouring and Kimberly could feel his discontent. Brett felt bad for coming across in such a negative way but it just crept out of him.

"This is not the Brett I know," said Kimberly with a straight face, looking at him intently.

"I know," replied Brett with a bit of a sigh, "but it just seems like I can't get on top of things these days."

Kimberly looked at Brett with a slight frown.

"Oi, you!" she said urgently, "I remember a young lad who thought he could do anything, who never let things get on top of him, don't you start feeling sorry for yourself and fading, you're bigger than that. If you ever wanted anything, you used to go for it. Where's the fire gone?"

Brett looked at her and a grin then appeared on his face, Kimberly always seemed to know what to say to him to make him feel better, for a moment he felt like he was a teenager again, that feeling that someone really knew who he was. She'd always been such a positive person.

Kimberly had never seen Brett like that before, she could tell that he was down. She didn't say anything about it because she didn't want to make him feel bad, but it saddened her. Brett was always such a 'cheeky chappie' and a gent, and he'd been that way since she'd known him. She hated to think that he was unhappy.

"Now you listen to me, bitch!" she said sarcastically with a grin. "'Man up and find your fire, you'll find your way out of this little rut because you're better than self-pity.' That's the kind of thing you would always say!"

Brett looked at Kimberly with a smile of reassurance. "Now come on, Kimberly," said Brett, "don't you be going getting worried about me, you know me, I'm OK, we all go through shit times, don't we? I'm still me old self."

"I know… you've got too much of a big head to let things get on top of you!" she replied with reassuring sarcasm.

"Well, I suppose I better let you get back to your pals, I don't want to steal you from them for the whole night!" said Brett.

"Yeah," replied Kimberly, "I know Bez must be missing you by now, here, take my number. Now I've seen you, I don't want to lose touch again!"

Brett didn't hesitate to get his phone out of his pocket and take her number.

"If you are ever in the area when you're out and about with your mates, I'm usually in the Empire on a Saturday night, so if you're ever about, pop in," said Brett.

"I may just do that!" said Kimberly.

"Now you take care of yourself," said Brett as he gave her a big hug.

He could feel the warmth of her body and she smelt just the way she used to. It took him right back and he didn't want to let go. They said their goodbyes but he knew in his heart that he would definitely see her again.

6

SCREAM

Brett was on his way to pick up Macy. As he arrived at Lisa's house he knocked on the door and awaited an answer. He was looking forward to seeing Macy and spending some time with her. He had been waiting a while now and there was no answer. He knocked again looking confused, still there was no answer, it didn't seem like there was anybody in.

Why would she go out? I told her the other day I'd be here to pick up Macy! he thought to himself.

He took his phone out of his pocket and rang Lisa but there was no answer. He tried and tried to ring her but there was still no answer. He was getting pissed off but also a bit worried. What if something had happened? He didn't know what to do. He didn't know whether to hang around or what.

He had a gut feeling that Lisa might be in the pub around the corner, the Turnstile, which sat on the edge of the estate and close to the Leicester City football ground. He knew Lisa would go in there sometimes and most of the cronies on the estate she hung around with would go in there. He hoped she wasn't in there with Macy. The pub was an absolute shithole and was known for trouble. It was nothing but a doss house for the lost souls of the estate. It wasn't the kind of place he would want Macy in, but the way Lisa was at the minute, he wouldn't be at all surprised.

He swiftly made his way through the estate with an etched look of frustration on his face until he came to the Turnstile pub door. He pulled open the door, which let out a loud creak, and looked around the pub eagerly. It was a typical estate boozer. A few of the local old fellas were propped up at the bar, and a few local heads turned in Brett's direction as he entered the pub. The air was filled with the many voices of the locals and their pub chat, locals that didn't seem fazed by the fact that the highlight of their week was sitting in a shit pub drinking the flat Carling beer that was always on offer.

Brett scanned the lounge and as he turned to his left he saw Lisa sitting at a table with Tara, another girl, and two white lads. He also saw Macy sitting there looking bored. Brett was pissed off not just at the fact that Lisa had not been at home with Macy ready for her weekly visit but also the fact that she had Macy in this shithole of a pub sitting there with her and her cronies. Lisa looked up to see Brett standing there and Macy also noticed her dad standing there.

"Daddy!" she shouted excitedly and she hopped off the

pub chair and ran towards him. Brett picked her up and cradled her in his arms giving her a big kiss on the cheek.

"How come you didn't have Macy ready for me at yours? I told you the other day I would be here at this time!" said Brett directly to Lisa with a slight frown.

Lisa looked a little bit embarrassed and looked around at Tara and the two lads at the table. She turned slightly red but also looked a little annoyed.

"Soz, I just nipped in here on the way to the shop, I just lost track of time," said Lisa with a slight shrug of her shoulders as if it was no big deal. Brett could see she wasn't far off from being drunk.

There was now an atmosphere at the table, Tara was looking at Lisa sort of half grinning childishly and the two lads just sat there in silence both now looking down on their iPhones. There was a long pause between everybody and Lisa didn't exactly jump off her chair to accommodate Brett.

"Well, do you think you could pop home and get Macy's night bag ready for me so I can take her please?" said Brett slightly snappily. He was now even more pissed off; he wanted to tell Lisa exactly what he thought of her but he resisted the inevitable showdown.

Lisa quickly finished her half a lager without even answering him.

"I'll be back in a minute!" she said to Tara as she got up off her chair.

As she made her way out of the pub she didn't even look at Brett. This annoyed Brett as he felt he deserved a bit more respect. He made his way out of the pub with Macy still in his arms and he couldn't hold his feelings in any longer.

"What is your attitude problem?" said Brett to Lisa with a scowl as they both walked the street en route back to Lisa's house.

"Don't start your shit, Brett, I'm sick of you thinking you can tell me how to live my life, you're Macy's dad, nothing more, don't keep thinking I have to explain myself to you all the time!" scoffed Lisa as she carried on walking.

Again, Brett was frustrated at Lisa's behaviour, she hadn't bothered to have Macy ready because she was at the pub, and she didn't even have the courtesy to properly apologise or show him the slightest bit of courtesy. He looked at Macy to see if she was OK as he struggled with her still in his arms. As he quickly walked to catch up with Lisa, he screwed his face and gritted his teeth as he made his way closer to her.

"I've told you before not to have my daughter in shitty pubs around slags and fuckin' chavs, can't you do it in your own time!" he growled quietly through his gritted teeth as close to Lisa's ear as he could get, trying his best not to alarm Macy. He just lost control and the frustration of Lisa's disrespect and bad attitude had got the better of him.

Lisa stopped on the spot. She had one hand on her hip whilst raising the other in a 'stop' gesture.

"Right, if you're gonna start thinking you can bully me and get aggressive you can go and see a solicitor and go through the courts to see Macy without having to contact me, because I'm not putting up with your shit all the time!" said Lisa sternly and clearly, and then she just walked on.

She knew she held all the cards and she also knew that Brett knew it. If he was to have to go through the courts for regular contact it could take a lot of time. This was a big fear of Brett's and she knew it all too well.

With those words from Lisa, Brett didn't have anything more to say. He knew how the system favoured women and that it could be a long and frustrating custody battle. He was angry not just because Lisa had sat with Macy in a shitty estate pub but because Lisa didn't even have the courtesy to apologise for not having Macy ready, and she didn't even answer her phone. If it wasn't for Brett guessing she was at the pub he would be left not knowing what was going on, it was like she just had total disrespect for him and she just did exactly what she wanted. He was a good dad but that didn't seem to matter to Lisa, but with those last words from her he was firmly back in his cage, but he knew now that he had to do something, he couldn't go on like this.

***

Brett and Macy were back at his flat, the time was approaching 10:30pm. Macy was in bed and Brett was cracking open a beer, relaxing, watching the telly when once again the neighbours began to play their music and once again it was loud. All Brett wanted to do was relax but he was now pissed off. Just last week he'd asked them politely to consider the fact that he has his daughter most weekends and they couldn't respect this. He'd had enough. He was at the end of his tether; the anger and frustration had reached boiling point. He'd had enough of everybody and their shit, he'd had enough of the entire planet at this moment and he just wanted to explode. He'd had enough of Lisa and what she had turned into and her disrespect, the neighbours downstairs, people like Glover and Kristian Bell.

Wouldn't it be nice if I just didn't give a fuck and bumped a few people into place? he thought.

But he did give a fuck. Raising Macy was his main priority and there was still an undying desire to show everyone that he would have his day. No matter how hard things seemed, he was determined to get himself on top somehow.

The music was pissing him off, but he decided not to go down to them this time, he didn't know if he would control his anger or if he could resist lashing out should an argument ensue so he left it, but if the music happened to wake Macy up and stop her from getting to sleep he would have no choice but to show them how pissed off he was. He just wanted peace.

***

That very next day Brett had decided to take Macy to the local funfair that was in the city. It was a nice day so he thought it would be nice to take her.

It was a fun day and Macy as usual had cheered him up. The sun was out so after the funfair they sat on the grass in the park with some sandwiches and sweets. The fair and park were not too far from where Macy lived so as it was a nice day Brett decided to walk Macy home. He hoisted her up on his shoulders, which she loved, but was very cautious clinging to his shaved head with her little hands. Lisa was getting ready to go out when Brett dropped her off. She looked tidy as she came to the door, made up for another night out. Brett gave Macy a big kiss as he said goodbye. Lisa didn't even say hello as she opened the door but Brett noticed Tara was in the house equally made up for a night out, both of them looked like they were ready to hit the town. Brett looked at Lisa as Macy made her way in the house and went to see Tara. It was comforting for Brett to see that Macy seemed quite fond of Tara as she went and sat on Tara's knee.

"So can I ask who is looking after Macy tonight, Lisa? Now, I'm not starting, I'd just like to know," said Brett to Lisa trying his hardest to sound reasonable to avoid a big argument.

"If you must know, she is staying at my mum's," replied Lisa sharply.

Brett was a little concerned as he knew that Lisa's mum was fond of a drink or two especially at the weekends, but what could he do? Brett looked through the door and blew a big kiss to Macy and said goodbye, again with a heavy heart.

Brett returned home to his flat and wondered what to do with himself for the night. He'd phoned Bez and Steve and they weren't out this weekend. He rang a few of the other lads as well that drank at the Empire but they were either not out for whatever reason or not answering their phones. Brett decided to go to the Empire anyway to see who was in there. He always knew someone in there so it was either that or stay at home and be bored.

Brett reached the Empire and had a look around. There were no lads in there he really wanted to spend time with but he was fed up. The last thing he wanted to do was sit and be lonely and worrying about Macy.

He ended up drinking with a lad named Richard Stokes or 'Stokesy' and a few of his cronies. Stokesy wasn't the most trustworthy bloke. He was one of those people that were out for themselves, not greatly liked but one of the local lads none the less. He was in his forties and spent most of his time in the bookie's or the pub. He sold a bit of coke, not big scale, just a few bags at the weekend for beer money. Brett wouldn't usually be drinking with Stokesy, he'd usually just say hello and have the odd chat but he just wanted to be out and not sitting in his flat.

After a couple of games of pool, Stokesy asked Brett if he fancied a cheeky line. Brett was glad of the offer. *Why the fuck not?* he thought. Stokesy knew what he was doing, though. He knew that Brett would get the taste for the coke after a line and most likely end up buying a bag, or in Brett's case having a bag and end up owing Stokesy money. And that's what happened, Brett got the taste for the coke and decided he wanted a bag. Snort away the tears for the night. Brett even ended up borrowing twenty quid from Stokesy as he'd run a bit short of cash. Brett polished off pint after pint and snorted line after line. He and Stokesy were laughing and joking as if they were best pals. Drinking, snorting and playing pool. Brett was drunk and coked up, it was a pressure release but he knew deep in his mind this particular night's drinking and snorting would come at a price.

The time had come for the bell to be ringing for last orders and Brett was in a bit of a state, as was Stokesy. There was time for one more pint though and Brett made sure he had it. After which, he bid Stokesy and a few of the other lads farewell and made his way out of the pub, £70 in debt to Stokesy, which he would have to pay back next week. Of course he couldn't afford it but the coke had tapped him on the shoulder and he obliged, to avoid another night alone in an empty flat.

Brett woke up the next morning with a hefty hangover and regretted getting so drunk and coked up with Stokesy. He knew that he now owed Stokesy money, and it was money he didn't have.

7

NO REST FOR THE WICKED

The stillness of Sunday afternoon haunted Brett's living room as the weekend was drawing to a close and he anticipated an early start on a Monday morning. He hadn't seen his sister Maria and his nephew Damian for a short while so he decided he was going to pay them a visit. Brett and Maria were close; even though they had different dads they were always close and would always massively confide in one another. On arrival, Brett noticed that Maria looked a little bit low and didn't quite seem herself, she was not very talkative and didn't greet him with the usual smile.

Maria was a good-looking girl and could look quite stunning when she made the effort. She had lovely light-brown, naturally curly hair and golden-brown skin. She was mixed raced, like Brett, but a little darker, and she had a voluptuous full figure, but today she didn't look particularly well. She was still in her night clothes and hadn't combed her hair and she was chain-smoking. Brett sat down on the settee. After a short pause Brett asked Maria what was the matter.

"Right then, what's the problem, what's on your mind?" said Brett to Maria in a direct but expectant fashion.

Maria gave a sigh.

"Well, it's just things getting on top of me, it's been a shit week, I'm skint and Kristian has been doing my head in!" replied Maria as she sucked away on her cigarette.

Brett just shook his head, annoyed.

"Why do you put up with his shit, Maria?" snapped Brett.

"He's hard work, you know what he can be like," replied Maria, sounding strained.

"Well, I'm at the end of my tether with cunts like him, he's a horrible, selfish prick, you and Damian would be better off if he just left you the fuck alone!" said Brett screwing his face. "Anyway, where is Damian?" asked Brett. "Is he upstairs?" Damian usually had an afternoon nap and it wasn't uncommon for him to be asleep upstairs when Brett visited in the afternoon.

"No!" said Maria with a sigh of frustration. "He's with Kristian. He's been with him since Friday. He was supposed to bring him back last night but he didn't. I've been ringing him and he just said he will bring him back in a bit, I've not heard nothing all morning and when I ring his phone he doesn't pick up, I told him I wanted

66

Damian back as I have plans and he just put the phone down on me!"

Maria's voice was breaking almost into tears as she spoke and Brett could see she was stressed about it. Kristian was doing things like this all the time but Maria didn't help herself, she put up with a lot from Kristian, but he was an intimidating man when he wanted to be, particularly when he didn't get things his way.

"One day that poor excuse of a man will get his comeuppance and I hope I'm there when it happens," said Brett.

Brett sat talking to Maria for a while. Maria cooked Brett a bit of dinner. Brett was a bit worried about Maria, he knew that she was struggling for money and he knew that Kristian's behaviour could really grind her down sometimes.

It came to around 6pm and Brett was getting ready to leave, he knew he had work in the morning and wanted to get settled early, when out of the blue, Maria's front door abruptly swung open. Brett was a little startled but before he had a chance to say anything, Kristian himself walked through the door and made his way into the living room with Damian in his arms.

"What, can't you answer your phone?" said Kristian to Maria sternly and looking agitated.

Maria had left her phone in the kitchen as she and Brett had been talking earlier. Kristian didn't even acknowledge Brett, he just looked at him and looked away as if he wasn't even there. Maria was annoyed with Kristian for being such an arsehole but Brett could also see she was a bit cautious.

"Excuse me! I've been trying to ring you all day, and you

didn't even give me a time when you were bringing Damian home," said Maria to Kristian.

Kristian handed Damian to Maria hastily, almost flinging him, which startled Damian and he began to murmur. Kristian asked Maria if they could talk in the kitchen, well, he didn't really ask, he just sort of told her he wanted to talk in the kitchen.

Maria left Damian with Brett whilst she spoke to Kristian in the kitchen. Brett could hear Kristian raising his voice at Maria, he couldn't quite make out what he was saying but he could hear Kristian swearing. Brett was getting pissed off, he'd had enough of Kristian. Why couldn't he just leave Maria alone? He was like a bad smell that you couldn't get rid of. Then just as soon as he had arrived, Kristian just swiftly made his way out of the door.

Maria walked back into the living room looking somewhat defeated, but she switched her attention to little Damian asking him how he was and making a fuss of him.

Brett gave Maria a look of disappointment as she had walked back into the room. He didn't say anything; he didn't need to, Maria knew exactly what the look was all about. She knew how Brett felt about Kristian and she knew how long he had felt that way.

Brett said his goodbyes to Damian and Maria and made his way out of the front door. He noticed Kristian was still parked outside in a big Range Rover. Kristian was talking on his phone. Brett also noticed a nice-looking lady sat in the passenger seat next to Kristian. Brett just looked away zipped his jacket up and began the walk home.

***

The next day, Brett was sitting in the Empire. It was drizzly and in the early evening. He had just popped in there for a quick pint or two after work. He'd been there for an hour or so when in walks Glover and one of his pals.

"Hello, Glover, what are you after?" asked Charlotte the barmaid as Glover made his way over to the bar.

"Can I have four pints of Stella, four double Jack Daniels and cokes, a couple of bottles of nice fizz and one for yourself, Charlotte, it's my birthday tonight, there'll be loads of us on it, why don't you come out later and join us?" asked Glover whilst pulling a wad of cash out of his pocket.

"I may just do that, thanks for the drink, I'll have a vodka and orange later," replied Charlotte with a cheeky smile.

Glover handed a few notes to his pal at the bar.

"Here, get these in, I'm off to the shitter," he said whilst handing the money over.

Glover walked past Brett staring at him as he walked by. Glover was his usual cocksure self but Brett just paid no mind and looked away. Glover eyeballed Brett but Brett didn't care, he wasn't interested.

Brett sat reading his paper and he noticed that people began drifting into the pub and were making their way to where Glover and his pal were standing. It looked like they were all out for Glover's birthday drinks. There was a mixture of guys and girls making their way in, the blokes were giving Glover the big pats on the shoulder and handshakes and the women were giving him the hugs and kisses on the cheek, they were making a fuss of him and you could tell Glover was loving it as he was filling the table up with drinks. There were some right good-looking women though and Brett was having a good look particularly at one of the girls who was gorgeous. She was sipping cava from a champagne flute and Brett noticed her gorgeous, prominent lips. Glover noticed Brett having a good look and cheekily grabbed the girl's bum and gave her a longish peck on those gorgeous lips. The girl just laughed playfully along with Glover.

"She's all right, ain't she?" said Glover to Brett loudly in cocky sarcasm in an attempt to make him feel small. Brett just ignored him as he could see by now Glover was in his element and had a crowd to entertain.

Brett decided he was going to make his way home, he'd had a few pints and there wasn't anything really worth staying out for, it was a Monday night and no one he knew was about and the sight of Glover and his cronies was all the encouragement he needed for him to fancy making his way home. Brett finished off his pint and made his way out of the pub.

Brett got back to his flat for the rest of the night in front of the telly alone.

8

ANOTHER STRAW

The next day, Brett had finished work early as he had an appointment at the dentist. He left the dentist around 2:30pm, which meant he would be early to pick up Macy for her weekly visit, so he decided to go to her school and surprise her coming out of the school gates. The school wasn't far from where Macy lived and he thought she would like it if he surprised her at school.

He got to the school gates and looked to see if he could see Lisa picking her up from school. He saw all the other mums and kids coming out of the school but there was no sign of Macy or Lisa. The last few parents and children left. In wonder, he made his way to Macy's classroom with a bemused frown.

As he looked in through the classroom door he saw the teacher, Miss Longley, tidying around in the classroom. He softly knocked on the door and Miss Longley turned to see who was knocking. She looked a little flustered as if she had had a busy day. Strands of her brown hair had loosened out of her usually neat ponytail. She saw Brett standing there and made her way over looking a little puzzled as she opened the door.

Brett greeted her politely.

"Hi, I'm Macy's dad, we've met before on a few occasions. Has Macy been in today?"

Miss Longley recognised Brett from a previous parents' evening earlier in the year and on the occasions that he had been to the school to pick her up. Miss Longley began to look discouraged.

"Macy has not been in since Wednesday, I'm afraid," replied Miss Longley, looking disheartened.

"Well, has her mum told the school why Macy is off, is she ill?" said Brett looking slightly concerned.

Miss Longley paused for a couple of seconds.

"I have to be honest with you, there have been some concerns with Macy's attendance these past few months, she has been having a lot of time off, especially on Mondays, and we rarely have good reasons for her absence, Lisa has had letters from the school regarding this. I'm not sure how aware you are of this but Macy's attendance is a bit of a concern," explained Miss Longley softly.

Brett frowned in anger and sheer disappointment, but he wasn't at all surprised, he knew that Lisa liked to go around the pub with Tara sometimes on a Sunday but it seems now Lisa's social life was impacting Macy's schooling. He began to get a heavy feeling in his chest and felt weighed down with the constant issues with Lisa. He was at that point now where he felt he was ready to blow, it was just one thing after another.

"I have not been aware of this but I will have a word with Lisa and see what the issue is. In future please contact me and let me know of any concerns," said Brett.

Miss Longley assured him that he would be contacted and be notified of all issues regarding Macy.

Brett made his way from the school to Lisa's house to pick up Macy. He was angry but he decided he wasn't going to lose his temper and get into an argument with Lisa, he didn't have the energy for it. But he was pissed off and he'd decided he wasn't going to take much more. He had to play it clever so he decided to keep his cool for now but maybe it was time for him to see a solicitor about official joint custody or even full custody. He didn't want to take Macy away from her mum but she wasn't cutting the mustard as a mum and it just wasn't good enough, if it wasn't one thing it was another.

He knew Lisa was regularly having people around the house smoking weed and drinking and using the house as a hangout and after-parties whilst Macy was there. He wasn't happy about Macy being left in the care of teenagers from the estate. He hated the fact that Lisa often had Macy in a rough estate pub whilst she was getting drunk with her pals and now Macy's schooling was starting to be affected because of Lisa's social life. It just wasn't good enough, but Brett also knew that school attendance reports and documented letters regarding concerns from the school would go against Lisa if he ever went to court for custody. He didn't quite know what he was going to do yet but he knew he had to do something.

9

WHERE KINDNESS FAILS

Brett was making his way to his flat with Macy after picking her up with a bag full of treats. He finally got to his street with Macy aloft on his shoulders. It had been a long wait for a bus so he was glad to be getting home. He reached down carefully in his pocket to get his front door key, carefully holding Macy's legs with his other arm, being extra careful not to drop her as he pulled the key out of his pocket. Once again, he could hear the music in the flat below his. It was loud and the bass was heavy; it was only around 4:40pm. But Brett hoped it was not another occasion where he would have to go and tell them to turn the volume down.

Here we fucking go again! he thought with a sigh.

As Brett got the key out of his pocket and began to

make his way towards the stairs of the flats he noticed the figure of a man walking swiftly towards him from the corner of his eye. As the man got closer he realised he knew him, it was a bloke called Terry Shepard. Brett had known him since he was a kid as he used to live on the street where he grew up.

He was a lot older than Brett, about in his late forties, and he and Brett had always got on. When Brett was seventeen and first started hitting the pubs, Terry kind of took Brett under his wing and made him familiar with all of the old haunts and the town's regular faces. Brett knew it was him as he was sporting his trademark rough-looking, thick, dark-brown beard. He had a reputation as a bit of a nutter when he lost his temper.

He wasn't somebody you'd go out of your way to mess around with but he wasn't a bully or a wannabe. He'd been in the army for years and it was common knowledge that some of the things he'd seen whilst serving had sent him a bit mentally unstable. Sometimes Brett would bump into him. Brett liked Terry, he was a morally driven bloke that would face off with anyone if he felt that they'd taken a liberty with him. Terry noticed Brett as he got to where he was standing.

"All right, Brett," he said quite sternly with an expressionless look on his face whilst reaching his right hand out to shake Brett's. Brett noticed his breathing was a little fast-paced.

"All right, Terry," replied Brett as he shook Terry's hand being careful to maintain balance of Macy on his shoulders. Terry looked pissed off.

"Brett, what cunt lives in this bottom flat here?" asked Terry referring to the flat of Brett's nuisance neighbours.

"They live below my flat, do you know them?" replied Brett.

"No, I don't know them, but they are gonna know me in a minute, my mum lives in the houses at the back of these flats and they've been keeping her awake for months with their music and noise. I'm gonna tell them it's gonna fuckin' stop!"

Brett was excited by this because he knew that if they gave Terry any lip they would quickly regret it.

"I tell you what, Terry, they are a bunch of little fuckin' chavs, mate, it's every week they are playing that music and making noise, I've been around to them a few times," said Brett knowing that these words would add to the frustration of Terry, but he felt glad, it was about time these degenerates were put in their place.

"Well good to see you, Brett, take care, you get yourself and your young one off, mate, because I'll blow my lid with these twats if they give me any mouth!" said Terry.

"All right mate, if you're ever about and you want to say hello, I'm in the top flat," said Brett.

Brett made his way up the grey concrete stairs but only to the next level, he wanted to hear what Terry had to say. He slowly lowered Macy down from his shoulders and waited to hear the action.

Terry banged the door loudly, continuously and hard with his fist. He was hitting it that hard the door was rattling against its wooden frame. After around ten or so seconds the door opened to reveal the same lad that Brett had previously had a word with. The lad looked confused, he was wearing his usual baseball cap and looked at Terry's cold, menacing features. Terry immediately smacked the baseball cap off the lad's head, making the lad almost jump out of his skin. Terry then grabbed him by the scruff of the neck.

"What the fuck are you doing?" shouted the lad in desperation, looking shaken and trying his best to struggle free.

Terry looked him dead in the eye whilst holding him in a vice-like grip with both hands. The lad wasn't backing down but this was just a half-hearted attempt to keep face until Terry opened his mouth.

Terry pushed his face right up against the lad's so they were nose to nose.

"My names Terry Shepard, you don't know me," said Terry calmly. The lad had clearly heard of Terry as he wasn't doing much struggling after hearing the words 'Terry Shepard'.

"My mum lives in one of the houses at the back of these flats and you have been keeping her awake with your fuckin' shit music and noise for a couple of months now, if she complains to me about it one more time I'm gonna come over here and smash the fuck out of you and anybody else that's in this flat! That means your fuckin' missus and every other cunt! My mum's a lovely old woman but I'm a nasty cunt and I mean what I fuckin' say, try me if you don't think I'm serious!"

The lad paused looking startled and had turned a shade paler than he already was. Terry just looked at him dead in the eye menacingly for a few seconds.

"DO YOU FUCKIN' UNDERSTAND YOU LITTLE TWAT!" shouted Terry loudly suddenly with his head still pressed up against the lad's.

The lad nodded, any bravado or ideas to keep face had now faded.

"GOOD!" snapped Terry cheekily, giving the lad a pat on the cheek.

Terry then walked off just as quickly as he came, the lad slowly picked up his baseball cap which Terry had earlier smacked off his head and sheepishly made his way back into his flat, with the music being turned off a few seconds later.

Brett, having listened intently, was now laughing as he made his way up the stairs to his flat. Macy in her childhood innocence was asking her dad why the man was shouting and swearing. Brett just told her he was playing and messing about. It had made his day that Terry had now put this lad in his place.

***

That evening, as Brett was settling for the night with Macy, there wasn't a single sound coming from the downstairs flat, not a voice or any music or dogs barking, just silence. You could hear a pin drop. Brett was happy but at the same time he was frustrated. Frustrated that his approach got him nowhere and that being polite and decent about a situation came to nothing whereas intimidation and fear and a fearsome reputation had worked a treat. Brett's kindness had been taken for weakness and this added to the heaviness of his heart.

10

CHEAP SHOT

The summer had begun to fade and the autumn was on the horizon. It had been a couple of weeks since Terry Shepard's intervention with Brett's neighbours and to Brett's relief there was still no noise or loud music coming from the downstairs flat. Brett had been to see a solicitor regarding joint custody of Macy but the discussions didn't go as he'd hoped. As he wasn't married to Lisa, he would have to approach her regarding joint custody and she would have to be an agreed party to such an arrangement. Failing that, Brett would have to go through the courts and contest Lisa for joint custody. Brett knew that any talk of this with Lisa would rub her up the wrong way as she didn't see any problem with her behaviour and things the way they were. Brett didn't know what to do for the best so things were just left the way they were, for now at least.

***

Brett was making his way home from work early on a Friday evening when he received a text message. A smiled beamed across his face when he saw that it was an unexpected text from Kimberly.

Fancy meeting for a drink later? read the text.

Hey you, that would be great, replied Brett. After some text message small talk, they arranged to meet in the Empire later that night at 8pm.

Brett got home and began to get himself ready, excited and looking forward to seeing Kimberly again. He got to the Empire a little early so he could knock a couple of pints down and loosen up a bit. He sat at a little table near the door so he could see Kimberly as she walked in. The pub was pretty busy with the usual regulars and people unwinding on a Friday night. Glover was also present in the pub again with his cronies and was acting his usual self being one of the most animated in the pub. Kimberly arrived and she looked gorgeous as usual. A big smile appeared on her face as she greeted Brett and she looked immaculate in an elegant maxi-dress. She had her hair up in a bun and she was wearing big bangle-style earrings.

"Hello!" she said, still smiling. She also looked a little bit nervous.

"Hello, how are you?" replied Brett warmly.

After the initial chit-chat Brett fetched some drinks from the bar and they began to talk.

The conversation flowed and they were hitting it off as they always did. Brett was actually trying his best to fish around to see if she was still with her boyfriend. He didn't want to ask directly but he was hoping that Kimberly had got in touch because she was interested in him. And then she hit him with it.

They were talking about work-related things when Kimberly mentioned Daniel. Daniel had come into the conversation because Kimberly had mentioned that he was tired from working long hours. Brett wasn't interested, he pretended to be by gallantly nodding his head along with the conversation but it was the last thing he wanted to hear.

Brett's mood had dipped a little, he couldn't think of anyone else he'd want to get to know again more than Kimberly. It was now obvious to him that Kimberly had friendship on her mind and nothing else. But in fact, unbeknown to Brett, Kimberly was thinking entirely the opposite. She'd in fact only mentioned Daniel out of habit. She hadn't stopped thinking about Brett since the night they bumped into each other and in reality things between her and Daniel were not good. She was kind of plodding along in the relationship but the flame had died. They were bickering a lot and the relationship appeared to have run its course. This actually became apparent to Kimberly the night she bumped into Brett. She didn't want to hurt Daniel; they shared a mortgage together and a lot of things would have to be sorted out should they break up, but she knew there wasn't a long-term future for them and she had made the decision that maybe it was time they went their separate ways. She was hoping Brett would show some interest as she felt too awkward to make the first move. She wanted to but she felt awkward and guilty because she knew she had a boyfriend sitting at home. So here they both were, both with a desire to tell one another how they felt, but both feeling too awkward to let each other know.

Brett was ready to go to the bar when he suggested they go elsewhere after the next drink. It was getting quite laddish in the Empire and Brett fancied moving on to somewhere a bit less of a local pub.

Kimberly was keen and suggested heading to the west end. Kimberly excused herself and made her way to the ladies'. As she walked to the toilet, a very tipsy Glover was propped against the bar with his pals. Kimberly couldn't quite get past Glover and his mob as they were taking up most of the room between the bar and the pool table, so she politely asked Glover if she could get by.

"Excuse me, please," she asked Glover.

Glover turned to her and you could see he liked what he saw as he gazed and looked her up and down.

"How about you squeeze past me?" replied Glover cockily still standing in the way of Kimberly.

Kimberly felt a little awkward but smiled out of politeness.

"If I could just get by!" she said with a hint of frustration.

"Don't be shy," said Glover standing up from the position he was leaning in to give Kimberly more attention. "Let me buy you a drink," he asked.

"No thanks," replied Kimberly with a little frown. "I just want to get by!"

Glover still wouldn't get out of the way and his pals were looking on, childishly chuckling.

Glover smiled. "I've not seen you in here before. I'd always remember a face as gorgeous as yours. Come on, let me buy you a drink," said Glover, trying to turn on the charm.

Kimberly could see that he was a bit drunk. He was getting a bit close and she could smell the whisky on his breath and it was making her cringe. Now he was becoming a nuisance. Brett could also see what was going on as he was standing at the bar. He was getting pissed off and he envisaged he would have to intervene. Glover looked over at Brett with a cocky grin. Then Kimberly with an impatient huff just hastily shoved passed Glover and made her way to the toilet. Glover wasn't used to this and it pissed him off, he'd also realised Kimberly was with Brett and he didn't like that either. Brett was agitated, he anticipated this leading to a confrontation and he didn't fancy his chances against Glover and his pals. He thought about leaving the minute Kimberly returned from the toilet but his pride wouldn't let him. Why should he leave because of someone like Glover?

Kimberly walked an alternative route on her way back from the toilet avoiding Glover and his cronies. She reached Brett at the bar with Glover looking on. Glover hated the fact Brett was with such a good-looking girl that had no interest whatsoever in him. For a split second Kimberly had looked at Glover in disgust during their exchange and this was also something Glover didn't like.

"Come on, let's go!" said Kimberly with slight agitation in her voice.

Brett had just got the drinks. Out of pride, he tried to reassure Kimberly.

"Don't worry about that idiot, just ignore him, we don't need to leave the pub because of him," said Brett with a confident smile.

Brett made his way over to the table with the drinks when Glover hastily walked by him heavily nudging into him, causing Brett to spill some of the drink out of the glasses, it was blatantly no accident. Brett managed to hold on to the drinks without losing them totally. Glover just walked off to the entrance of the pub, grinning. Glover pretended to be taking a phone call on his phone but it was obvious he was trying it on and trying to make Brett look small. Brett could hear a few of Glover's pals cackling over at the bar. Kimberly saw what had happened and was urging Brett to just leave the pub but again, out of pride, Brett insisted they stay to finish their drinks. Brett was shaking the spilled drink from his hands whilst mumbling obscenities under his breath; he was angry but knew the odds were stacked against him if he was to retaliate. Glover then put his phone in his pocket and made his way back into the pub. Glover approached Brett who was clearly pissed off and still mumbling his discontent.

"You got a problem, mate?" said Glover to Brett directly standing with his hands on his hips.

Kimberly had hold of Brett's arm by now and was urging Brett to "leave it" but Brett wasn't having any of it. The odds may have been stacked against him but he wasn't letting Glover have it all his way that easily. This behaviour was typical of Glover, it was sheer bully-boy tactics and it was mainly because Brett had a nice-looking girl on his arm who had shunned him and had no interest in a bloke like him whatsoever.

"I think you're the one with the problem, mate, just leave it out, hey? Nobody wants any trouble," said Brett to Glover with a frustrated frown. Glover looked somewhat surprised.

"OK, mate, no trouble, hey," replied Glover holding up his hands in a gesture of peace.

Brett was surprised at this but he smelt a rat, why was Glover being so decent about it? This wasn't like him. Brett kept his distance and backed off a little making sure he was out of harm's way. He then turned to walk away to put an end to the situation.

This was Glover's opportunity to show his true colours and as soon as Brett was completely turned away Glover quickly stepped forward and cheekily gave Brett an almighty slap to the side of Brett's face hitting his jaw.

It was a cheap shot but it stunned Brett tremendously. It was a big slap that caught Brett flush. The force of the blow and sound that it made was enough to draw a gasp from the pub regulars. Brett's head shot back to the position of him looking up at the ceiling and he lost his balance and fell awkwardly to the ground. Kimberly, looking concerned and horrified, quickly went down on her knees to see if he was OK. Brett was hastily trying to get back on his feet with all the pub revellers looking on. When he got to his feet Kimberly was standing in his way, ready to stop him from retaliating. Brett half-heartedly attempted to push by

Kimberly, but she grabbed him tightly by the waist. Glover hadn't even stood long enough to see Brett drop, he just casually walked back to the bar where all his boys were standing ready to pounce but still managing to chuckle at Glover's antics, apart from one of them who was shaking his head as he stayed seated on his bar stool.

"Come on, mate, that was a bit out of order," said the lad to Glover. Glover just laughed it off.

"I'll tell you what's out of order, me fingering your mum later!" replied Glover to his mate as he cackled at his own joke.

Brett was gritting his teeth with a look of intense rage as if there was fire behind his eyes. Kimberly was holding him by the waist begging him to leave the pub with her. Glover was now stood over at the bar looking at Brett menacingly whilst brazenly standing with an empty pint glass held upside down in his hand looking ready to ram it into Brett's face. Brett knew the best thing to do at this moment was to leave it, despite him being so angry, but he wasn't finished with Glover and little did Glover know how his actions would haunt him in the future. Brett left the pub with a concerned and upset Kimberly, and with Glover taunting him as he left.

"Yeah, that's it, take your little girlfriend and fuck off!" shouted Glover with a chuckle.

Brett's lip was bleeding and Kimberly was trying to tend to it with a napkin from the bar as they swiftly walked from the pub car park.

"It's OK, Kimberly, just leave it!" said Brett sternly, eager to walk on.

"Oh Brett, don't feel bad, there was nothing you could do, he hit you with a right cheap shot, you did the right thing walking away," said Kimberly pleadingly.

Brett looked totally downbeat and the air was filled with silence as they walked on.

"I think we should call it a night, hey?" said Brett, feeling defeated, with his ego in tatters.

"Oh please, let's not let the night end like this because of a twat like that," replied Kimberly.

Brett turned to Kimberly gave her a smile and grabbed her, giving her a big hug.

"Don't worry about it, I'm fine, but I'm not in the mood to carry on drinking, it won't do me any good. We'll meet again soon, hey?" said Brett looking directly into Kimberly's eyes with a total look of sincerity on his face.

Kimberly reluctantly nodded her head as she surrendered to Brett's wishes.

"OK," she muttered and gave Brett a reassuring smile.

Brett walked Kimberly to the nearby taxi rank and made sure she got in a taxi for the journey home. He promised her he would be in touch and she left him with a long, reassuring hug. He wanted to see her again but as far as he knew she was settled with her boyfriend Daniel, and he felt pretty small having been smacked to the ground by Glover. He wondered if there was any point to seeing her again because he knew he wanted more than friendship. He had no idea she felt the same way. He waved at her as her taxi pulled off. He watched it disappear in the distance with a sigh and he wondered if he would ever see her again.

11

WINDOW SHOPPING

In the week that followed, Brett decided it was time to dish out some payback to Glover. His frustrations had become so intense he felt as though his heart was going to explode and Glover was going to be the recipient for his release. Being skint, being lonely, all the bullshit with Lisa, worrying about Macy, seeing his sister ground down by Kristian and his bullying, was all part of the frustration he was determined to unload. The world no longer made any sense to Brett.

He was adamant he was not going to let Glover get away with what he'd done so he planned an attack. He wanted Glover to know how it felt to be on the receiving end and felt he deserved it. Even the likely event of repercussions did not deter Brett from wanting to go through with revenge.

His anger had taken over and every time he tried to talk himself out of it he would just remember how he felt that night at the Empire. He knew the location of Glover's car dealership and had seen Glover locking up at around 6pm on a few occasions when he was on the bus from work.

The dealership was on a main road called Blackbird Road facing the Blackbird pub about two miles from the city centre, however the entrance to the office was at the back of the building leading onto a side street, so Brett thought out a plan of action. Brett decided he was going to ring the office of the dealership at 5:45pm and pretend he was a customer interested in the black BMW 3-series on display and wanted a look at it. This would make Glover hang around a bit later and give Brett a clear opportunity. Brett armed himself with a cosh and a can of mace he'd bought in a pub when he was drunk one night the previous year. This was extreme for Brett but Glover was a big guy and Brett wasn't taking any chances; he justified this by constantly thinking of the cheap shot Glover had given him so he made the phone call hastily to stop him from talking himself out of it. It was all set for 6:00pm. Glover was all too happy to accommodate what he thought was a potential sale late in the day, not knowing that it was actually Brett ready for an ambush.

***

The hour came and Brett made his way to the dealership. He stood on the corner across the road in an old black jacket he had with the mace secretly tucked away in his left pocket.

The cosh was in his right hand ready to be sprung and laid into Glover. He planned to smash the cosh around Glover's shins making him drop to the ground and then give him a few more whacks whilst he was down. The mace was just extra backup.

Brett could see Glover alone through the office window. Glover was drinking a mug of tea or coffee whilst checking his watch. Brett waited, thinking things through one last time. He planned to walk over to the office and on his way use his mobile to ring Glover's office phone, then when Glover went to answer the phone he was going to walk in the office and take him by surprise with the cosh just like Glover had taken him by surprise.

This was it, Brett's heart was pumping with adrenaline as he was about to make his way to dish out some rough justice. There was no turning back now. But then the strangest thing happened, just as Brett was a second from walking over to exact revenge a bus pulled up at the bus stop a little further down the road and a woman in around her late twenties stepped off the bus with a little girl of, say, about four years old. The woman was telling the little girl off, shouting and swearing at her, and the little girl was crying whilst being hurried along with the woman pulling on her arm. It was an exhibition of bad parenting and Brett felt sorry for the little girl. The little girl reminded him of Macy and in an instant all of his anger vanished. All he could think about was Macy.

"What the fuck am I doing?" he thought. He had a responsibility to Macy and he'd be damned if he was going to get himself locked up or in a war with Glover. He was a dad first and anything after that had to come second.

He was not going to let Macy down no matter how tough things got. And that was that. Brett sighed but made his way home. Glover would never know how close he had come to a tremendous beating that day.

Brett never spoke of that day to anyone except his sister Maria. Days later he was stood in the kitchen of her house telling her about everything whilst she was smoking a cigarette. She looked at him with a look of disappointment whist shaking her head.

"Brett, how could you put yourself in that position? What would have happened if you hadn't seen that little girl at the bus stop? You could have got yourself in so much shit!" said Maria to Brett.

"I know, but I was so angry, Maria, I can't remember the last time I was that out of control. He made me look a right twat in front of Kimberly and everyone in the pub. He deserves a good beating. He was lucky!" replied Brett intensely whilst nodding his head.

"Yeah, but he wouldn't have just left it like that would he? He would have come back after you, then what?" said Maria as she was stubbing out her cigarette in the glass ashtray.

Brett nodded along with Maria with a raise of his eyebrows; he knew that Maria was right and it was just what he'd been thinking all along. Maria appeared to be getting on a lot better just lately. She'd explained to Brett that Kristian hadn't been about too much and that he was lying low as a warrant had been put out for his arrest. Maria didn't know too much about the details, just that the police were looking for him. This made Brett happy of course and he hoped that the police soon caught up with Kristian and locked him up for as long as they could. Just a couple of months or so with Kristian out of the picture and Maria was already looking a lot better.

Brett could see it in her eyes; she seemed to have got a bit of her spark back. Brett was even more pleased when Maria explained that she had started seeing someone. And to Brett's surprise, it was an old friend of his, a lad named Martin Bale. Brett knew Martin from when they used to play football together when they were thirteen years of age. They played for a local team called Aylestone Park and although that was a long time ago, Brett used to bump into Martin occasionally. Brett quite liked Martin; he was a funny lad, always had a smile on his face and once he got talking he could talk the hind legs off a donkey, but he wasn't a threat to anyone, totally different to the kind of person Kristian was. Martin liked a beer and was a bit of a lad. Brett was pleased that maybe now Maria would have a chance to move on with her life.

12

SAME SONG

It had been a while now since Brett had seen Steve and Bez. This was mainly because Brett was trying to save money and he didn't feel like going in the Empire after what happened with Glover. He'd also deleted his Facebook account. He'd had a few people he knew from the Empire messaging and asking him what happened with Glover and he couldn't be arsed with it. He was also just sick to death of the whole self-indulgence of Facebook.

***

It was Saturday and Steve had phoned Brett earlier in the day to arrange a night out. Brett arranged to meet Steve and

Bez later that night but instead of meeting in the Empire, he arranged to meet them both in town. The three of them met in the Walkabout bar in the city centre and they were going to head off to Aquis House.

The summer nights had turned to autumn evenings but town was still busy. The three of them stood in the Walkabout bar and during conversation Steve mentioned that he'd heard what had happened with Glover and had been trying to ring Brett about it. In truth Brett had been ignoring Steve's calls and just texting him back with excuses saying he'd ring him back; this was mainly because he didn't want to talk about the whole Glover episode. Steve was reluctant to bring it up as Brett hadn't mentioned it to him and he figured that it was probably a sore subject but he was intrigued as he'd only heard second-hand information from locals in the Empire.

"So what's all this then about Glover knocking you out, mate, why didn't you tell us anything?" asked Steve as he took a sip of a bottle of Budweiser.

Brett looked at Steve and rolled his eyes. Obviously through second-hand information the event had been exaggerated.

"First of all there was no knocking out! He gave me a slap when I wasn't looking, it was a proper cheap shot and he had all of his boys with him and I was on my own, just me and Kimberly!" said Brett directly with a raise of his hand.

"What was that over?" asked Bez

"Well, it was down to the fact that he tried it on with Kimberly and she more or less told him to fuck off and he couldn't take it!" replied Brett with a shrug of his shoulder.

Bez and Steve both shook their heads.

"He deserves to get banged out for that, the prick, don't you fancy offering him a straightener?" said Steve with a grimace.

Brett looked at Steve dismissively and gave a sarcastic chuckle.

"Have a straightener with him! Let's say I beat him then and put him on his arse and did the cunt in front of his boys and everyone hears about it, do you think he'll leave it there? Well, he won't, will he? You know that, he'll come back and he's got an army of silly wannabe twats to back him and Mitchell Webb in his corner! You're my boys, do you fancy going up against that lot every time you walk in the Empire or town?" said Brett smugly with a gallant raise of the eyebrows, purposefully not mentioning the fact that he was only seconds away from laying into Glover with a cosh.

Steve and Bez didn't really respond, they just looked at Brett a little sheepishly, they knew what he was getting at. They were no shrinking violets, they would always be ready and willing to stand should things get on top, but logically, did they really fancy becoming embroiled in an ongoing feud with Glover and his cronies and of course Mitchell Webb? The answer was no and this is what Brett was spelling out to them.

"Look lads, fuck Glover, he's a prick, he's not worth it, I've got other things to think about. One day he'll get what's coming to him and I'm definitely not getting you pair involved in anything," said Brett calmly.

"Yeah, but you know we've got your back, mate," replied Steve whilst giving Brett a pat on the back.

"I know that, lads, but a twat like him just ain't worth it. Don't get me wrong if he starts again and thinks he can bully me every time he bumps into me then he can think again and somewhere down the line I may call on you, but for now, fuck him. I'm not giving him another thought in my head," said Brett, and with that he was eager to move the conversation on.

By the time they got to Aquis House, they were all nice and tipsy. The hype of Aquis House had died down a little since the summer so thankfully there wasn't a massive queue but it was still a buzzing atmosphere in there and plenty of eye candy for the lads to look at.

As the night grew older and with more alcohol inside him, Brett was losing his inhibitions enough to start trying it on with a few of the ladies but yet again he was either saying the wrong thing or had lost his touch because he wasn't having much luck, but he wasn't becoming frustrated in the same sense as before. He was actually beginning to look around at some of the girls and he wondered why he even bothered.

Most of them were dressed like wannabe glamour models showing off as much flesh as they could. Their faces were coated in bronze foundation along with the cartoon-like drawn-on eyebrows. There was the constant flashing of phone cameras for the endless group selfies that were being taken next to tables littered with expensive bottles of alcohol that were being brandished and exposed ready for the next 'mad night out' Facebook posts.

Almost every girl just looked like a clone of one another and in the rare event that he managed to strike a conversation with any of them they all seemed to be working in beauty salons or selling beauty products. Underneath the make-up and the posing and pouting Brett could feel the insecurity within them and the desperation of trying to live up to the image of the girls in the glossy magazines, the celebrities, and reality TV stars. They were looking for high rollers, men with money and status to fulfil their idea of being a twenty-first century girl. What chance did a guy like Brett have to find a nice, genuine girl in this day and age?

At times like this, there was only one girl that came to his mind, and that was Kimberly. She was a breath of fresh air, and with the confidence that the night's intake of alcohol had given him he decided he was going to ring her. He knew she had a boyfriend and he knew it was wrong of him to make a move but he just needed to know if there was any chance for them to start afresh or if she had any feelings for him.

He told Steve and Bez that he was going to the toilet as they were loitering at the edge of the dance floor.

He reached the toilet and made his way into a cubicle, swiftly avoiding the African toilet attendant who was asking him if he wanted to "freshen up for the ladies". He fumbled around for his phone, took it out of his pocket and searched for Kimberly's number. He hesitated for a few seconds as it was late but *Fuck it*, he thought.

He put the phone to his ear and waited for it to ring. A pre-recorded woman's voice sounded. "The mobile you are calling is switched off, please try again later."

He took the phone from his ear and looked at it with a blank expression for a second then disappointedly put his phone in his pocket and made his way back to the lads.

13

TEENAGE KICKS

September became October and Brett hadn't seen that much of Steve and Bez over the past few weeks. He'd begun to spend more time with an old friend called Kieran after a chance meeting as he was making his way home from work. Kieran and Brett were once very close as teenagers but had drifted apart over the years. Kieran was a hustler in every sense of the word. He was always thinking of ways to make money, from insurance scams to dodgy banknotes, you name it. There was always an illegitimate way he was making a nice bit of cash. He worked as a forklift truck driver but always had his hands in a few pies.

Brett liked Kieran a lot. They'd had some great times

as teenagers, both clumsily unaware of the seriousness of the world around them as they hung around on the streets cultivating their teenage kicks. They shared everything back then, cans of high-strength lager, weed, clothes, even girls, but teenage kicks don't last forever.

Kieran was a tall lad standing around 6ft 2in. He was mixed raced although his skin was a shade or two darker than Brett's. He was usually neatly unshaven and had those eyebrows that gradually meet in the middle and converge to form one big eyebrow. Kieran always seemed to be on top and never seemed to take life too seriously or let things drag him down. Kieran had your back and that was one thing for sure. He didn't care about names or reputations or any of that, if somebody took a liberty he would be swinging his fists and if you were with him and somebody took a liberty with you it would be no different. In some ways Brett wished he was a little bit more like Kieran, but Brett could never be a hustler, he just wasn't made that way.

On the rare occasions in the past when he had sold a bit of weed he just got sick of the running around or people knocking on his door, and he hated constantly having his mind on making the money for the next batch, it just wasn't for him. All he wanted to do was earn a good living doing something meaningful but Brett knew all too well it just wasn't as simple as that. Kieran had recently begun dabbling in the coke game again and was keen to get Brett involved but Brett just couldn't be doing with the hassle and of course the fact that if he managed to get caught he'd be heading to prison. It was very tempting though. He saw the nice clothes that Kieran was always kitted out in, and the sleek BMW that he drove, and he always had a good bit of cash to spend, all of the things that Brett was finding so hard to attain.

14

ENOUGH

Brett had arranged to meet Kieran and go for a pint or two after work. They were meeting on Narborough Road which was a busy main road in Leicester's west end. It was a Wednesday and Brett had had a particularly stressful shift at work. One of the service users, a chap in his late fifties named John Hammond, had become abusive and threatening towards Brett. John could be quite nasty and foul if things weren't going his way or if staff were not performing duties fast enough for his liking, like sorting out his medication boxes or helping him tune in his television. Brett had come very close to losing it with John but managed to keep his cool. By the time he'd finished his shift he was fatigued from the sheer frustration at the impatience and utter lack of gratitude from some of the service users.

***

On his way to meet Kieran, Brett thought he'd pass by and say hello to Maria as he was a little early and she lived in the west end. As Brett was walking along Maria's street making his way to her house he noticed Kristian walking out of the front door. Brett screwed his face in disgust at the mere sight of Kristian. He stopped walking hoping that Kristian wouldn't spot him. Kristian was fast-paced as he jumped in his car and swiftly drove away. Brett's face was still screwed in frustration as he marched over to Maria's door. Did this mean that Kristian was back on the scene? What about him being wanted by the police?

Brett grabbed the handle of Maria's front door and barged his way in. He noticed Maria straight away standing in the kitchen. She was leant against the kitchen worktop in her nightgown sort of hanging her head with her hair half covering her face. The kitchen was filled with the pale blue smoke of the cigarette that was between her fingers. She looked surprised when she noticed Brett. Brett could tell that this was the Maria he would encounter when Kristian was back in the mix. She wasn't sparkling like she was a while back when Kristian was out of the picture. And she had that usual dim look in her eyes.

"Oh, are you all right, Brett? If I knew you were coming I would have got dressed," said Maria faintly.

"What was Kristian doing here, Maria? Don't tell me he's back on the scene," said Brett looking puzzled.

Maria didn't answer, she just dropped her head a little and let out a sigh as she sheepishly stubbed out the cigarette in the glass ashtray.

Brett knew the answer. The reluctance to reply and the sigh from Maria was confirmation that Kristian had his feet back under the table. Brett just looked at Maria and shook his head.

"So what about Martin then? Has Kristian scared him off?" snapped Brett with a disappointed look on his face and his arms folded.

Again Maria didn't answer. Like a schoolgirl that had been caught smoking by the headmaster, she just half hung her head.

Brett noticed that Maria wasn't looking upward, as if she was hiding her face. He tilted his head and moved his face closer to hers. Maria tried to turn away and it was then that Brett noticed her upper lip was fattened and there was dry blood on the underside of it. On closer inspection he could see red marks on her neck and bruising on her cheekbone and underneath her left eye. It looked as though she had been roughed up and was looking sore. Maria knew Brett had seen the marks so she began to quietly sob.

The uncontrollable anger in Brett felt like it was going to erupt out of his body. The pilot light had been lit.

"What the fuck have you let him do to you?" said Brett with a growl through his gritted teeth. "Look at your fuckin' face, Maria!" snapped Brett again with the growl now turning into a loud bellow.

Brett softly grabbed Maria's chin trying to get a closer look but Maria was just moving his hand away and still whimpering softly.

"Everything you say is right, Brett. You're right, OK, you're right," said Maria submissively through her sniffles.

She wasn't even going to try and explain her way out of it or justify anything; she knew Brett was right. The truth was, she felt trapped by Kristian. He'd roughed her up a few times and it was no coincidence that Maria was looking roughed up just after having someone else in her life.

"That's it, I'm gonna kill him, I'm gonna fuckin' kill him!" shouted Brett as he let fly at the kitchen wall with his fist.

As soon as Maria heard that, her mumbled sniffles turned into stern words.

"No Brett, you're not gonna do anything, you're not getting yourself into loads of bullshit because of him, I promise you, I'll deal with it!" uttered Maria finally turning towards Brett and looking him dead in the eye, no longer in shame of revealing her bruised face.

Brett sighed painfully with the frustration still etched on his face.

"Why do you keep letting him back into your life, Maria, why?" whined Brett with his hands spread out in frustration.

"He just grinds me down, Brett. He threatens me, he says he's gonna run away with Damian, he turns up out of the blue and it just grinds me down, so I suppose I just give in!" said Maria.

"But you have to stand firm and not let him get away

with the bollocks, phone the police, get an injunction out on him, the law is on your side, there are things you can do, Maria!" replied Brett with a fatigued, strained tone in his voice.

"But he's Damian's dad, Damian loves him. How am I gonna feel the day I have to tell Damian he can't see his dad because I got the police on to him?" said Maria shrugging her shoulders.

Brett just let out a massive sigh in frustration.

"Oh here we go with the 'he's Damian's dad' bollocks, who are you trying to kid? He's no dad, he just turns up when he wants. What fuckin' kind of dad busts his kid's mother's lip open and blacks her eye knowing his own kid has to look at his mum like that? Damian will be better off without him and you know it. You're just making excuses!"

After those words from Brett, there was just silence. Maria didn't have anything to say. Brett just stood there looking at her with total sadness in his heart. All of his anger had just turned to sadness by the fact that his sister was standing before him bruised and sore at the hands of someone like Kristian. Maria was bruised and so was Brett's soul.

"You have to do something now, Maria, else it will just get worse. I will support you and be here for you all the way but you have to make the steps to get this cunt out of your life," said Brett looking at her pleadingly.

Maria raised her head slowly and she was steadily shaking her head in agreement. There was a fixed look of determination in her eyes that Brett noticed straight away.

"You're right Brett, fuck it, I'm gonna do it, I've had

enough!" said Maria firmly with her eyes still red and puffy from her tears.

Brett looked Maria dead in the eye and he knew she was serious. He didn't have to question her, he knew that when she really needed to be, she could be very strong and determined. And that's what Kristian knew deep down, that's why he liked to keep her on edge. But Maria hated seeing the sadness in Brett's eyes and she adamantly promised Brett she was going to get Kristian out of her life for good.

After hanging around a little to make sure Maria was all right, Brett eventually left Maria's house and made his way to meet Kieran. They met in a pub called Hogan's Bar, which was surprisingly busy for a Wednesday night. Kieran could see that Brett had something on his mind and asked him what the matter was. Brett explained the whole situation with Maria and Kristian.

Kieran didn't like Kristian either. Kieran was keen for Brett to take out some retribution on Kristian and get involved himself if need be. He told Brett that Kristian had taken a massive liberty and he should do something to make sure Kristian thought twice before abusing his sister. Brett knew Kieran was right, but he also knew what was at stake should he inflict any damage on Kristian. Brett was starting to think that maybe it was time to put Kristian in his place, come what may.

15

TEARDROP

Macy was not her usual self as she sat down with Brett watching TV. Brett had been deep in thought about Maria since the whole Kristian situation a couple of days before but now Brett's attention was solely on his daughter. She had a bit of a temperature and was not as talkative and chatty. Brett was concerned. He gave her some ibuprofen and plenty of water, which seemed to take her temperature down, but he was being very vigilant for any worsening in her condition.

After checking her temperature over the next hour or so he was satisfied that it was OK and he took Macy to bed and tucked her in for an early night.

***

The following day Macy seemed a bit better but still not one hundred per cent her usual self. She didn't have a high temperature but Brett thought that maybe she was coming down with a cold or something. Lisa had told him that she wanted Macy back early that day as she wanted to take Macy out for dinner.

Brett made his way to Lisa's house with Macy. He didn't go by bus as he usually did. He decided to get a cab as he thought it would be better for Macy as he could see she was still a little under the weather.

The taxi pulled up outside Lisa's house and Brett noticed that Lisa's friend Tara was stood outside the front door taking a call on her phone. Brett paid the taxi driver and helped Macy out of the car and then carried her to the front door. Tara said hello to Macy as Brett tapped the front door that was ajar with his fist and then made his way in, with Tara noticeably not acknowledging Brett. Lisa was sat on the settee on her laptop and was a little startled as Brett walked through the door.

"Hiya, babe," said Lisa to Macy as she looked up at her. Lisa then went into the kitchen and swiftly placed the laptop on the kitchen table before making her way back to the living room.

"Hiya, Mummy," said Macy softly as she held her arms out for her mum. Brett began to explain that Macy hadn't been too well.

"She had a bit of a temperature last night, and she's not been her usual self today. I've given her some ibuprofen medicine but keep an an eye on her," explained Brett as he handed Macy over to her mum.

Macy immediately sank her head into her mum's shoulder and Lisa could see that she looked a little more tired than usual and was a little warm. Lisa placed Macy down onto the settee.

"Have a lay down, hey, I'll make you some warm milk," said Lisa to Macy as she laid her head onto a cushion that her mum had positioned for her. Macy smiled and nodded her head.

"She'll be fine. I reckon she's just a bit overtired," said Lisa to Brett as she made her way into the kitchen to warm up some milk for Macy.

Brett followed Lisa into the kitchen.

"Are you taking her out for dinner? Maybe it might be better just to keep her at home tonight being as she's a bit under the weather," said Brett to Lisa almost pleadingly.

Tara then popped her head around the kitchen door after finishing her phone call outside.

"I'll meet you in the Turnstile at half eight then," said Tara to Lisa enthusiastically.

"Yeah, see you later. Don't be late!" replied Lisa giving Tara a little wave.

Tara gave Lisa a little wave with a raise of the eyebrows and then made her way out of the house saying goodbye to Macy as she left. Brett wasn't too impressed.

"I thought you were taking Macy out for dinner?" said Brett looking bemused.

Lisa gave a slight frown as she placed a cup of milk into the microwave.

"Well I'm gonna take Macy out tomorrow for dinner," she replied.

Brett knew that Lisa was out for another night's partying and this didn't sit well with Brett, especially as Lisa had asked him to bring Macy back early. He was also wondering who would be looking after Macy whilst Lisa was no doubt getting pissed. Macy hadn't been well either so now the alarm bells were ringing.

"Lisa, Macy's coming down with something, it's obvious she's not well, I'd feel more comfortable if you stayed home tonight to be honest," said Brett as unconfrontationally as possible.

Lisa sighed and rolled her eyes.

"Look Brett, if you're gonna start telling me what to do, just go please, I can't be doing with it!" she replied looking at Brett directly with a shake of her head.

"I'm only thinking about my daughter, I've been with her this past day and I'm telling you, she's not been herself!" replied Brett looking right back at Lisa.

Then Brett had an idea.

"I tell you what, I'll take Macy back to mine she can stay with me, wouldn't that be better?" said Brett enthusiastically.

"It's all right, I've sorted it," replied Lisa almost immediately in a flat tone.

This made Brett sigh with frustration.

"Well, who's looking after her tonight then?" snapped Brett. Lisa then slightly screwed her face and looked at Brett with a complete look of disdain.

"I don't know why you think I have to keep explaining to you, you piss me off! You're always making out I can't look after my own daughter. Just leave please, I can't be doing with it," said Lisa holding her head in frustration.

Brett again sighed in total agitation. He placed his hands on his hips and bowed his head a little. It was then he noticed what was on the internet search on Lisa's laptop that was placed on the kitchen table. It read: "Exchanging properties from Leicester to London on the social housing scheme." The alarm bells didn't just ring within Brett when he saw this, they shook his body from his feet to his head. He walked over to the kitchen table and turned the laptop around to face Lisa.

"You planning on moving to London?" said Brett in an agitated whisper.

Lisa flushed a little red. It was easy to see that she didn't want Brett to see what was on the laptop. She became annoyed and walked over slamming the laptop screen down.

"I was having a look. I'm not gonna stay in Leicester forever, I've been thinking about it for a while. There's nothing in place yet so you don't have to panic!" said Lisa sharply.

Brett couldn't believe what he was hearing, and the total inconsiderate attitude from Lisa. The feeling of overwhelming anger took him over.

"If you think I'm gonna sit back and let you fuck off out of town with my daughter you can think again!" said Brett in a deep tone whilst pointing his finger directly at Lisa.

Lisa took a deep breath and folded her arms with an expression on her face that made her look quite sure of herself.

"Who do you think you are, telling me what to do and how I can live my life? Let me tell you something, I can go and live wherever I want, and there's nothing you can say or do about it," she bellowed with a smug uncompromising smirk etched on her face.

Brett paused. He didn't know what to say but the anger surged through his body and there was nothing else he could feel. He looked straight at Lisa in sheer disgust as he imagined launching himself at her. Lisa continued to stand there with her arms still folded and the same smug smirk still displayed across her face. At that moment Brett hated every part of Lisa from her head to her toes. His fists clenched as he stepped towards Lisa. Lisa quickly responded by pointing her finger and stepping back defensively.

"If you fucking touch me I'm calling the police! Go on, hit me then, and see if I don't. Then you'll never see Macy, will you!" she scowled.

Brett was breathing heavily as the anger consumed him. Lisa continued to goad Brett.

"Go on, hit me! Hit me!" she snapped as she cruelly chuckled at him.

The anger inside Brett finally took over him. Almost uncontrollably he grabbed Lisa by the neck of her T-shirt and forced her backwards up against the wall. Lisa didn't try to fight back she just continued to goad him whilst still smirking. Brett pressed his forehead against hers.

"If you take my daughter away from me I'll make it my life's ambition to fuck you up one way or another, don't think for one second that I will let you get away with it. Every minute of every day I will be thinking of a way to make you pay for it!" growled Brett softly as he tightened his grip on the neck of Lisa's T-shirt.

Lisa just smiled and then spitefully spat in his face. She

was determined to let him know that she wasn't afraid of him. Brett swiftly wiped his face and let go of Lisa's T-shirt and made his way out of the kitchen with Lisa berating him, telling him he wasn't a man and that he was nothing but a bully as he walked. Brett looked at Macy and he noticed that she had fallen asleep.

"See you soon, baby," said Brett to Macy as he gave her long kiss on her forehead. He noticed that her head was quite warm.

Brett made his way out of the house, giving Macy one last glance as he left. As he walked, Lisa walked out onto the doorstep.

"Don't come back to my house. Come back here again and I'm phoning the police. And I AM moving to London and if you don't like it, it's tough. Don't ring me either, you can fuck off, if you want to see Macy from now on, do it through a solicitor!" spouted Lisa before she slammed the front door, still angry at the way Brett had grabbed her by the scruff of the neck.

Brett walked on, ignoring her words. He was cut up inside, hurting and angry because he knew now that he had damaged the link between him and Macy. As he walked on he felt his bottom lip tremble and felt a teardrop roll down his cheek.

16

PANIC

Brett was sat in his flat waiting for Kieran to pick him up. Brett was feeling anxious as he'd earlier fallen asleep on the settee. It had only been a few hours since the run-in with Lisa and he'd had a horrible dream that he'd turned up at Lisa's to pick up Macy and Lisa had moved house taking Macy with her without warning, as though she'd skipped away in the night. In the dream Brett had looked through the window and seen that the house was bare of any furniture and was totally empty. This dream had made Brett feel unsettled and all he could think about was Macy.

Brett and Kieran had planned a night out in Nottingham. Brett wasn't in the mood to go out and party anymore. He knew that if he rang Kieran and cancelled, Kieran would just talk him into going so he decided just to go along with the plan and try his best to put things to the back of his mind. When Kieran arrived he could see that Brett wasn't quite himself. Kieran questioned Brett and asked him what the problem was. Brett told Kieran about the whole situation with Lisa. Kieran managed to make Brett feel a bit better.

"Listen, mate, she'll never stop you from seeing Macy. She's got it too good with you having Macy every weekend. She never has to worry about a babysitter when she goes out and she gets a weekly break. She won't give that up. Don't worry about it, mate, she's just mouthing off and letting off a bit of steam," explained Kieran to Brett reassuringly as they both talked over the situation as they sipped on cans of Red Stripe in Brett's kitchen.

"But what if she does actually move to London?" asked Brett looking downbeat.

"Brett, it will take a while for her to move to London, it won't happen overnight. Don't worry too much about it. It's probably just a big idea. When she realises how much hassle it is to move to another town, she'll probably forget about it. In the meantime sort something out with a solicitor. You have some rights as Macy's dad. It might be hard but be ready to fight," said Kieran with in an encouraging tone of voice.

"I just didn't want it to come to that, mate. I just wanted to keep it sweet and raise my daughter with no hassle," replied Brett with a sigh.

"She's not given you a choice, bruv. You've tried your best to keep things sweet but she just keeps taking the piss by the sound of things. You can't keep taking her shit.

Maybe it's time you bit the bullet and did things the official way. Maybe things will turn out better. Sometimes things like this happen for a reason, bruv," said Kieran as he gave Brett a big pat on the shoulder.

Kieran could say the right words to make Brett feel stronger. It was like that when they were teenagers. Kieran would always have fight in him.

The two of them left Brett's flat just after 8:30pm. Kieran explained that he was going to pick up a friend of his, a guy named Franny whose actual name was Kevin Francis but everybody just called him Franny for short. By the time they picked up Franny, Brett was thinking about texting Lisa and trying to smooth things over. Kieran noticed Brett keep looking down at his phone.

"I know what you're thinking," said Kieran to Brett as he drove along the motorway. "You want to text Lisa and try to sort things out. I'd Leave her, bruv, if I was you, give her a few days. Let the dust settle. She'll only spout off if she's still pissed off and start another argument."

Brett nodded along half-heartedly but he wanted to see how Macy was, so decided to text Lisa.

How is Macy? Is she feeling better? I just want to know how she is as she wasn't too well earlier, said Brett in a text message to Lisa. There was no reply. Brett could see on the notifications that the message had been read but this was probably Lisa's way of making him pay for what happened hours earlier.

The three of them reached Nottingham and Kieran parked his car in a side street he knew on the outskirts of the city centre. Franny began to talk to Brett a bit more and had become more animated since leaving the car. Kieran had formally introduced them in the car earlier but the mood was a little sullen. The mood had lifted as the promise of pubs, alcohol and the atmosphere of the weekend hit them as they walked the streets passing other revellers as they walked.

Franny was known as a bit of a loose cannon, he drank hard and he spent hard and on a night out that was guaranteed. He was a game lad and like Kieran didn't take any shit from anyone. He only stood about 5ft 9in but always had a little mischievous spark in his eye. Franny could be a handful when he'd had a few drinks in him and would be quick to let his fists fly at the first sign of anybody taking a liberty.

They hit the first bar and Franny was eager to hit the shots on the first round. Brett couldn't help but check his phone to see if Lisa had sent him a reply but unsurprisingly there was nothing. Brett was trying his best not to think about the situation with Lisa but it wouldn't leave his mind. After a couple more shots Kieran had the idea of moving on to a club called Pryzm. Brett and Franny were keen and were more than welcoming towards the idea.

The atmosphere was good when they got to Pryzm and Brett began to relax a bit more and try to forget about his troubles for the night. He was still checking his phone every now and again but he was starting to feel a bit tipsy. He noticed the battery on his phone was getting flat so he put it in his pocket and was determined not to look down at it again.

Franny grabbed Brett's hand and placed the all-too-welcoming bag of cocaine in it and gave him the welcoming gesture with a nod of his head. Brett looked down and saw the white powder glistening in the small button bag. The image was very welcoming to Brett and he didn't waste any time thanking Franny before eagerly making his way to the gents.

Brett made his way into one of the toilet cubicles and placed the toilet seat down before sitting down. He wanted to be alone with the coke and savour the ritual. He made sure the cubicle was locked and then held the bag aloft, level with his eyes, to view the amount of coke that was in the bag. To Brett's delight, there was plenty. He wasted no time in carefully tipping a small pile of the white powder into the crevice he'd made between his thumb and the back of his hand. Once he was satisfied he had enough, he lowered his head and took a powerful loud snort. He held his head back ensuring none of the powder would fall out of his nose and then gave another sharp snort. He then brushed and wiped his nostrils with his fingers ensuring that no white powder would be visible once he'd left the toilets.

He made his way back to Kieran and Franny and felt nice and ready to see what the rest of the night would bring.

Brett was having a good look around and he noticed a lad he knew in the distance sitting in the VIP lounge. It was a lad by the name of Beresford Jenkins. Brett was around eight years older than him and had known Beresford since he was seven years old. Beresford had grown up on the same street as Brett and Brett would always stick up for him if he was getting any stick from anyone on the estate. Beresford had hit the local headlines in the past few months as he was an upcoming footballer who had been in Leicester City's youth team. He'd recently had a place in the starting line-up in the senior squad in a cup game and had scored two goals. He seemed to be enjoying his new-found fame as he sat surrounded by people. Brett hadn't seen him in a long time and was eager to go and say hello and congratulate him on his recent success.

"Hey, there's Beresford Jenkins in there, in the VIP lounge, I know him. Let's go and chat to him, he'll get us in the VIP lounge," said Brett to Kieran and Franny eagerly.

Kieran and Franny looked over. They recognised Beresford from the recent headlines and the TV reports so they were eager to go along with Brett.

"I've known this guy since he was a kid," said Brett as they made their way toward the VIP lounge.

The club was crowded and it was hard to get to the entrance of the VIP lounge. There were two bouncers standing outside as well that were only letting people in with passes. Brett got to the door and it was obvious the bouncers were not going to let them in without passes so he was trying to get the attention of Beresford who was sitting near the front of the lounge. Brett was looking over the bouncers and waving his hand.

After a few seconds Beresford saw Brett, even though he was preoccupied with the large group of people he was with. Brett was confident that Beresford would be happy to see him and was expecting the big hug and pats on the shoulder to follow anytime soon. But to Brett's surprise, Beresford just nodded his head then gave Brett a very swift wave and then just looked away. At first Brett thought

Beresford didn't recognise him but he'd glanced at him a second time and again just looked away continuing with the conversation with a young lady from his party. Kieran and Franny looked at Brett looking somewhat bemused.

"I thought you knew this guy!" said Kieran looking puzzled.

"Well I do but obviously his new-found fame has gone to his head!" replied Brett with a look of disappointment on his face.

The bouncers then explained to Brett that he had to move on from the VIP lounge as they were blocking the entrance. Beresford saw Brett being asked to leave by the bouncers but again just turned his head and carried on his conversation with the young lady. Brett was hurt by this and baffled by Beresford's attitude. The only explanation that made any sense to Brett was that the little bit of new-found fame that Beresford had recently achieved had gone to his head.

Brett made his way to the bar with Kieran and Franny in tow. Kieran commented on what a twat he thought Beresford was.

For a split second Brett thought he saw Bez standing at the bar. It was only when he got closer that he realised that it wasn't Bez but just someone who resembled him. This made Brett think about Steve and Bez. He hadn't seen them in a while and realised he was missing his good pals. He planned in his mind to get in touch with them the following day.

Brett felt his phone vibrate in his pocket. He swiftly pulled his phone out of his jean pocket and looked down at the screen. He didn't recognise the number so he was reluctant to answer it but something was telling him to answer. He answered the phone with a dubious frown.

"Hello," said Brett in a flat tone.

"Hello, is that Brett?" said a young girl's voice frantically.

"Who is this?" said Brett

"It's Chantelle, Lisa's friend, I've been trying to ring Lisa but she won't answer her phone… It's Macy, she is ill, I think I need to ring an ambulance!" said the girl in a stupor of utter panic and sounding tearful.

Brett's entire body flushed over with sheer panic and instantly his heart began to pound.

"What do you mean? Where's Macy? What's wrong with her? What's wrong with her?" Brett shouted. He marched out of the main room of the club unaware of the people he was knocking as he stomped his way through and made his way outside.

"I don't know!" shouted the girl, by now bursting into tears. "She is red-hot and I can't seem to wake her up. Her skin is red and I don't know what to do!"

"Ring an ambulance… ring a fuckin' ambulance!" shouted Brett, his voice now broken in terror.

Kieran and Franny had by now realised that there was a situation and were wondering what was wrong and began to make their way out of the club to join Brett.

Brett didn't have to ask the girl on the phone where Lisa was, she was obviously out partying whilst leaving Macy at home with Chantelle, the teenage babysitter from the estate.

Brett managed to calm himself a little to try and gain some control of the situation.

"Now listen to me, Chantelle, check that Macy is

breathing! Is she breathing?" said Brett, his own breathing now shallow and quick.

"Yes, she is breathing. I've laid her down on the settee, I can see she is breathing," replied Chantelle frantically, still clearly tearful. Brett tried his best to be as calm as possible.

"Now listen to me, Chantelle" said Brett loudly and clearly. "I'm in Nottingham, I will get there as soon as I can, you need to do exactly what I say. Take Macy's clothes off down to her pants, and then lay her on her side, then get a flannel soaked in cold water and place it on Macy's head. Keep the temperature in the room as cool as possible and ring an ambulance straight away! Do that quickly right now. Do all that in the order I have told you to!"

"All right, I'll do that now!" replied the girl, her voice sounding a little calmer.

"Do it now! Right now! I'm gonna come off the line for a minute and ring my sister, she only lives down the road, I'll get her to come to you and I'll ring you back on Lisa's house phone. Ring the ambulance, do it now!" said Brett, his voice now strained with the horror that had taken over him.

"All right!" replied Chantelle.

Brett finished the call and desperately tried to search the contacts on his phone to get Maria's number. His hands were shaking so much he almost dropped his phone. Maria's number appeared on the screen and he pressed the call button and quickly placed the phone to his ear as it began to ring.

"Please answer, Maria, please," he whispered to himself as the tears began to form in his eyes.

Maria answered with a mundane, "Hiya." Brett had never been more pleased to hear her voice.

"Maria, listen to me, you've got to get to Lisa's house. Macy is there with a babysitter and she is ill, the babysitter has just rung me and she is ringing an ambulance!" said Brett quickly with his voice still clearly strained.

"What!" said Maria sounding horrified. "What's wrong with her, is she all right?" Maria's voice was now also sounding strained.

"Maria, I haven't got time to explain, I've got to ring the babysitter back now. Please get to Lisa's, please, Maria I'm begging you!" said Brett in total desperation.

Brett didn't hear anything back. Maria didn't say anything and he noticed that the line was dead. As he looked at his phone screen he saw that the phone was dead the battery had run out.

Total intensified terror now overtook him. He felt sick. It felt like the black night sky was caving in on him and he could feel a crushing sensation on his lungs as if he couldn't breathe properly. The panic made him feel like he was drowning. At this point Kieran and Franny had made their way out of the club to find Brett and made their way to him as they saw him outside the front entrance of the club. Kieran could see the horror in Brett's eyes and asked Brett what was wrong. Brett explained the situation the best he could and Kieran wasted no time getting Brett to the car. The three of them paced through Nottingham city centre almost sprinting to get to the little side street where the car was parked. They jumped in the car possessed by the mission of getting Brett to his daughter.

"I have a charger that's in the car, it's in the glove compartment; plug it in. It takes a while to charge though!" said Kieran as he sped out of the side street like a rally driver.

It was a desperate situation. Without phone power, Brett couldn't ring Chantelle the babysitter or Maria. Kieran asked Brett if he knew any of the numbers off by heart so he could ring them from his phone, but Brett didn't know any numbers off the top off his head. Brett opened the glove compartment and hectically rummaged around looking for the iPhone charger. Once he had found it he plugged it in. There was nothing else he could do, he just had to sit and wait for the charger to do its work.

Kieran didn't know what to say, he was just concentrating on the road trying his best to get Brett to Macy. Franny didn't say a word either, he just sat feeling helpless.

Brett began to hold his head in his hands. The feeling of helplessness was driving him crazy. All he could think about was his baby. He kept checking the phone to see if there was enough power to make the call but the red line at the bottom of the battery display contributed to the sheer despair of the situation. Kieran had explained to him that the charger takes a long time to charge from the car. This was the last thing Brett wanted to hear.

The next few minutes were the longest minutes of Brett's life. Every few seconds he looked down on his phone to see if there was enough life to make the call. Five minutes passed, then ten, then twenty then thirty, but this seemed like a lifetime to Brett. At last the screen of Brett's iPhone lit up and Brett had never been happier to see the Apple symbol appear. Brett furiously tapped the screen to get Maria's number and call her.

He made the call but to his dread the phone went straight to the answerphone. This was due to poor reception. Brett let out a moan of frustration. He then tried to ring Lisa's house phone but there was no answer. The panic felt like it was ravaging his body as he couldn't seem to control his breathing. Brett tried to ring Lisa's phone but to no avail, Lisa wasn't answering. Kieran's foot hadn't been off the accelerator as they approached Leicester from the motorway. Then to Brett's relief his phone rang and he saw Maria's name on the screen. He quickly answered, his voice shaking with dread. He closed his eyes as he waited for information from Maria. It had now been over an hour since Brett had last spoken to her.

"Brett, don't panic, Macy's OK, she's awake, we're at the hospital!" said Maria quickly, in order to avoid Brett's panic.

Brett began to cry as a sense of relief came over him. He was a broken figure. Macy had got to the hospital quickly as Lisa's house was literally a minute's walk from the hospital. What Maria hadn't told him was that she had carried Macy over to the hospital as she knew this would be quicker than an ambulance. Maria had left Damian at her next-door neighbour's house as she was a good friend of hers and she had got to Lisa's as quickly as she could, which didn't take long as she only lived a few streets away.

"Is she OK? What's wrong with her? Put her on the phone," said Brett with his voice broken by stress.

"She is with the doctors, Brett, but she was awake. She

is gonna be OK. The doctors have said she has a severe case of tonsillitis," said Maria reassuringly.

Again the feeling of sheer relief overcame Brett.

"Are you sure, Maria? Is she OK? Are you sure?" asked Brett with his voice still croaked and shaky.

"Brett, she is poorly, I'm not gonna lie, but the doctors managed to wake her and they have said it's tonsillitis. She'll be OK, she's in the best place, she is with the doctors and she is awake!" replied Maria.

"Thank you! Thank you so much, Maria. I'll be down the hospital soon, I'm coming straight there now. Make sure you are with her. Make sure you stay with her. Ring me if anything changes, stay with her!" said Brett sternly.

Brett didn't like the idea of Macy being ill and alone with the doctors. He wanted someone she knew with her.

"I promise you, Brett, I will ring you if there is any change, don't worry just get down here as soon as possible," said Maria with a hint of encouragement.

"OK. Make sure you ring me if there is any change. I'll see you in a minute," replied Brett sounding calmer.

"Brett, I promise you, I will, I'll see you in a bit," said Maria.

With that, Brett hung up. The tears had stopped and he felt reassured. He was desperate to get to the hospital to see Macy. Kieran and Franny were eager to find out how things were and Brett explained what the situation was.

Kieran had made short work of the journey from Nottingham to Leicester and now it wouldn't be too long before Brett was finally at the hospital. Brett felt a little bit of solace as he looked at the familiar Leicester roads from the car. His feelings of sheer dread and terror were now also being overtaken by the feeling of anger. He was livid with Lisa. He'd warned her that Macy wasn't well but she went out partying anyway, and in the state of emergency nobody could get in contact with her as she wasn't answering her phone. Macy was in hospital and nobody could get in touch with Lisa. She hadn't even returned the calls. There was no more immediate news from Maria so in Brett's mind no news was good news but this was the final straw. He'd had it with Lisa and at that moment he'd decided that he was going to fight her for full custody of Macy. Even if it meant a massive battle, he was going to get custody of his daughter and he was now determined that nothing would stop him.

17

THE DEATH OF BRETT KELSO

Brett almost fell out of the car as he was in such a hurry to get to Macy as Kieran dropped him off at the Leicester Royal Infirmary car park. Kieran had asked him if he wanted him to go with him but Brett declined. He assured Kieran he would ring him later and said his goodbyes to him and Franny. Kieran told Brett to make sure he rang him. Brett quickly made his way to the main reception on foot. He knew where the children's accident and emergency department was and began to pick up the pace and jog. He jogged through the main entrance and made his way to the children's department. He approached a plump-looking middle-aged woman at the desk.

"I'm looking for Macy Kelso! She was brought here over an hour ago!" said Brett, out of breath.

The woman tapped away at her keyboard and looked at the computer screen with Brett fidgeting as he impatiently waited for instructions from the woman. After a few more clicks on the keyboard and a gaze at the screen the woman broke her silence.

"Macy Kelso, I believe she's in emergency response. If you walk to the end of this hall, turn right, and it's right in front of you," said the woman as she directed Brett.

Brett didn't even say thank you, he quickly made his way to the end of the hall and turned right. He saw Maria straight away sitting in the corridor outside a room. Maria was sitting eerily still as he looked at her. He almost ran, and she turned to the right to face him as he called her name. She immediately burst into tears and covered her face with her hands. On seeing this, Brett ran to her.

"Where's Macy, Maria?" said Brett, almost shouting as he got to her.

Maria just couldn't stop crying. The kind of cry you'd hear when someone was in immense pain, it was almost a scream. Brett became instantly agitated and again, panic and dread surged through his body as he grabbed her and began to shake her.

"Where the fuck is Macy, Maria? Where is she?" shouted Brett.

Maria tried to hug him.

"Oh God, Brett, oh God!" Maria wailed.

Brett wasn't interested, he just carried on shouting and shaking Maria, asking where Macy was. On hearing the commotion, two doctors made their way out of the room that Maria had been sitting outside of in the corridor. One of them tried to guide Maria away and the other was trying to speak to Brett standing in front of him directly. Brett looked at the doctor's eyes through his glasses. His attention was now solely on the doctor as he noticed the empty look in his eyes. Brett couldn't speak. He just couldn't find the power to even speak. He could hear Maria's cries become a little fainter as she was guided into a room by the other doctor.

"Mr Kelso, there's no easy way of telling you this, but I'm afraid Macy passed away eight minutes ago, I'm so sorry, we did everything we possibly could!" said the doctor softly as he looked directly at Brett with a sullen look etched on his face.

Brett looked at the doctor, confused. This wasn't real. This couldn't be happening. *Tell me what's really happened*, Brett thought to himself. The world had stopped turning at that moment. It was a dream. It was obviously a dream. Brett was going to wake up any second. He'd heard the words but he wanted to be sure that he'd heard the doctor rightly.

"What do you mean she's passed away?" said Brett looking confused whilst shaking his head.

"I'm so sorry," replied the doctor with the same empty look in his eyes.

Brett realised it wasn't a dream and he wasn't going to wake up. He felt his body shudder and his breathing accelerate uncontrollably. He opened his mouth to scream but there was no sound. The entire world closed in on him. The shock and the disbelief crippled him has he stepped back and slumped onto the plastic chair in the corridor. The doctor slowly sat next to Brett. Brett's body couldn't function properly. He tried to talk but he stuttered. Then the question hit him. *How? How did she die?*

"What happened? Maria said she had tonsillitis! She had tonsillitis!" said Brett his voice strained with frustration and confusion.

The doctor paused for a few seconds before leaning forward and poignantly looking at Brett. Brett was just looking into the distance in total shock.

"Mr Kelso, my name is Dr Mann, I myself worked on Macy. I'm afraid Macy had a case of bacterial meningitis. She did have a severe case of tonsillitis, which was confirmed almost immediately after her arriving at the hospital, but unfortunately she wasn't showing any typical signs of meningitis and I'm so sorry to say that by the time the meningitis was picked up, it was too late. The bacteria had spread into her blood causing septicaemia and her heart suffered toxic shock and she went into cardiac arrest. We tried our very best to revive her, but after repeated desperate attempts we were not successful. I believe it's accurate of me to say that she didn't suffer any prolonged pain or discomfort," explained the doctor softly looking directly at Brett.

Brett was still staring away from the doctor and into the distance. He began to sob with his head in his hands uncontrollably. He wailed in pain, and all that could be made of him was the shaking of his hands and the violent bobbing off his shoulders as he sobbed.

"Where is she? I need to see her!" said Brett, disorientated by the sheer pain he was feeling.

The doctor held his hand out in the direction of the little room on the corridor.

"She is here," said the doctor softly as he walked toward the room.

Brett followed him, taking a massive deep breath in between his cries. The doctor stood at the edge of the bed with his head held a little low. As Brett walked into the room he couldn't take in any of the surroundings. Immediately he saw his little daughter lying on her back with her mouth slightly open. Her face looked a little red but she looked peaceful. Her hands were by her side and Brett could tell that there was no life in her body. On seeing her, he let out a massive cry and lunged forward onto the bed grabbing her and hugging her whilst pressing his face against her cheek. She was slightly cold, but Brett still imagined her waking up.

"Oh, my baby, my baby girl!" cried Brett over and over again through his sobs.

The doctor respectfully left the room to leave Brett with his daughter. Brett held Macy and just sobbed and sobbed. Maria entered the room and at the sight of Brett with his daughter cradled in his arms she again began to wail in sorrow and sob. She walked forward and leaned down next to him, putting her hand on his shoulder. Brett knew she was there.

"You said she had tonsillitis!" said Brett through his cries with his face still pressed against Macy's cheek.

This made Maria cry even more.

"That's what they told me. Everything changed so quickly!" whaled Maria with her face scrunched up in pain.

Brett didn't say anything further. He just sobbed and sobbed whilst clutching Macy tightly.

The minutes slowly crept by. Minutes that then turned

into an hour of nothing but stillness and the sound of groans of sadness and pain. Brett was now sitting on a chair at the edge of the hospital bed holding Macy's hand in total disbelief that he was never going to see his daughter's beautiful smile ever again. He would never hear her call him "Daddy" again. He was never going to tuck her into bed. He was never going to give her a cuddle on his settee ever again. It just didn't make sense, this just couldn't be happening.

The doctors had spoken to Maria briefly outside of the room to explain procedures of after-death care, but they were in no rush. Maria, still very upset with her face looking puffy and swollen, raised the issue of contacting Lisa. Brett didn't even want to hear Lisa's name being mentioned. Hate had now infected his soul. He was adamant that it was Lisa's lifestyle that had contributed massively to Macy's death. He told her not to go out and party that night as he had concerns over Macy's health. He offered to look after Macy that night but Lisa refused. If Lisa had been at home with Macy, maybe Lisa would have acted quicker than the sixteen-year-old that was babysitting. Maybe if Lisa had answered her phone when the babysitter rang in the first place, it would have saved more time.

Lisa must have by now seen all of the missed calls on her phone so why hadn't she acted in a responsible manner and made contact? These were the only things that were going through Brett's mind. The fact that Lisa had the cheek to plan a move to London with Macy hadn't been forgotten. But none of that mattered now. Macy was dead and Brett couldn't do anything to save her. It was as if he always knew something like this was going to happen somehow.

Maria, as much as she disliked Lisa, had tried to ring her to tell her to make her way to the hospital but again the phone had gone straight to the answerphone. Maria left a message telling Lisa to get to the hospital as there was an emergency with Macy, her voice clearly shaken on the recorded message.

The doctors and the after-death care personnel had again spoken to Maria as another hour had passed. Brett was adamant that he was not leaving Macy. Maria, still visibly upset and not really knowing what to say, had explained to him that he had to try his best to let go and that sooner or later procedures had to take place. Brett told Maria that he would never let go. Maria sat with Brett and didn't really know what else to say. Brett again cradled Macy in his arms and gave her a massive kiss on her head as the tears streamed down his cheeks and he whimpered desperately. It was at that moment that Brett heard Lisa's voice in the corridors of the hospital.

"I need to find my daughter, Macy Kelso!" Brett heard a concerned Lisa shout to the staff in the hospital.

Brett gently laid Macy down onto the bed and said goodbye with a final kiss and again pressing his face against her cheek. Brett could feel that Macy was now cold. He didn't want her to feel cold. He raised his head and looked down at her one last time. He knew Lisa was now here and he didn't want to be anywhere near her. Maria knew that Brett was ready to leave the room and she again began to sob. As Brett left the room taking one last look back at Macy as he left, he saw a desperate-looking Lisa at the top of the corridor with her friend Tara also looking desperate and concerned. Lisa looked at Brett with a look of almost relief on her face. She quickly ran towards Brett. Brett could see that she was half-cut and dishevelled.

"Where's Macy? What's happened?" screeched Lisa as she reached Brett.

Brett looked at her in disgust. He could see the sorry state of her make-up that had run down her face and he could smell the foul stench of stale Pernod on her breath. Brett just looked at her, and then without warning spat straight in her face just as she had spat in his. Lisa was shocked but she somehow knew from Brett's actions that there was something seriously wrong.

Brett just walked on, never turning back to look at Lisa. He could just hear her screeching in desperation as she made her way towards the room where Macy was. Brett walked past Lisa's friend Tara and also looked at her in utter disgust. Tara was sheepish and seemed to hang her head, as if in shame. Brett then made his way down the corridor and didn't know what to do with himself once he saw the hospital entrance. He then collapsed and passed out. The shock, the heartache and the immense pain had taken their toll on his mind and his body. His heart was shattered into a thousand pieces and he had simply shut down.

18

FRIENDS LIKE THESE

It didn't take long before the news of Macy's tragic death hit the streets. The first thing Steve and Bez did was go to see Brett at his flat. Brett had spent a night in hospital after he had passed out on the night that Macy had died. He'd discharged himself the day after and, despite pleas from Maria to stay at her house, he made his way back to his flat.

Steve and Bez were by his side sitting with him not knowing what to say, but just being the good friends they were and being with him. Brett was silent just giving 'yes' and 'no' answers and spending most of the time staring into space. He was holding the dressing gown that Macy would wear when she was at his flat and every now and again he would bury his nose in it as it still carried Macy's scent. Steve and Bez kept looking at each other in concern, wondering what they could do to help him.

"Brett, I don't mean to talk out of turn here, mate, I really don't, but wouldn't it be better for you to be staying at Maria's? It's not gonna do you any good sitting here all by yourself!" said Bez softly as he looked down at Brett with his hands in his pockets.

Brett looked up at Bez, his eyes looked lifeless and drained.

"I feel like I'm walking away from her if I leave here. Her things are here. This is where we used to sit and watch films. I feel like she is still here with me. I can't leave!" replied Brett.

Bez didn't know what to say, again he looked over at Steve wondering if he would say something, but Steve was at a total loss.

"Well, I tell you what, I'll stay here with you for a few days if you like, mate. It might be better than you being on your own," said Bez as enthusiastically as he could with a nod.

Brett looked up at Bez and smiled through the pain that was written all over his face. Bez stood up and put his hand on Brett's shoulder. Bez stood there looking at him awkwardly not knowing what to do, then Brett put his other arm around him and hugged him tightly.

"You are one of my best friends in the whole world and you always will be," whispered Brett in Bez's ear.

A wave of sadness took over Bez in a way like never before, and he hugged Brett back tightly before bursting into tears. On seeing this Steve rose to his feet and put his arms around them both so the three of them were in a huddle. The tears had built up in Steve's eyes as he grabbed the both of them tightly.

19

THE PAINFUL LAST KISS

Brett refused to have any correspondence with Lisa in the days that followed. Maria was to liaise with her with regards to sorting out Macy's funeral. All of Brett's wishes were put forward by Maria and Brett would only talk to the funeral directors without Lisa present. Kieran had been to see Brett and had given Brett £1000 towards Macy's funeral. Brett refused to take it at first but Kieran wouldn't take no for an answer. Steve and Bez had also contributed £1000 between them and raised a further £700 in donations from a lot of the local people that had known Brett over the years. A lot of the lads from the Empire had also donated a few quid. This touched Brett immensely and even at this point of uncompromising hurt and pain he realised that there was still some good people out there.

On the morning of Macy's funeral, Brett was sat on the end of the bed in his boxer shorts looking down at the floor. Staying at his flat had become too much for him as the days passed and he was staying in Maria's spare room. He hadn't had a wink's sleep and he just couldn't believe that today was the day that he was going to lay his little Macy in the ground. It was a cold late October morning and he could hear the world around him moving and carrying on.

The sound of the refuse lorry reversing on the street, the sound of people de-icing their car windscreens getting ready for the drive to work. The world was just carrying on and it didn't seem right. He'd spent the past week at Maria's in the spare room. Maria had been everything a sister should be and more. She had been a tower of strength and had taken care of everything that Brett had not been strong enough to see through.

The funeral car was arriving at Maria's house at 10am to take Brett and Maria to the funeral home to see Macy, and then onto the cemetery. Brett had insisted that Steve, Bez and Kieran were present with the two of them in the funeral car. Brett had shunned any family members when Maria asked about them.

"Fuck 'em. None of them have been there for us! Where the fuck have they been all these years?" These were the words Brett would say to Maria whenever she brought up the topic of their family. Maria didn't mention their mum, Anne. Brett and Anne had had a massive falling-out a few years ago and Brett had vowed never to talk to her again.

Anne had been an alcoholic throughout Brett's childhood and let's just say her children's welfare was not her number-one priority. Anne would always put men and alcohol before Brett and Maria when they were growing up and Brett had left his mum's house when he was just fifteen years old. Maria would still see her mum every now and again but only out of a sense of duty that Maria carried.

At Brett's request, Lisa had to get a separate funeral car. He didn't want to be anywhere near her during the funeral.

The car arrived five minutes early. Steve and Bez had arrived at Maria's house with half an hour to spare but they were all still waiting for Kieran. It wasn't unusual for Kieran to turn up right at the last minute but to Brett's relief he was there in the nick of time. As the five of them sat in the car nobody could find any words of comfort for Brett. No words could make any sense at this moment in time so the car was just filled with silence. Brett was wearing a pink tie and a small pink rose in the lapel of his black suit jacket, the pink being a tribute to Macy, as it was her favourite colour. Brett had requested everybody wear a little bit of pink as a tribute to her. Maria also had a small pink rose worn on the breast of her dress. Steve and Bez both wore pink ties and Kieran wore a pale-pink shirt.

As Brett stepped out of the car at the chapel for the service at Gilroes Cemetery, he could feel his legs shaking and felt as though all of the breath had been sucked out of his body. He kept telling himself that he had to be strong for Macy. Bez was the first to stand near him and ask him if he felt all right. Maria held him by the hand, and every so often she would give his hand a squeeze as if to remind him that she was there. Brett could see the people standing outside the church. There were more people than he had expected and the colour pink was a prominent sight that shone from the people that were gathered outside the chapel. He could see staff members from Macy's school, and a lot of people he knew from the New Parks estate where he had grown up.

Brett knew that Lisa's car and the horse-drawn carriage that was carrying Macy's coffin were only a short way behind him. He couldn't bring himself to look at Macy's coffin for too long before now, but as he got to the chapel door, he knew that he would have to. People began approaching Brett to pass on their condolences but Brett couldn't even find the strength to say any words, he just gently nodded his head. Kieran stepped over and politely asked people to leave it for now, as he could see that Brett wasn't in any frame of mind to be acknowledging people.

Brett could hear the slow-paced clippety-clop sound of the two horses that were pulling along the carriage followed by the sight of the horses with the pink plumes of feathers on their heads gently bobbing as they walked. As the horses turned, the uncompromising, sad sight of Macy's coffin in the carriage was apparent for all to see. Macy's coffin was a beautiful pale-pink colour with her name carved on one side and the word 'Princess' carved on the other. The carriage was followed by the car carrying Lisa. The carriage came to a stop with the funeral car behind it. Brett could hear the wailing of Lisa and others as the car doors opened. Lisa stepped out with her mum and Tara either side of her with their arms around her. Lisa was in floods of tears and looked a complete sorry state. Lisa's older sister Becky followed them out of the car.

As Brett looked at Lisa, the hate inside him burned. As far as he was concerned, Macy could very well still be alive if she'd been more responsible. Brett would never forgive her for not letting Macy stay the night at his when he asked. As soon as he saw that Macy was ill he would have taken action. He would have raced her to the hospital. There would have been no wasted time. There wouldn't have been the hour wasted when the babysitter was trying to contact Lisa. There wouldn't have been the time wasted of the babysitter not knowing what to do. Brett was going to let Lisa know exactly what he thought of her and not hold back. He would now have his turn to tell Lisa what an uncompromising, irresponsible bitch she had been. Every little thing that she had done was going to be repaid. Of course, she didn't know that yet, but Brett was driven by the thought of him handing her the comeuppance she deserved.

The moment had come. The pall-bearers were now making their way to the back of the carriage. Brett had wanted to carry the coffin with Steve and Bez originally, but he didn't think he would be able to keep himself together. He watched in heartache as Macy's coffin was slowly lifted out of the carriage. The pall-bearers carried Macy's coffin by hand at the handles as it was a somewhat smaller coffin than that of an adult. As the pall-bearers approached the chapel entrance, Brett swiftly made his way behind them. He let out a cry. Maria then hurried to him and grabbed his hand once again. Lisa made her way over to be behind Macy as she was taken into the church. She was close to Brett and he could smell her. The smell of her usual perfume filled the air and just the scent of Lisa fuelled the hate that he was feeling for her at that moment.

As they made their way into the church with the mourners following behind, the chapel was filled with the sound of the song 'Let It Go' from the Disney film *Frozen*, which was one of Macy's favourite songs. This made Brett wail out in pain as all he could think of was the way in which Macy would sing it using her hairbrush as a microphone when she stayed over at his flat. Maria held onto Brett even tighter as she could feel him quiver with the agony of the pain he was feeling. Brett made his way to the front of the church on the left side.

Maria, Bez, Steve and Kieran followed. Lisa and her family made their way to the right side at the front of the chapel. Cries echoed throughout the chapel as the vicar commenced the service.

Brett was in a daze during the service. He just looked at Macy's pale-pink coffin in disbelief that she was in there. Tara was stood at the altar reading out a poem she had written in tribute to Macy. Brett wasn't at all interested. To him, Tara was just a slag mate of Lisa's that had got in on the act as far as he was concerned. She was one of the influences in Lisa's life that contributed to Lisa being such a shit mum and he had no time for her.

As the service concluded it was time for the worst moment. Listening to the song 'Chandelier' by the artist Mia was going to kill Brett and he knew it. This was the song that he chose for Macy and the song that would play as her coffin was carried out of the chapel. Macy would dance all around his living room singing the song at the top of her lungs cutely mumbling the words that she didn't know.

The pall-bearers sullenly made their way over to Macy's coffin with their heads bowed. They lifted the coffin and slowly began to walk. The song played. Brett fell to pieces and almost dropped to his knees at the opening of the song. Steve and Bez rushed to him and held him up. He managed to stay on his feet and walk forward, crying out in pain. At the site of this, Maria also began to cry uncontrollably. Kieran placed his arm around Maria. And they walked forward, following Macy's coffin out of the chapel.

At the graveside, Brett felt as though he was in a dream as Macy's coffin was lowered into the ground. The site of his little girl being placed into the soil just didn't seem real. This was it. He would never see his little girl again. He managed to compose himself enough to place a single red rose onto her coffin.

As the minutes passed and the graveside service was concluded, people were beginning to make their way out of the cemetery gradually until there was just Brett, Maria, Kieran and Steve and Bez standing at the graveside, along with Lisa, her mum, her sister, Tara and a few of Lisa's other friends. Brett said his last goodbye to Macy by tearfully blowing her a kiss. Then he poignantly made his way back to the car, feeling empty and soulless as the car drove out of the cemetery gates.

20

INTO THE DEVIL'S EYES

Brett, Kieran, Steve and Bez went back to Maria's after the funeral. Brett didn't want a wake. He knew he wouldn't feel like being in a pub surrounded by people drinking after the funeral, and being around people drinking and socialising just didn't feel right. Brett didn't feel like being around anyone but he didn't feel like he wanted to be alone either. Kieran had bought Brett a massive bottle of Courvoisier brandy which Brett wasted no time in starting to knock down neat by the glass. After an hour or so Brett suggested that the lads go home as he wanted to try his best to get some sleep. He was mentally exhausted but he had no intention of going to sleep. It just felt like the lads were hanging around not really knowing what to say so he thought it best they be out of their discomfort and go home.

Brett sat alone sipping the brandy in the living room. Maria had fallen asleep on the settee. Brett was beginning to feel drunk. He was getting fidgety and didn't know what to do with himself. He decided to go for a walk. He left the house leaving Maria asleep on the settee. It was cold out but the cold didn't bother Brett like it usually would. He didn't care. He was walking the streets with his head down not concentrating where he was going. The screeching of a car slamming on the brakes to avoid running him over as he wandered onto the road was just enough to wake him out of his stupor. He carried on walking, not even knowing where he was headed. Then, as if by fate, he raised his head and he realised he was just around the corner from the Turnstile pub. Brett knew that Lisa would be in there as she had organised a wake there herself for Macy. He knew she would be in there with her usual crowd of chav mates and at that moment he decided he was going to pay her a visit.

Brett made his way towards the pub. He decided to walk around to the bar entrance as he knew Lisa and her cronies would all be in the lounge where they usually were. The bar was usually the room where the old boys of the estate would sit.

As he walked in the pub there were just a couple of people sat in the bar area. It was quiet but he could hear that it was busy in the lounge. He stood at the bar and ordered a brandy. He could see through to the lounge and he spotted Lisa straight away sitting with Tara and two other girls. Lisa looked drunk but that was nothing unusual.

There were people approaching her and hugging her and giving her drunken pub hugs. Brett looked on at Lisa with her pals. The kind of pals that treated a funeral almost like a night out and another excuse to get pissed, or so Brett thought. This made him grimace at the sheer sight of them all. Brett kept his head a little low and stood close to the wall, occasionally hiding his head behind the beer pumps, wary that he could be spotted by Lisa or any of her pub pals. He didn't want to cause a massive scene on the day of Macy's funeral, but he was itching to get Lisa alone and look into her eyes. He was fixated on her, just waiting to see if an opportunity for him to get her alone would present itself.

After many long minutes, Lisa arose from her seat, not looking in the most agile state but managing to stand. She then began to walk toward the lady's toilet which was located at the side of the bar. Brett looked on eagerly, almost ready to pounce. Lisa walked into the toilet, carelessly flinging the door back behind her, and Brett almost swooped over, grabbing the door and following her in. He was now right behind her and she hadn't even noticed as she attempted to walk forward to the cubicle.

"Hello, slag," said Brett in a devilish tone with a wicked smile on his face.

Lisa turned around to see Brett standing there.

"Just you stay away from me!" snapped Lisa in a panic. She could sense that Brett was out of his mind at that moment. The ball was in his court now, and she now held no cards.

"Speak again, and on your life I will smash your fuckin'

face right into that mirror!" said Brett calmly with a malicious gaze whilst pointing over to the large mirror on the wall.

Lisa said nothing but she began to tremble in fear. She didn't know what Brett was going to do.

Brett took a step closer. Lisa was too scared to move. She saw the look in Brett's eyes and it was as if he was possessed by the devil. She winced as he moved closer. There was no bravado from her this time.

"Don't worry, I'm not gonna hurt you today! Out of respect for my daughter on the day of her funeral, I'm gonna let you walk out of here and go back to your slag mates," said Brett in a chilling tone as he moved even closer to Lisa, his eyes bulging and lighting up like hundred-watt light bulbs. "But let me tell you something, me and you have some unfinished business, don't we, and soon I'll catch up with you again, and I'm gonna make sure you get exactly what you deserve. And I promise you, my face is gonna be the last one you'll see! I was the nice guy, the soft touch that you fuckin' abused, well now that lad who used to put up with your shit is gone, good ol' Brett the mug is gone forever! The monster is awake, and he owes you, big time!"

Brett moved even closer to Lisa and again she winced, frozen with fear. The look in Brett's eyes and the chill in his voice made him look twice as big and twice as capable. He was a scary sight to behold at that moment. She was just praying that someone would walk into the toilet. Brett chuckled maliciously as he callously looked Lisa up and down. He just stood there for a while knowing how scared she was. He was getting a kick out of her fear and the fact that he knew that she felt totally powerless. He looked her up and down again and he could see her trembling as the tears built in her eyes. This made him tick almost as if he was feeding off of her fear. Now the boot was on the other foot.

"Now, I want you to remember everything you've ever said to me! All the times you threatened me with not seeing Macy, the times when you mouthed off at me and verbally abused me, the move to London you were trying for when you planned to TAKE MY FUCKIN' DAUGHTER AWAY FROM ME! I want you to think about all of that before you die, because if it wasn't for you being such a fuckin' degenerate, pisshead slag, our daughter would still be alive!" growled Brett as he moved his face even closer.

Lisa flinched and almost lost balance as she desperately tried to move her head back. She had to place her hands on the cubicle door to stay upright as she nearly fell back.

Brett looked her up and down one last time before he slowly turned and walked out of the toilet. Lisa then broke down in tears out of the relief that she was still in one piece.

21

PLEASE – PART TWO

It was Friday afternoon, a couple of weeks after Macy's funeral, and Brett had popped back to his flat. He'd been staying at Maria's but now he wanted to go back to his flat to see how it felt.

In his mind he'd already decided to give his flat up. He couldn't live there anymore knowing the times he'd shared there with Macy, but he knew that he would have to face it sooner or later. There was an eerie silence as he placed the key in the door. A few letters slipped under the door as he pushed it open. He walked down the hall and looked into the little box room that he'd made into a bedroom for Macy. It was too much. He let out a groan as the tears filled his eyes as he placed his hands over his face. He quickly walked back to the front door and picked up the mail that was on the floor. He then went into the living room. He sat on the edge of the settee and began to reluctantly open his mail. As he was doing this he noticed music coming from the downstairs flat. Terry Shepard's mother had moved off the estate into a bungalow and the music was back. Once again it was loud, very loud, that same old repetitive pumping bass-line that used to drive him around the bend, and once again Brett was going to pay the lad downstairs a visit.

Brett gallantly walked into the kitchen and rummaged around in the kitchen drawers. The claw-hammer he was looking for was soon in his hand. He tucked it down the back of his trousers by the handle leaving the head of it sticking out of the back of his jeans. He carefully made sure the jacket covered it and then made his way out of the front door almost in a charge. He jogged down the concrete staircases in malicious glee. He got to the door and gave it a knock. After a few seconds the door opened to reveal the same lad that Brett had encountered before. The lad looked at Brett with a sigh and a slight roll of his eyes. He then folded his arms. Brett's face tightened and he looked straight into the lad's eyes.

"If you don't shut that fuckin' row up I'm gonna come in there and smash that fuckin' stereo to bits!" said Brett nodding his head with a slight smile looking totally sure of himself.

The lad looked surprised and then frowned.

"Who the fuck do you think you are?" said the lad, looking dumbfounded.

This was what Brett was waiting for. Brett smiled before smashing his forehead straight into the lad's nose. It was a flush shot almost making the sound of two snooker balls hitting one another. The lad fell back and was flat out on the floor. Brett walked in the doorway where the lad lay and kicked him in his ribcage repeatedly. The sound of the air being hoofed out of his body could be heard with every boot. Brett slammed the front door then made his way down the hallway towards the living room. The lad's girlfriend had arisen from her seat to see what was going on. She began to scream as she stood in the living room with the view of her boyfriend curled up on the floor in agony. Brett grabbed her by her face.

"Shut the fuck up," he snarled. "If you try and leg it, your boyfriend dies," he shouted as he pulled the claw hammer out of his jeans.

On seeing the hammer and the crazed look in Brett's eyes the girl didn't need to be told twice. She just stood there with her hands over her mouth in despair as her chest pumped panicked air from her lungs.

Brett then made his way over to the stereo and vigorously began to take it apart with the claw-hammer. By the time Brett had finished he was out of breath. The lad was by now on his knees in the hallway desperately trying to get to his girlfriend. Brett, now breathing heavily, casually sat down on the settee.

"Get me a glass of water," he said calmly to the girl whilst pointing in the direction of the kitchen with the hammer. The girl nervously ran to the kitchen and frantically filled a glass with tap water. She walked into the living room and handed it to Brett. Her hand was shaking so much she almost dropped the glass.

"Now fuckin' sit down!" said Brett looking directly at her. The girl did as she was told and sat down. Her brightly dyed blonde hair looked strained, the ends matted with the sweat that the fear in her had produced.

The lad was now in the living room on his feet, his mouth and nose pouring with dark blood. He was desperately holding his stomach. He began to say the word "please" in a hoarse tone, obviously in a great deal of pain. Brett stopped him from saying anything further by callously raising his hand.

"Funny old word that, isn't it? The word 'please'. I remember when I used to knock on your door and say the word 'please'. Can you remember that?" said Brett calmly with that same slight malicious smile.

Brett then downed his water in one gulp before throwing the glass across the living room smashing it on the floor making the girl jump almost out of her skin. The lad knew what Brett was getting at. He didn't say anything, he was just praying that Brett had proved his point. Brett slowly got to his feet and walked over to the lad, his girlfriend now in a fit of uncontrollable sobs. The lad looked fragile and still in total pain and discomfort. Brett bent down as he reached him.

"If I ever have to come here again for any reason, I swear the claw end of this hammer will be embedded into your head. Now do you understand?" said Brett up close to the lad's face. The lad nodded and Brett noticed his lips quiver in fear.

Brett then walked out of the flat as calm as a swan gliding across a quiet lake. Again Brett was feeding off the fear. The feeling of totally being in control with someone at his mercy strangely fulfilled him in a way he never expected. The pain he was feeling over losing Macy was that great it was almost as if it had turned into hate. Brett was now in control. The reason he had for living was gone, and the twisted cruel irony was that, in a strange way, he'd never felt more liberated.

22

PRESENCE FELT

Rumour had it that Lisa had swiftly left Leicester. Maria had heard from some friends that Lisa had just packed up and left. This wasn't a surprise to Brett as she had left a voice message of foul abuse on his phone a week or so before. She'd actually threatened him on the message saying that one of her Scottish uncles had paid someone to give him a punishment beating. Lisa could be a foul, nasty bitch and this particular message was in retaliation for how Brett had threatened her in the Turnstile pub on the night of Macy's funeral. Lisa obviously knew that she was leaving town when she sent the message and this was the reason for such bravado.

After hearing this message Brett had been to Lisa's house

but it was empty. Once again Lisa's cheek and disrespect had driven him crazy. Even after all she had done, she was cheeky enough to start threatening him. Brett was driven by the thought of finding her one day.

Brett had become fidgety lately. He wasn't sleeping very much and he'd become very twitchy as if there was a massive ball of energy violently trying to burst out of his body. He'd moved into the spare room at Maria's and given up his flat. He couldn't keep still, and would become violently agitated when trying to rest. To use up this energy he was constantly doing press-ups or sit-ups or punching a punchbag that he'd hung up outside on the wall in Maria's backyard. Sometimes he'd even punch the wall outside until his knuckles bled. Physical pain didn't seem to hurt him anymore. It was strange. He could feel the pain but it was almost like he wanted more when he felt it. A rush of adrenaline followed pain whenever he felt it. Nothing compared to the mental and emotional anguish he had felt since losing Macy; physical pain had lost the discomfort.

Steve and Bez had popped round to see Brett every week since the funeral and Kieran and Franny had been regular visitors too. Brett had sat around for a few weeks thinking about nothing but Macy, but now he no longer had anything to lose, he was eager to see how society would cope with a man with no fear, and totally free to settle every score with no thought of consequences.

***

It was the weekend. Steve and Bez had talked Brett into going to a charity boxing show which was being held at the Republic nightclub in the city centre. Steve and Bez had watched Brett wallow in anguish for weeks so they were determined to get him out. Brett actually wanted to go, he wanted nothing more than to bump into someone who had caused him misery in the past and let them know that the tables had now turned and things would be different. Two people in particular were not far from his thoughts with regards to this. Kristian Bell was high on the list. Kristian hadn't been about much. He'd sent Maria a few text messages but once again he was keeping his head down because there were still issues with the police supposedly looking for him. Kieran had told Brett that he'd heard through the grapevine that Kristian was in Amsterdam.

And there was also Glover. Brett had begun to fantasise about what he was going to do to Glover. The fear was gone, fear didn't exist.

It felt different being out and about in town to Brett. The world had changed. He looked at people out on the town having a good time, laughing and enjoying themselves, and he was thinking that he would never laugh like that again and truly feel it. The town smelt different, the beer tasted different, the people didn't look the same. To everybody else, everything was exactly the same as it was before, but to Brett, the world had changed.

The three of them got to the Republic nightclub and it was packed by the time they got in there. It was a big night. There was a special guest who was going to be appearing during the show. A celebrity gangster-type character named

'Big' Jim Bowers. He was quite a well-known figure from Coventry and once proclaimed himself as 'Coventry's hardest man'. He came with the usual shit that these so-called celebrity hard men come with, like being featured in a Danny Dyer series on hard men, and having a book published detailing his years of running the doors of Coventry and a short-lived bare-knuckle boxing career. This was the kind of stuff that Brett had come to despise, but he was in there now and was just going to see how the night panned out. He was looking out for Glover, his eyes peeled for the mere sight of him. It was a typical sort of vibe really, the usual lads out. A lot of half-arsed wannabes as usual and the pretend glamour-model girls that follow them around.

Brett did eventually notice Glover. He was standing ringside with none other than Mitchell Webb. Brett's eyes were glued to him. His heart was pumping and the adrenaline was beginning to flow with excitement. Steve noticed the situation and also noticed the malicious look on Brett's face.

"Brett, forget it, mate. You're not in the right frame of mind to kick off with him," said Steve to Brett with a slight shake of his head.

"I'll see how I feel!" replied Brett with a cocky grin. Steve didn't react but he was concerned for Brett.

As the night went on, Steve and Bez noticed the difference in Brett. His eyes had changed. It was as though he was looking through you when he spoke to you. They were sort of lifeless. When Brett was walking to the bar, instead of saying "Excuse me," or trying to squeeze past people, he just nudged them aside. People had looked over at him and

161

a few looked like they were going to say something, until Brett looked back at them. You could tell just by looking at him that he was fearless.

There was an announcement from the MC in the boxing ring. 'Big' Jim Bowers was going to make his way into the ring and do a charity auction. The money raised was going to the LOROS hospice in Leicester. There were various things in the auction, like signed Leicester City shirts and signed photographs of boxers like Ricky Hatton. Jim Bowers was quite a sight to behold. He was around 6ft 4in and weighed around twenty stone. He'd been in better shape in all honesty but he was still a sight to see, the guy was huge. He looked the part. He had a bald head and a jet-black beard, with hands the size of spades that you could notice as he grabbed the mic. The crowd responded warmly to him; it seemed to be in awe of him because of his notoriety and the fact that he'd been on the TV. He looked even bigger when he was in the centre of the ring stood next to the MC.

After the auction he answered a few questions from some people at ringside as part of a Q and A. Once he'd finished the Q and A, the ring announcer was back on the mic.

"Now, is there anyone here who thinks they can go three rounds with 'Big' Jim Bowers?" said the ring announcer with a smile.

Jim Bowers played up to the announcement by walking around the ring puffing out his chest.

"If there is anyone who can last three rounds with Big Jim, there's a £500 cash prize," said the ring announcer again with jest-like enthusiasm.

This announcement appeared to take the crowd aback. People were looking around for anyone who dared to get in the ring and have a go. Jim Bowers continued to play his part by shadow boxing as he stood in the ring, and the sight of his quick, big fists and the total ferocity was enough to quash any ideas from anyone in the crowd. You could hear the excuses from some of the so-called hard men as they joked that they were too pissed or too well dressed and such things. The ring announcer gave it one last attempt to try and tempt a would-be giant slayer by giving a countdown.

"Right then 10… 9… 8… 7… 6," bellowed the ring announcer.

Brett looked at 'Big' Jim Bowers and for no reason other than the frequency of hate rising up within him, decided he would be the one who stepped up. He began to take his jacket off. Steve and Bez saw what Brett was about to do.

"Are you off your fuckin' head?" said Steve as Brett handed him his jacket. Bez was just speechless.

"Yeah, fuck it, let's go and have it with the cunt!" replied Brett cockily before swiftly walking forward.

People saw Brett making his way over to the ring and the ring announcer was quite surprised to see someone take up the challenge. A few people began to cheer Brett on as he hurried to the ring. He struggled a little as he climbed onto the ring apron, but he had a hand from a couple of people who were ringside.

The ring announcer, looking surprised, put his arm around Brett as people looked on aghast that someone was as eager as Brett to take up the challenge. Brett was holding his hands out looking at the crowd, not believing that there was no one else in the whole place that had taken up the challenge.

"Well, folks, it looks like we've got a challenger after all," said the MC to the crowd as he walked Brett to the centre of the ring.

"What's your name, fella?" asked the MC with a smile as he aimed the mic towards Brett's mouth.

"Brett Kelso," replied Brett clearly, with a smile of his own.

"And where are you from?" asked the MC.

"Here in Leicester, New Parks," replied Brett.

There was a cheer from a portion of the crowd on hearing the words 'New Parks'.

Brett had no fear whatsoever. Even the size of Jim Bowers was nothing in his eyes at that moment. What pain could be worse than what he'd been through?

Jim Bowers walked to the centre of the ring after being summoned by the MC. He looked down at Brett with his hands on his hips. Brett smiled at him, calm and collected, as if he had just stepped out of the shower. This surprised Jim Bowers and he knew from that moment that there was absolutely no fear in Brett.

Brett was a big enough lad, but even his sixteen-stone frame was engulfed by the huge Jim Bowers. The MC stepped between them and made a couple of wisecracks about them having to wait before they got stuck into each other. Brett was enjoying the stand-off, his adrenaline was pumping and he just wanted to lay into Bowers and destroy his face. The MC explained that Brett would be in the red corner and the rounds would only be a minute and a half long, as it was an exhibition. Brett nodded and walked over to his corner. He was quickly allocated a cornerman by a few of the organisers. The cornerman was a small old silver-haired chap, introduced to Brett as John.

John gave Brett a pat on the shoulder and swiftly told him to remove his top and T-shirt. Brett looked at John a little taken aback at this request. Brett frowned before removing his top and T-shirt and handed it to John who then handed it over to a chap at ringside. John then held up a vest and gestured Brett to bend his head so he could put the vest on him. Brett looked down at the white acrylic vest. It was a little tight, with the words 'Braunstone ABC boxing' emblazoned in the centre in bold red writing. John was then handed some boxing gloves from a steward.

"Here, try these on lad!" said John as he grabbed Brett's left hand.

As John fiddled to get the black boxing gloves on Brett's hands, Brett could see they weren't a perfect fit. They were a bit tight and the leather was solid, as if they hadn't been used much. They felt good on Brett's hands and he felt ready, like a pressure cooker ready to blow. He looked over at the other corner and he saw 'Big' Jim Bowers with his gloves on as he turned and faced Brett's corner. Jim Bower's gloves looked big and cushiony in comparison to Brett's. John the cornerman then moved close towards Brett to give him some instructions.

"Have you boxed before, lad?" asked John.

"I did a bit of training when I was a teenager on and off for a couple of years, but don't worry, he's going down!" replied Brett whilst grinning. John chuckled at him.

"Keep your hands up, cover that chin, keep moving and just pop that jab out when you can. Don't do anything daft or wild," said John in Brett's ear.

Brett cheekily patted John on the head.

"Don't worry, he's going down!" said Brett. Again, John chuckled.

"Just get back here in one piece," said John with a smile and a slight shake of his head.

"Ten seconds!" shouted the MC as the referee made his way into the ring.

John sprayed Brett's face with some water from a water bottle and then attempted to place a gumshield in Brett's mouth. Brett refused by shaking his head.

"Don't need the gumshield," said Brett.

"Suit yourself," replied John with a shrug of his shoulders.

There was an electric atmosphere in the place. People looked on in intrigue as 'Big' Jim Bowers stretched in his corner. Steve and Bez were in awe of Brett, not quite believing that he had stepped in the ring to go toe to toe with 'Big' Jim Bowers. Bowers' corner told him to take it easy and coast a bit before putting the pressure on. They took Brett for what he was, a chancer that didn't really have a chance.

The MC began to hype up the crowd before the first bell went and then it was time. 'Ding ding', that all-familiar sound of the boxing bell.

Bowers steamed out of his corner at Brett as Brett casually walked to the centre of the ring. Bowers swung but Brett managed to slip the punch. Bowers began to unload but Brett covered up well and took the shots on

166

the arms and elbows. Brett was forced back against the ropes as he grabbed Bowers. The sheer strength of Bowers, and the weight of him stacked on top of Brett, stretched the ropes, making them look like they were going to snap. Brett grabbed Bowers' arms and leaned down and spoke in Bowers' ear.

"I thought you were supposed to be a hard man. You punch like a pussy!" said Brett with a cackle.

This frustrated Bowers who then broke free of Brett's hold. Bowers was grunting and snorting like some sort of mad bull. Any intention of taking it easy on a random chancer like Brett was now out of the window. Bowers was ready to unload again but Brett just smiled at him. Bowers charged forward and began to unload. This time he caught Brett with a hard right hand to the stomach. It was a hard shot, enough to draw a gasp from the people at ringside. Brett felt the blow, it hurt him, but at the same time gave him satisfaction. It was strange; it was like the pain gave him a charge.

"Come on, hit me again!" shouted Brett.

Bowers kept swinging lefts and rights, catching Brett on the arms as Brett covered up. Brett was stuck to his spot. John his cornerman was shouting at him to move and "Get away from the ropes," but Brett leaned back on the ropes taking Bowers' shots to his body whilst grabbing his head and taunting him. Bowers then showed his true colours. In a fit of rage, he brought his head down and butted Brett right in the bridge of his nose. The pain was immediate and the blood ran out of Brett's nose like water from a tap. There was an 'ooh' from the crowd as they beheld the dirty tactic from

Bowers. The referee stepped in and berated Bowers for the headbutt. He was about to disqualify Bowers.

Brett was livid and in a split second all of the pain he had felt within the past few months turned into sheer hate. The memory of Macy laying there in the hospital bed bombarded his brain. He let out a roar of pain and the hate and rage completely over took him. He launched a big right hand at Bowers who was caught unaware as he was arguing with the referee. The shot stunned him tremendously. Brett then unleashed a flurry of lefts and rights with ferocious speed. Bowers tried to cover up but it was no use; Brett was like a man possessed by a demon as he laid into Bowers whilst screaming out. It was like all of his pain was being released at that one moment and Bowers was the recipient. A big right from Brett caught Bowers flush on the chin and Bowers crumbled and dropped down to his knees. Brett continued the onslaught and Bowers must have been caught by at least ten hard shots to the head. Bowers fell to the right onto the canvas and was now out cold.

Brett had taken out the 'Big' Jim Bowers in one round. There was a tremendous roar from the crowd and Steve and Bez were jumping up and down and hugging each other in wild excitement as they had witnessed Brett take apart the 'Big' Jim Bowers.

A big guy from Bowers' corner jumped into the ring and ran towards Brett, angered at the fact that Brett hit Bowers whilst he was on his knees. Brett could see the guy running towards him and with the same speed and intensity flung everything he had at the guy. The guy couldn't put up much resistance and he too crumbled to the canvas.

All hell began to break loose as more of Bowers' team began to jump into the ring. Organisers and security jumped into the ring and surrounded Brett so nobody could get to him. Police officers who were present at the event also made their way into the ring. The ring was packed with people and the atmosphere in the place had now changed from electric to frightening. The sight of the police was enough to gradually calm things, and people's attention had turned to Bowers, who was out cold but twitching awkwardly where he lay. The MC was on the mic urging everybody to stay calm. Brett looked over at the MC and rushed over to him and grabbed the mic. The MC wasn't going to argue with Brett as he had just witnessed what Brett was capable of, and the look in Brett's eye sent a shiver down his spine.

Brett put the mic to his lips as people looked on in awe and disbelief at the total ferocity Brett had just displayed.

"Where are all the fucking gangsters? Where are all the fuckin' hard men in here? Load of wankers!" shouted Brett snarling like some sort of wild animal. He was a scary sight to behold with his eyes wide, shining like headlights, and the veins bulging out of his neck.

"Come on, where the fuck are ya?" snarled Brett again before throwing the mic to the ground, which made a deafening thump in the speakers.

There was a silence from the crowd as Brett made his way out of the ring looking for his T-shirt and top. People were looking at Brett in astonishment. Anybody who'd never heard of Brett Kelso would now remember the name.

23

PAY DAY

A couple of weeks after the night at the Republic nightclub and people were still talking about this chap called Brett Kelso who'd taken 'Big' Jim Bowers apart. It meant nothing to Brett. Brett's attention was now focused on Glover. The night at the Empire, when Glover had slapped him to the ground when he was with Kimberly, was etched in his mind.

***

Brett made his way to the Empire on a particularly bitter-cold Thursday night. He was by himself. He looked for Glover the moment he walked in the pub but there was no sign of him. Brett pulled up a stool to the bar and ordered a brandy. He sat there with his head bowed and looked over at the door every time somebody walked into the pub, hoping it was Glover.

Brett could then feel someone's presence as he sat sipping his brandy. There was a tall lad standing next to him.

"All right, mate, are you Brett, the lad who done that Jim Bowers at Republic the other week?" said the lad with a hint of excitement as he held out his hand.

Brett just looked at the lad calmly.

"Fuck off!" said Brett flatly as he then turned his head and took another sip of his brandy.

The lad's face dropped.

"What's that all about?" asked the lad looking deflated.

Brett turned his head, looking frustrated.

"I'll tell you what it's all about, I've been drinking in this pub for fifteen years. I've seen your face in here for about the past ten of them years. Not once have you acknowledged me in that time. In fact, you're usually running up to Glover licking his arse! Well carry on and keep away from me!" snapped Brett as he then turned away.

The lad then sheepishly walked away.

Brett waited and waited but there was no sign of Glover. He stayed until last orders and still Glover hadn't made his way into the Empire.

He went to the Empire the following night, then the night after that. All of the usual people that were usually in the Empire had shown their faces at some point, everyone except for Glover, and Steve and Bez for that matter.

Brett was frustrated as he made his way out of the

Empire on this cold Sunday night. He wanted Glover that bad, it was as though electricity was surging through his veins at the mention of his name. He grimaced as he walked to the car park, disappointed that another night had passed without payback. Then, as he made his way, he noticed a black Mercedes pull up outside of the pub. Brett looked over and behold, Glover was in the driver seat. Pure excitement surged through Brett at this moment.

Glover made his way out of the car with a pretty, petite girl making her way out of the passenger seat. Glover began walking towards the entrance with the girl alongside him. Brett then realised that the girl with Glover was indeed Abbey, the girl that had ignored Brett at the arrival of Glover and his cronies months ago in the Empire. Brett then swiftly turned around and made his way back towards the entrance of the Empire with his hands in his pockets. This was it. The moment that Brett had wanted was now here. There were no nerves, no butterflies, just hate.

Glover made his way to the bar and Brett was right behind him. As Glover stood at the bar with Abbey, Brett walked past, purposefully nudging him just as he'd nudged Brett on the night he was with Kimberly. Glover was a big guy, but the sheer force Brett had hit him with made him lunge forward. Glover screwed his face in rage and then turned to look at Brett who was standing there casually with his hands in his pockets.

"What you looking at, you big, ugly, flat-nose cunt, and what's a good-looking slag like that doing with a fat, ugly wanker like you?" said Brett cockily.

Glover looked at Brett in total disbelief with a scowl. He

didn't say anything he just quickly reached for one of the few empty pint glasses that had been left on the bar. Glover lunged forward towards Brett and swung with the glass. Brett moved out of the way with the glass just skimming his head.

Glover wasn't the quickest and the momentum of the swing he took made him lose balance and fall against the bar. Brett then smashed Glover with a big right hand to the head then just unleashed with lefts and rights in a fit of ferocious intensity. Glover had dropped the glass and he attempted to grab Brett. Again, the hate had taken over Brett and he cried out in rage. All that Brett could feel was the abundance of hate. Glover desperately tried to make a grab for Brett. Brett grabbed Glover's face and pressed his thumb as hard as he could into Glover's eye. Glover could do nothing but bring his hands to his face to protect his eye as he grunted in pain. Brett then smashed Glover ferociously with a flurry of lefts and rights until Glover tumbled to the ground. Again, the image of Macy's lifeless body hit Brett's mind and he began to stamp on Glover's face as he lay flat on his back.

"You bastard, you fucking, no-good bastard!" snarled Brett again and again as he continuously smashed the soul of his foot into Glover's face.

Abbey stepped back looking on in sheer terror. "Somebody do something!" she shouted.

Glover's arms were now laid out and he was now in the crucifix position and totally unconscious. Brett was out of breath as he gave Glover's face one more laboured stamp. The few Sunday-night regulars looked on in disbelief, a couple of them made a half-hearted attempt of approaching Brett but the look on his frenzied face made them think otherwise. Glover's face was now a total mess of broken teeth, blood and snot.

"That's enough, he's had enough. I'm calling the police!" shouted Jan the landlady, who before now was in no particular rush to quell the carnage as she too was no big fan of Glover.

Brett looked over.

Glover was a mess but Brett was suddenly calm. Abbey was now crying as silence filled the pub. Brett looked over at her.

"Why the fuck is a girl like you into that piece of shit?" said Brett as he walked over to her.

Abbey winced as Brett got up close to her.

"You silly little girl," said Brett sarcastically.

Abbey was shaking. Brett looked at her shaking his head.

"Find a nice guy, you stupid cunt!" said Brett before turning away.

Brett then took a big sigh before walking over to where Glover lay unconscious. He then callously laughed as he unzipped his flies and then, after fidgeting around a little, began to urinate on Glover's face. Brett continued to laugh as the piss rained down on Glover, some of it falling into his mouth. Brett then began to whistle as he was pissing, as if he were standing at the urinal in the gent's toilet. He shook the last bit of piss down on Glover before casually zipping up his flies. People looked on in shock and utter disgust, but fear and a general dislike of Glover stopped them from getting involved. Brett then just made his way out of the pub.

24

PRISON OR DEATH

The word was that Glover was in the hospital with a broken nose, broken teeth and his jaw wired up. The police had investigated the incident but Glover never said anything about Brett. Glover may have been an arsehole but he didn't give Brett up to the police, and out of fear and the old-school values of the New Parks estate, neither did anybody who witnessed the incident in the Empire that night. Brett knew that Glover would come back at him but he didn't care. He didn't care if he lived or died, life had become nothing to him. As far as Brett was concerned, society was now at his mercy, because he had absolutely nothing to lose.

***

Brett was sat in Maria's living room in the late afternoon. A few days had passed since the incident with Glover. Maria was out with Damian. Brett was just sitting there in the silence, staring into space. He would do this a lot lately, particularly when nobody was around. He would just slip into daydreams, thinking about Macy. Brett noticed his phone ringing. He pulled it out of his pocket and looked down at the screen, he didn't recognise the number. He was intrigued.

"Hello," said Brett as he answered the phone.

A deep husky voice replied. "You've taken a massive liberty with Glover and it's gonna be put right!" said the voice.

Brett guessed rightly that it was Mitchell Webb.

"Glover's big enough and ugly enough to look after himself, but if you fancy getting involved, you can be next," said Brett in wicked excitement as he sat up from his chair.

"Are you for real? You're in way over your head, mate," replied Mitchell.

"Mitchell, let's put this into perspective, mate" said Brett cockily. "You're nearly into your fifties, you've a good life, a great-looking wife, you've made your money and you've gone legal. You've got nothing to prove. But let me tell you, all of that will be put into jeopardy if you fuck with me, because I've got fuck all, and I promise you, all I'm living for is the screams of no-good cunts in my ears. People like Glover and others like him are nothing but prey to me. Do you really want to put yourself at risk for an arsehole like Glover? because you will have to kill me to stop me. Do you want that pretty wife of yours visiting you in prison for the next twenty-five years or identifying your body at four in the morning? Those are your options, my friend!" said Brett chillingly.

Mitchell couldn't quite believe what he was hearing but he knew Brett was serious. Deep down, Mitchell knew that Glover had taken massive liberties with a lot people and had been nothing but a vicious bully boy. Out of duty he stood for Glover and took it upon himself to try and muscle Brett, but at that moment he knew Brett was a different kind of animal, and he knew that a conflict with him would go all the way to the end of the line, wherever that would be. It would either be the cemetery gates or a prison cell. Mitchell was a hard man but his heart wasn't totally in this one, and Brett could sense it.

"You've got some fuckin' front, I'll give you that!" said Mitchell, angered by Brett's reaction.

"Nothing to do with any front, mate. I'm ready to die… are you?" said Brett coldly.

Silence filled the air, and there were no more words. Mitchell hung up the phone.

25

HEADHUNTING

The streets were always watching and the whisperers were always whispering. Brett's name now came with a tag, and that that tag was fear. The word had gone around that there was a new gun in town, and that gun came in the form of Brett Kelso. The stories of the frenzied attack on Glover and the demolition of *the* 'Big' Jim Bowers had circulated, and from each pair of lips that spoke of these events came the added extras that only added to Brett's new reputation. But Brett didn't need any gossip for people to start to fear him. Over the next few weeks, his actions alone were the true testament of his new character.

He was now like an out-of-control locomotive that was ready to smash through anything that came in his way. The number of people on the receiving end of Brett's punishment was growing. If Brett saw anyone who was known to be a bully or somebody that fancied themselves as some sort of big-time Charlie, he would look for an opportunity to put them in their place.

A good example of this was when he was waiting for a taxi at the end of a night's drinking in town with Kieran and Franny. Brett had begun to spend more time with Kieran, and Franny was always in tow to join them.

As the three of them waited in the packed taxi rank, Brett noticed a guy by the name of Gary Redshaw. Gary Redshaw was a person who thought very highly of himself and liked to think he was something special. He was a party boy and was very popular due to the big parties and massive club nights he organised. He'd promoted a lot of big house music events in and around the Midlands and liked to portray himself as some sort of playboy. Famous footballers and known glamour girls would attend his events and for a lot of people his parties were some of the hottest tickets in town.

Gary usually surrounded himself with muscle. Due to the money his events brought in, he had a known crew of heavies ready to pursue his interests. This contributed to his over-inflated ego. Brett had never liked him. He was arrogant and cocksure of himself and he was well known for his poor treatment of the people that helped him promote his club nights. These were usually young lads that held him in high regard and he would take advantage of this. Gary also had his pick of the pretty young girls. The type of girls that saw a man like him as some sort of prize and too immature to realise that the guy was nothing but a massive arsehole.

Brett sat in the taxi rank looking over at Gary. Gary was acting his usual self, cocksure and loud, talking as if he was the most important person in the room. He was with a group of people, a mixed group of guys and girls that looked like they were ready to party. Brett looked over at Gary with a frown. Franny, who was more than a bit drunk and half-slumped on his chair, commented on what a wanker he thought Gary was.

Brett looked on and noticed Gary make his way out of the taxi rank. As he walked out of the taxi rank he looked over at Brett and gave him a look of complete disdain, a cocky side glance. This was all the invitation that Brett needed and he soon followed him.

As Brett made his way out of the taxi rank he noticed Gary had walked around the corner to the almost-empty little side street to have a piss up against the wall. As Brett walked past him closely, he whispered the word "Cunt" clearly so Gary could hear. Gary screwed his face and turned to Brett.

"What did you just say?" said Gary as he hastily buttoned up his flies looking both angry and bemused.

"I said you're a cunt!" said Brett loudly with a cocky smile.

"What! Do you want it, yeah?" replied Gary as he menacingly marched forward with his fists clenched.

"Yeah, let's have it!" said Brett in fiendish glee as he ran forward towards Gary.

Gary didn't have a chance as Brett ferociously unloaded on him with tremendous speed, fuelled by the uncompromising hate and rage that burst out of his body.

A tremendous flurry of blows rained down on Gary as he slumped to the floor, trying to hold onto Brett to keep him up as he went down. Brett finished him off with a knee to the face, leaving Gary violently twitching on the cold concrete.

Brett was treating his new lust for violence like sport, and a week or so later, on a wet Thursday night, his actions were about to take a more sinister turn.

***

Franny was dropping Brett home after they had hit a few pubs. Kieran had got a taxi home earlier as he didn't fancy getting drunk and having a hangover for work the next day, but Franny and Brett had stayed out. Brett was trying his best to drink away his pain but the main escape from his anguish now came from the punishment he dished out to the people he felt deserved it.

As Franny was driving along the outskirts of the city centre, Brett, who was sat in the passenger seat, noticed a lad that he knew walking along the street. It was a lad named Tom Conrad. He was younger than Brett, around twenty-five, but Tom Conrad and his antics were well known. Tom had got a reputation for himself as a vicious menace. He was a burglar and a thief, and he also had a regular crack cocaine habit. He'd been a major headache for a lot of people in the west end of Leicester and there was a long list of people that he had troubled.

The last Brett had heard of Tom Conrad was a few months back when he'd heard that Tom had gatecrashed an eighteenth birthday party. It was the eighteenth birthday party of the daughter of a chap that Brett had known for a long time, a chap by the name of Billy McIntyre. Brett liked Billy, he was a lively and funny bloke and he would always make Brett laugh whenever he bumped into him.

Brett had heard that Tom Conrad and a group of his cronies had gatecrashed Billy's daughter's eighteenth birthday party at the west end working-men's club. Tom began to get rowdy and cause trouble and Billy asked him to leave. Things began to get heated and Tom and his boys ended up giving Billy a beating. Billy was left in a pretty bad way and sustained a broken eye socket and cheekbone and was left unconscious with his daughter and her party guests screaming in terror.

This left Brett livid. Billy's fighting days were behind him as he was well into his fifties. At the time Brett couldn't get involved as he had Macy to think of, but that was then.

The beating Tom had given Billy was just the tip of the iceberg. Brett had also heard that Tom was in the middle of burgling a house when he was disturbed by the owner, who was a sixty-two-year-old woman. When the woman began to scream and become hysterical, Tom held a Stanley knife to her face and threatened to slash her to ribbons. The police couldn't get a positive identification on Tom and there were no witnesses so he was free to swan around as he pleased. Billy didn't go to the police either as he was scared of any retaliation that could be aimed towards his daughter. Billy was also 'old school' and would rather settle things without the police being involved.

As Brett looked on at Tom as he walked, he decided it was time for Tom to be made an example of.

It was late and the streets were almost empty. Tom turned left onto the side street as Brett gazed at him. Brett explained the situation to Franny who, in true Franny fashion, was eager to be involved in dishing out any punishment once he'd heard what a toerag Tom Conrad was. Brett asked if Franny had any tools in the car. Franny explained that there was an old spanner under the passenger seat and half a can of petrol in the boot that had been in the car for months. Franny slowed the car down a little and turned into the side street. They both kept a keen eye on Tom. Tom turned and looked at the car as he noticed it had slowed down.

"Excuse me," shouted Brett as he lowered the passenger seat window.

Tom looked over, lowering the hood that had been draped over his black baseball cap.

"You talking to me?" said Tom with a scowl, his pale face and weasel-like features doing nothing but angering Brett more.

"Yes, mate, do you know where Elizabeth House is?" replied Brett pretending to need directions.

Tom walked over to the car with his hands in his pockets. He looked a bit dubious at first but leaned down to the passenger car window and began to give directions. As he was pointing towards the direction of Elizabeth house he glanced at Brett realising that he recognised him.

"Hey, don't I know you?" said Tom.

Brett looked at Tom intensely.

"Yeah, I think you do, I'm a mate of Billy's!" said Brett angrily as he made a grab for Tom.

Brett had a firm grip on Tom's jacket. Tom began to struggle and shout at Brett, demanding, "Get the fuck off me!"

"Drive the fuckin' car, Franny!" shouted Brett.

This caught Franny by surprise but he quickly released the brake and put his foot down on the accelerator. Tom shouted like crazy as the speed progressed and he struggled to break free. Brett began to laugh as Tom's legs desperately tried to keep up with the speed of the car. Franny also began to chuckle as he tried to keep the speed at a level that Tom could maintain on his feet.

"Speed up, Franny, speed up!" shouted Brett as he laughed loudly.

Franny put his foot down a bit more and Tom lost his footing. He screeched loudly as he bumped the floor and his legs scraped the road. Brett could hold on no longer as the force pulled Tom from his grip. Tom tumbled and rolled into the road. Franny slammed on the brakes and he and Brett both looked back at Tom sprawled in the middle of the road. Tom was moving but in too much pain to make a get-away.

Brett told Franny to reverse to the spot where Tom lay.

Franny was cautious of any passers-by that may have witnessed what had just happened but there was no one around, apart from a few people walking down the main road in the distance. Brett got out of the car when they reached Tom. He grabbed the big spanner from underneath the passenger seat. The force of the drag had pulled one of Tom's shoes from his feet. His left leg was bleeding quite heavily through his shredded jeans and there was a tremendous graze below his knee. His head was bleeding as well, but Brett couldn't make out the wound as there was quite a bit of blood.

Tom was groaning in pain holding his leg whilst shouting obscenities at Brett and Franny.

"So you like threatening old women with Stanley knives, do you?" said Brett coldly as he looked down on Tom.

"What the fuck you on about?" shouted Tom, his words strained with pain.

Brett turned to Franny, who was now looking a bit nervous as he was wary of witnesses and any cameras that may be viewing their actions.

"Come on, let's get him in the car and take the mouthy bastard for a ride," snapped Brett.

Franny quickly made his way around the car. Tom began to shout and swear at the both of them. This angered Franny, who then began to lay a few boots into him.

"Let's just get him in the fuckin' car!" said Brett.

They grabbed Tom and tried their best to bundle him into the back seat of the car. He was struggling but in too much pain to fight the both of them off. Brett began to get frustrated as Tom fought and struggled so he smashed his left shin hard with the spanner. Tom screamed in pain and reached down to grab his leg. This made it easier for Brett and Franny to bundle him into the back seat. Brett got into the back seat with Tom, who was now grinding his teeth in pain. Brett smashed him a few more times viciously with the spanner, which subdued any fight that Tom had left in him.

"Shut the fuck up!" snarled Brett as he laid into him.

"Right, let's get him up to Markfield, we'll take him up to the woods," said Brett to Franny.

Franny was a little reluctant. Franny could be volatile, but pub brawls and straighteners were more Franny's thing. This was kidnap, and Franny knew the possible implications of such actions, but he was not the type of lad to back out and leave a mate to sort things out by himself, so even though he was reluctant, he went along with Brett's wishes. They were in this together now.

Franny began the journey to Markfield. Tom's persona had now gone from anger and shouting obscenities to pleading for his release. It was no use. Brett callously told Tom that he was bored of listening to him and again began to lay into him with the spanner.

There was a lot of woodland around as they approached the village of Markfield, and it was a very eerie scene as they reached the outskirts of the village. It was pitch-black as Franny pulled up and parked the car at the side of the woods on a winding country road. Franny still didn't know exactly what Brett had in mind.

"Right, get out of the car!" said Brett to Tom.

Brett leaned over Tom and opened the car door. Tom slowly crawled out of the car, still bloodied and in pain as he murmured. Brett gestured Franny to get out of the car and follow Tom. Brett also got out of the car. The silence filled the dark air and all that could be heard was the wind through the trees as the three of them stood there feeling like the only three people alive on this lonesome country lane. The cold of the wind bit them as they stood in the silence.

"Take your clothes off!" said Brett to Tom in a very direct manner.

"What! I'll fuckin' freeze to death out here. Come on, please!" pleaded Tom desperately.

Brett smiled.

"What happened to the big dangerous lad that likes to beat fifty-odd-year-old blokes up at birthday parties? And the bloke that likes to threaten to slash old women's faces?" said Brett, his smile now turned to a scowl as he looked Tom in the eye. "Now either take your clothes off or I pour petrol all over you and set you alight!"

Brett angrily then stomped to the boot of the car and fetched the can of petrol.

Tom, who had just managed to lean up against the car, didn't know what to do. It was bitterly cold and he couldn't bear to take his clothes off, but Brett didn't look like he was messing about and the sight of the petrol can in Brett's hands was enough to make him reluctantly begin to take his jacket off, but he was in no hurry to take off the rest of his clothes.

Franny looked over at Brett with a grin as Tom slowly slipped off his jacket.

"Put your jacket in the car!" said Brett.

As Tom reluctantly turned and threw his jacket into the car, a Stanley knife fell out of the jacket pocket. Brett and Franny noticed it as it tumbled to the ground. Brett made a reach for it whilst placing the can of petrol on the ground.

"Right, just take your clothes off, else I start carving you up!" said Brett as he pointed the knife at Tom's face.

Tom didn't know what to do. Even a lad who was as

callous as he could be knew the seriousness of the situation he was in. He didn't fancy being naked in the cold in the early hours in the pitch-black night on a long empty country lane.

"Please! Don't leave me out here. For fuck's sake, lads, come on, I could die out here!" pleaded Tom.

Brett began to get frustrated. He grabbed Tom by the T-shirt and began to swipe and simulate slashing him with the Stanley knife. Tom cowered feebly. In sheer frustration Brett then picked up the can of petrol and quickly screwed off the lid before tipping the contents all over Tom as he kneeled helpless on the cold ground. Franny looked on wondering whether Brett was actually going to set Tom alight.

"All right, all right," said Tom, holding his hands up defensively as he was now soaked in the petrol, the scent of which now filled the air.

Tom then slowly took his soaked clothes off, struggling as he was still in pain. He was a pathetic sight. His pale, naked body shivered as he sat scrunched up trying to hug himself to keep warm. Brett and Franny burst out in laughter as they looked at him sitting pathetically, looking helpless with his teeth chattering as the cold wind hit him. Brett asked Franny to put Tom's clothes in the back seat of the car.

Brett then asked Tom if there was anybody he wanted to ring to say goodbye to before he died.

"Get on your knees!" said Brett in a quiet tone.

Tom realised he was going to die. He couldn't make a run for it as his legs were in too much pain. In sheer terror, he lost control of his bodily functions and began to urinate and shit himself as he anticipated how fire overcoming his body would feel.

"Don't kill me! I'm begging you, don't kill me!" pleaded Tom with his eyes filled with tears.

Brett then burst out laughing again.

"Franny, get your phone and take a photo of this cunt!" said Brett cruelly.

Franny, who was now chuckling at the fact that Tom had shit himself, wasted no time in taking a series of photos of the pale, naked Tom, whose legs were covered in shit and blood. Tom didn't care about any embarrassment. He realised he was never going to see daylight again. He was never going to wake up on a sunny day and look forward to what the day may bring. He was never again going to feel the taste of a nice, cold beer. This was it.

"Come on, Franny, let's go," said Brett.

Franny was now in hysterics but managed to make his way back in the car. Brett looked at Tom.

"Good luck finding your way home. If I hear of you in Leicester again, we're coming back to this spot!" said Brett as he made his way to the passenger seat of the car.

Tom felt a sense of relief that he'd never felt before. A few seconds ago he was certain he was going to die. Now, even though he was out in the country, naked and covered in petrol in the pitch-black cold night, he'd never felt more happy to be alive. Franny, who was also relieved that he wasn't an accomplice to murder, started the car and drove off, leaving Tom naked and alone at the back of woodland. Franny was still laughing as he drove.

"Fuckin' hell, Brett, for a second there I really thought you were gonna kill the cunt," said Franny with a chuckle.

"So did I!" replied Brett.

Franny looked over at Brett, realising he was deadly serious. Brett looked forward, expressionless, as he stared into the road. The two of them didn't say one more word to each other for the whole journey back to Leicester.

26

A FEAST OF FRIENDS

Steve and Bez didn't like what Brett had now become as the months passed. They knew he was still in great pain over Macy, but they both felt like they had lost their friend. Brett was now a person with a notorious reputation that commanded fear. People began to think he was mad and out of control.

His infectious smile was long gone but the monster was clear in his eyes. He was now like a devilish clown that invited confrontation and took great pleasure in dishing out pain with intense severity.

Every time they saw him just lately, there would be someone on the receiving end of a beating.

Brett would never intimidate or bully people, but if he

thought that somebody needed to be made an example of, he wasted no time in dishing out punishment. An example of this was when the three of them had recently popped into town for a drink one evening. As they attempted to walk into the Terrace Bar, the bouncer stopped them with the words "Not tonight!" When Brett asked what the reason was, the bouncer's response was a stern, "I don't need a reason." Brett reacted by headbutting the bouncer and then laying into him. Brett thought back to occasions when bouncers had smugly turned him away in the past and made him look silly.

As the bouncer hit the ground, Brett laid the boot in until the bouncer was motionless. He then laughed and taunted him as he lay on the ground.

This was typical of Brett just lately; anybody that was arrogant enough to treat him or his friends with disrespect would be hit so hard that the rest of the city would hear about it.

Another example of this was when the three of them had recently been to the Soar Point pub to watch Leicester City play Chelsea. There was a big red-haired chap in the pub who was being a bit loud and brash, singing football songs. He was being a bit of a nuisance, bumping into people as he cheered throughout the game, and had spilled his pint close to where Brett was standing. Brett told him to stay out of his way to which the chap responded by telling Brett to "Fuck off". He would later regret these words when Brett followed him to the toilet, leaving him unconscious and bloodied on the toilet floor.

Brett was also snorting unseen amounts of coke at every social outing.

The irony of all of this was that people now seemed keen to give Brett opportunity and put money in his hand. His pockets were now always full.

People who promoted big-scale music events were keen to have Brett's name associated with their promotion. This would stop anybody with any ideas of promoting a similar night to rival theirs from doing so. It would also deter any potential troublemakers from attending the events. Brett would receive a chunk of the money made from the promotion.

People had also started asking Brett if he would act as a debt collector. People that had been ripped off were eager to get Brett to chase the debt and they would offer Brett half of the money. Brett wouldn't get involved in just any old dispute, but if it was something that compromised his morals then he would be more than happy to settle any scores.

There was a case with a local chap named Mark McNess. Mark had paid a contractor named Mick Garrett to build a big extension on his elderly mum's house. Mick had completed half of the work and then left the extension half finished. He'd been paid in full but refused to complete the work, leaving Mark's mum unable to return to the bungalow because of health and safety concerns. Mark's mum was devastated and her health deteriorated. She ended up in a care home never being able to return to her beloved bungalow. Mick Garrett had a long line of people that he'd left thousands of pounds out of pocket with half finished work on their houses.

Brett found out Mick Garrett's address and paid

him a visit first thing in the morning as Mick was taking his beloved Staffordshire bull terrier for a walk. Brett confronted Mick about the money he was paid for the work. Mick tried to be brave and front Brett with his bull terrier viciously growling at him. Mick then had the horror of helplessly watching a growling Brett begin to hack away at his beloved bull terrier with a small machete that he'd concealed behind his back. Brett laughed as he wiped the blood from the machete onto the terrified Mick's jacket, with the dog whimpering beside him.

Mick was warned that he'd be next if he didn't pay back all of the money that was owed, plus interest. Within two days of Mick enquiring about Brett he'd paid back all of the money to Mark, and Brett's fee was £5000 of the money that was paid back.

People were now eager to be in Brett's favour; it seemed everybody wanted to be his friend. When he walked into a pub, people would try and talk to him and shake his hand. He ignored most of them. He knew that most people were just trying to lick his arse and he despised that kind of shallowness in people.

Women also seemed to be very eager to get to know him lately. He would see them whispering and looking over as he walked to the bar. Brett would always make sure whoever he was with would never have to put their hands in their pockets and it was as though these women could sense the status, and this ticked their boxes. Brett treated these sort of women worst of all. He could feel the shallowness oozing from them as they easily made themselves available to him.

He would take them back to hotel rooms, hardly talking

to them and being rude as he made his way to the room. He would coldly tell them to take their clothes off, and then give them a quick, rough shag, after which he would immediately tell them to put their clothes back on and tell them to leave. If they protested, he would become agitated and call them vicious names and just tell them to fuck off. In his mind, why should he treat these women any differently?

A while back, women wouldn't give him the time of day, but all of a sudden they were all over him. As far as he was concerned, they deserved to be treated like pieces of shit.

Brett was now one of the most feared men to walk the streets of Leicester, and this meant that amongst the 'feast of friends' that surrounded him, there were a few people waiting in the wings that were eager to do him damage. He was now a prized scalp that certain people would love to take, and Glover was also ready for retribution.

27

AMATEUR ASSASSIN

Brett had decided it was time to move out of Maria's and into his own flat. He'd only stayed there so long because he wanted to protect her from Kristian, but Kristian hadn't been anywhere to be seen for months and rumour had it that he was still in Amsterdam evading the police.

Brett was also conscious that there would now be people out for his blood after the beatings he had dished out. He didn't care who was out there planning retribution, he was actually excited by it, and the thought of going to war with anyone was actually gratifying for him.

Kieran was over at Maria's giving Brett a hand with a few of his things. Brett's new flat was a stylish little apartment on the outskirts of the city centre. He and

Kieran had planned to take Brett's things to his new flat, and then they were going to Loughborough to collect a debt from someone who had ripped off a couple who had paid for a big lavish wedding in an estate on some Leicestershire country grounds. The chap who hired out the estate had pocketed the cash and then pretended to be bankrupt, only to be found to be operating under a new business name. The couple had to cancel their wedding and were left massively out of pocket so Brett was going to enjoy settling this one.

Kieran and Franny had been accompanying Brett on a few of his collections recently and Kieran was trying to talk Brett into going more legal as a security firm and collections company. Kieran was shrewd and could be very business-minded, but Brett wasn't really interested in any legality.

As Brett and Kieran were ready to set off in the car, they noticed the sound of a powerful engine revving behind them. Kieran looked in the rear-view mirror and he noticed a black motorbike pulling up close to his car. Brett then noticed the motorbike pulling up next to him on the passenger side. Kieran smelt a rat and quickly turned on the engine. It was too late. The helmeted motorcyclist pulled out a black single-barrelled sawn-off shotgun and swiftly aimed it towards Brett. Brett didn't move, he just smiled. This shocked the assailant who couldn't believe that somebody could be so calm in the face of death.

The hesitation from the assailant gave Kieran time to scramble the car into gear. The assailant then shouted the muffled words, "This is a present from Glover!" Kieran got the car moving but he was too late to evade the shot.

Glass had shattered everywhere and blood had splatted over the passenger side of the front windscreen. The assailant screeched off. Neither of them heard the shot until what seemed like seconds after the blood and glass had splattered the car. There was a deafening whistling sound in Kieran's ears as he tried desperately to gain composure. He looked over at Brett, who was slumped forward onto the dashboard.

Kieran pulled him back to check the damage. Brett was unconscious and his chest and neck were covered in blood. Kieran could make out what looked like lots of deep little holes in Brett's chest. He quickly gained composure and began the desperate drive to the hospital. Brett looked lifeless as he slid down in the passenger seat.

"Come on, Brett, don't fuckin' go out like this, mate!" shouted Kieran as he swerved through traffic.

He wasn't that far from the hospital, but that didn't stop him from ignoring the traffic lights and all of the other road users. He got to the front entrance of the Leicester Royal Infirmary in quick time. He slammed on the handbrake and jumped out of the car.

"I need help! There's a man here been shot, somebody fuckin' help me!" screeched Kieran as he ran around to the passenger side, desperately trying to keep Brett upright.

Kieran continued to shout at the top of his lungs. An ambulance team and two hospital porters were soon coming to his aide but nowhere near quickly enough for Kieran's liking. They lifted Brett out of the car and onto a wheeled stretcher. Kieran could see the extent of the wound from the shotgun spray as they cut off Brett's T-shirt. A big patch of a hundred or so deep little holes covered the left side of Brett's chest. The paramedics seemed to be sticking all sorts of instruments to Brett as they rushed him through the doors on the wheeled stretcher.

"We've got vital signs!" were the words from one of the paramedics as they rushed Brett through the accident and emergency reception with people looking on.

On hearing these words, Kieran dropped to his knees. The stress of the situation had exhausted him. He knew that Brett was still alive, but how alive was not yet clear. Kieran watched from a distance as the paramedics disappeared with Brett down the corridor.

28

LAUGH NOW, CRY LATER

Brett realised that he was in hospital as he awoke to the surroundings of a hospital room. He felt drowsy as he tried to lift his head. His body felt heavy as he tried to lift himself up. He looked down at his body and he could see his left arm and shoulder were heavily patched up. His chest was also patched up and he felt tremendously uncomfortable.

He looked to his side and noticed that a drip was attached to the back of his right hand. It was then that he felt somebody sitting next to him. He looked to his right to see Maria sitting next to the bed. She looked pale and her eyes looked puffy and he could tell she had been crying. She had a very sad expression on her face as she looked at Brett intently. She didn't say any words. Brett was confused as to what day it was and how long he'd been unconscious, but he wasn't confused about the incident. He knew exactly what had happened and he knew that it had been Glover behind the trigger.

Glover had taken a bit of a slide down the pecking order since the beating from Brett. People weren't quite treating him the same. It's hard to carry as much weight when everybody knows you were lying unconscious with someone pissing into your mouth. Glover found out the hard way just how plastic and shallow people can be and his ego was in tatters. So much so that he wanted Brett dead. Glover had let everybody know that it was him that had organised the shooting and was going around saying "Who's laughing now?" Even though Brett wasn't dead, Glover was satisfied that his retribution had claimed back some face... for now.

29

KISS OF LIFE

Brett had sent a reluctant Maria home after urging her not to worry. He'd been in the hospital for three days after some surgery to remove shotgun pellets from his shoulder and chest. He'd been drifting in and out of consciousness after the surgery as he was on strong painkillers.

The doctors had explained to Maria that the shotgun pellets had missed any vital organs and that the pellets didn't spread properly to cause maximum damage. This was a combination of the shotgun not being properly sawn off and the fact that Kieran moved the car very quickly. A yard or so closer and Brett would have probably been dead. Kieran had saved his life.

Brett was eager to discharge himself from the hospital.

He was about to start making preparations when he had a visit from Steve and Bez. They both looked very sombre as they walked into the room. Brett was happy to see his two good friends. There was an awkward silence as they both sat down.

"We knew this would happen," said Bez with a concerned look on his face.

Steve poignantly nodded along with what Bez was saying.

"We want Brett back, mate. We hate to see you involved in all of this shit. We don't want to see you dead at the hands of somebody like Glover," said Steve, almost expressionless.

Brett frowned and looked away from them both. He didn't want their concerns or any pity. He then turned back to look at them.

"My reason for living is gone. She died, and I died with her that night. This world sucked all of the goodness out of me. The only goodness I had left died when my baby girl died," said Brett with a scowl as a tear rolled down his cheeks.

Bez was choked on hearing Brett's words and almost crying himself. Steve couldn't think of anything to say to respond to Brett. He just looked over at Bez, waiting for a response.

"Well, we think that the old Brett is still in there. And we're not giving up on him. Yeah, Macy died, but she lives on in you. She wouldn't want her dad to just give up and steam his way to an early grave," said Bez gallantly. It was almost like a battle cry, the way that he clenched his fists as he spoke.

Brett didn't respond, he just turned his head. He didn't want to hear any talk of moving forward and living on. He just wanted to hate.

"Anyway, we've brought someone to see you," said Steve with a hint of promise.

Brett was intrigued.

"Who?" he replied.

Bez then got out of his seat and opened the door to reveal Kimberly standing awkwardly in the doorway. She looked upset but still looked her pretty, sanguine self. She couldn't bring herself to look Brett in the eye. Steve was the first to notice that Brett looked pleasantly surprised, and for a split second he could see Brett's eyes, not the soulless eyes that had recently replaced them.

There was a silence that filled the room, like nobody knew what to say. Then Bez spoke.

"We'll leave and let you two catch up," said Bez softly as he looked at Steve and gestured that they should leave with a flick of his head.

"Listen, mate, we'll see you soon," said Steve as he patted Brett on the shoulder.

Brett cried out in pain as Steve had accidentally hit Brett's fresh shotgun wound. Brett then began to laugh at Steve's clumsiness, with Steve apologising whilst quickly moving his hand away from Brett's shoulder. Bez also had a laugh about it. This was a rare laugh between the three of them in recent times.

Bez gave Brett a 'thumbs up' before the two of them quietly left, both giving Kimberly a friendly kiss on the cheek as they left the room.

Again, there were a few seconds of awkward silence before Kimberly spoke.

"I don't know what to say to you," said Kimberly as she finally looked Brett in the eyes.

"It's good to see you," replied Brett with a smile.

Kimberly gave a forced smile back.

"I'm so sorry to hear about Macy," said Kimberly softly whilst looking down to the floor and slightly shaking her head.

Brett didn't say anything for a few seconds. He didn't respond to Kimberly's condolence.

"I tried to ring you a while back, but it went straight to answerphone," said Brett as he looked at Kimberly intently with an expressionless look on his face.

"I lost my phone and all my contacts. I tried to get in touch with you on Facebook," said Kimberly, sounding downbeat.

Brett gave a sarcastic scoff. "I came off that bollocks a while back."

Kimberly's pretty face was now scrunched in pain as she fought back her tears. She couldn't bear to see Brett in the sorry state he was in. She took a deep sigh.

"We should have tried harder to find each other," she said, slightly raising her voice.

"Well, none of that matters now, does it?" replied Brett flatly.

"I'm here now," said Kimberly as she walked forward and grabbed Brett's hand.

"It's too late now, Kimberly. There's not much of the old Brett left," replied Brett as he looked up at her.

"I can still see him in your eyes," said Kimberly as she stared at him.

"I'm afraid that's just a shadow," replied Brett, almost expressionless.

"People's spirit can fade, but a person never truly loses their true essence!" said Kimberly as she grabbed Brett's hand a little tighter.

Brett frowned in frustration.

"I never lost my essence. Society stole it from me," replied Brett. He then screwed his face in discontent.

Kimberly couldn't think of any more words to say. She sat on the edge of the bed and continued to hold Brett's hand.

"Have you come here to tell me there's hope, Kimberly? Or to tell me that I can find a way to live again?" asked Brett.

Kimberly paused for a second.

"Bez got in touch with me on Facebook. His message was two months old before I saw it. He wanted somebody to talk to you. He and Steve are scared you're going to end up dead, Brett! When you ended up in here, I told them I would talk to you, but not just for them, for me too!" said Kimberly pleadingly.

"Kimberly, there's nothing you can say, I am going to die, and I'm going to make sure of it. My days are numbered, because before long somebody will have no choice but to end my life. That's my plan. Call it a prolonged suicide, if you like," said Brett coldly.

"You're in a lot of pain and grieving, I can't imagine the pain you're going through, but that's grief talking, that's not you!" said Kimberly with her voice sounding strained.

"She let her die, and I couldn't do anything to save her!" said Brett suddenly with his voice croaking in agony. "She let her die because she was a shit mother," shouted Brett, his eyes filled with tears. "And this society kept Macy with that unsuitable mother! I tried to get custody, I wanted her with me, where she'd be looked after, but the law gave me no chance!

"I did everything society told me to do. I did a job that was all about helping people, and that job left me skint. I struggled paying my weekly bus fare to work! Women wouldn't give me the time of day, but now, ever since I've become this monster, the women are falling over themselves to sit on my lap, I have three drawers at my sister's house filled to the brim with £20 notes, and wherever I go, people can't seem to do enough for me, that's how fucked up things are. When I was a nice guy, doing good things, I didn't stand a chance.

"The irony of me losing Macy is that, in a fucked-up way, I'm free! I'm free to right all of the wrongs of a society that chews up good people and spits them out!" Brett followed his words with a pained sarcastic snigger.

Again, silence filled the room. Kimberly couldn't find any words of solace.

"There is still goodness in this world, Brett. There are still good people out there!" said Kimberly.

"I'll tell you where the good people are, the real good people, they're depressed and skint, or sitting alone contemplating suicide, or on mental health wards, that's where the good souls are! The cunts of this world are doing all right, but trust me the real good people are out there, suffering!" growled Brett in reply.

Kimberly softly shook her head and began to well up inside. She now realised that Brett had lost all hope, and she knew that there was nothing she could say to bring him back. She then fiddled around in her handbag and pulled out a pen. She ripped a piece of scrap paper from an old envelope that was in her bag and scribbled on it with the pen. She placed the piece of paper in Brett's hand.

"Here's my number. I've been working in Bristol these past few months on a temporary contract. I'm going back there on the 27th of May to live, as they have just offered me a permanent job. If you want to see me before I leave, then get in touch," said Kimberly.

She then leaned down and gave him an unexpected kiss on his lips, after which she warmly rubbed the side of his face as she looked into his eyes empathetically. She then turned around and walked out of the door. Brett could still taste Kimberly's lips as he watched her leave. It brought back memories of what it was like to be kissed by somebody who meant it, and for a second or two, Brett felt alive, but only for a second or two.

30

COLD STEEL

It soon became apparent that Brett being shot had only enhanced his reputation. He had taken a shotgun blast and was out of the hospital within a few days as if it was nothing. Within the underworld mentality, taking a bullet and living to tell the tale was like a hallmark of status. Brett wasn't interested in any of that, but the people around him could feel this. Franny had noticed that, even when he wasn't with Brett, people were now going out of their way to talk to him and to offer him favours. Franny enjoyed this and he enjoyed the notoriety.

Kieran also found that this level of fear and notoriety had its advantages. Kieran and Franny were both genuine mates, but they couldn't help but revel a little in the notoriety.

When they walked into a bar with Brett, the amount of whispers, looks, and people eager to shake their hands was as though a Hollywood star had entered the room. Brett didn't respond to it in the slightest and soon made himself somewhat unapproachable.

Brett had also become involved in a new venture in the few weeks that passed. He was now 'taxing' heroin dealers with none other than Terry Shepard and a guy named Johnny Hammill. Taxing heroin dealers of their drug money could be very lucrative, especially if, like Brett, the fear of any comebacks was non-existent.

Terry had always been a well-known nutcase and his years in the army and knowledge of firearms made him dangerous and formidable, but Johnny Hammill was from Belfast and well known to have links in the Belfast underworld. It was common knowledge that he'd been associated with the Ulster Volunteer Force. This kind of association sent shivers down the spine of anybody who found themselves on the wrong side of him, especially in a city like Leicester.

Terry Shepard and Johnny Hammill had known each other for years and had first met in Belfast when Terry was stationed there serving with the British army.

Terry had recently been in touch with Brett when he'd heard that he'd been shot. Terry had picked up on Brett's recent notoriety so he offered Brett the chance to get involved in the 'taxing'. Brett had always liked Terry and was well aware of Terry's low opinion of heroin.

Terry had already targeted the dealers he wanted. These weren't street dealers locally pushing out bags on the street, these were people that were earning tens of thousands from the large distribution of heroin.

Johnny Hammill was a big, fair-haired bloke. He always had this stone-cold look in his eyes and he spoke with a very strong northern Irish accent. He had no remorse for any act of violence that he'd ever carried out. It was as though he was programmed for war and brutality. No matter the punishment he'd dished out, he would always feel more than justified in doing so. His mind was that conditioned for brutality that he had this strange way of bringing you around to his way of thinking. He was very good at justifying the brutality that he had been responsible for.

The first dealer on Terry's list was a British Pakistani guy named Tariq Ali. It wasn't a secret that this bloke was a big-time smack dealer, but he made an effort to use lucrative businesses as cover and to launder some of the money.

Johnny had been watching him for a couple of weeks and getting to know his habits. He lived with his wife, who was a dental technician. Johnny noted that Tariq would usually get home around 4pm. His wife would arrive home around 5:30pm.

Tariq lived in a big mini-mansion-style house in the Knighton area. His neighbours included Tom Meighan, the lead singer from the rock band Kasabian, and the Leicester City reserve goalkeeper. The plan was for Johnny to puncture the tyre of Tariq's wife's car at her dental practice. This would delay her getting home. Johnny had also noted that Tariq was a big drink driver and he spent most of his days at the plush Melton bar and restaurant on the city's Melton Road. This played into Johnny's hands, as he knew it would be easy for the three of them to bundle Tariq around if he was half-cut.

***

The planned day was at hand, and it was around 4pm. The road was quiet and Johnny had changed the number plates on a blue Ford Transit van. The three of them also wore shabby work clothes and hard hats so nobody would bat an eyelid at the sight of them sitting just outside Tariq's driveway.

Johnny told Brett that things like this always worked better in the daytime. Brett was surprised by this but Johnny explained that the public don't notice as much in the day. They are busy going about their business and there is a lot of life around and the buzz of things like traffic noise, whereas at night-time when things are quiet people notice noises and they notice people lurking around and faces that don't belong. Johnny explained that it was the way he'd always done things, so Brett was happy enough to go along with the plan.

The three of them sat outside the house in the van awaiting Tariq's arrival. They were going to wait for him to open his front door and then rush in behind him. They were confident. Brett didn't care about the workman disguise, he didn't even want to wear it, but Johnny and Terry insisted.

Terry suddenly placed a gun in Brett's hand as they waited, as though he was handing him an everyday item like a pen or a lighter. It was a Ruger 9mm. It felt heavy in Brett's hand and he could feel the cold steel against his skin. Brett felt the cold metal in his hand and felt the kind of power that a loaded gun in your hand brings.

Like clockwork, Tariq pulled up to his drive around 4pm in his Mercedes. He was on his phone as he pulled into his drive. He didn't bat an eyelid at the three of them sitting there in the Transit van as he lazily got out of his car. He looked around his mid forties. He didn't fit the stereotype of a big-time drug dealer with his beer belly pushing over the belt of his trousers as he walked.

Brett was thinking how greedy he looked as he walked forward with his stubby sausage fingers holding his car keys, and he meant greedy in every sense of the word.

"Right fellas, let me do the talking," said Johnny sternly as they watched Tariq approach his front door.

As Tariq put his key in the front door the three of them slowly walked behind to the right so they were just out of his eye-line. He walked in and attempted to close the door behind him, but Johnny quickly bumped the door open hard with his big shoulder, knocking a surprised Tariq back into the hallway. Terry and Brett quickly barged in, slamming the door shut behind them. Johnny then pointed the pistol in Tariq's face.

"Make one sound and you will die, here, today, on this spot!" said Johnny sternly.

Tariq immediately put his hands in the air.

"All right man, all right!" said Tariq sounding jittery as he looked directly at the barrel of Johnny's gun.

Terry and Brett also drew their guns but stood there calmly with them held down by their sides.

Johnny ordered Tariq into the kitchen and firmly told him to sit down on a chair.

"My name's King Billy, formerly of Belfast's Ulster

Volunteer Force. We're here to tax you of proceeds made from the distribution of heroin within the community. If you fail to comply you will be punished as we see fit, and the consequences will be dire for yourself and members of your family!" said Johnny directly in his coarse Belfast twang.

These words sent a chill down Tariq's spine. When he heard the words 'Ulster Volunteer Force', he realised he may not be just dealing with some local thugs that had chanced an opportunity to rob him of his cash.

"Listen, if you want money, it's no problem, I have around nine grand upstairs, you can take it," said Tariq frantically.

"Nine grand is not sufficient taxation for someone at your level of distribution!" said Johnny looking straight into Tariq's eyes.

Brett enjoyed the way that Johnny went about his business. It was almost formal and official, the way he put his words together. He said it so directly and in a way in which you had no reason to doubt him.

Johnny then asked Terry to have a look around for the 'cutlery'. Terry wasted no time and soon found a collection of kitchen knives on a knife stand on the worktop. Terry then took the two biggest knives from the stand.

Tariq's stomach sank and he began to panic when he heard the word 'cutlery'.

Without warning, Terry then began to cut Tariq's shirt from his body with the knife. He did it rather brashly and clumsily so Tariq could feel the cold blade on his skin. Tariq began to breathe heavily.

"All right, fellas, all right, I'll get you more money,

there's forty-odd grand at my other house," said Tariq as he imagined what a cold blade in the stomach would feel like.

Tariq explained that he owned another property that he rented out to his brother-in-law just a short drive away, and that the house was currently empty as his brother-in-law was in Mumbai for a wedding. Tariq explained that the cash was in a safe that was cemented into the garage floor. Johnny soon persuaded him to hand over the keys to the house and the safe and to also give him the alarm code.

Once Johnny was satisfied, he sent Terry to the address in the van. Johnny coldly warned Tariq that if things didn't run smoothly and Terry wasn't back within forty-five minutes then he would start to slice him in ways that would make his organs spill out of his stomach whilst he was still conscious to see them. On hearing this, Tariq was like putty in the hands of Johnny. It was then that Tariq's phone begun to ring and vibrate on the kitchen table.

"Answer your phone and pretend that everything is hunky dory, and do a good job or I promise, you will be watching your own intestines spill out of that gut of yours," said Johnny.

Tariq answered the phone. It was his wife on the other end of the line. She explained that she would be late from work as she had a puncture. She stated that she'd called the roadside recovery to get it sorted. Tariq did a good job of not raising any suspicion. When his wife asked why he sounded a bit low he just told her that he had a bit of heartburn. By now he just wanted the ordeal to be over.

The simple things in life seem to stand out when you

feel that your life is at risk. Sitting on your doorstep on a spring afternoon with a cup of tea watching your kids play is the kind of thing you think about when you think that you may not see the next day, and these were just the kind of thoughts that were going through Tariq's mind.

Terry arrived back at Tariq's house after being gone for around forty minutes and he was looking very pleased with himself. He had a bin liner and it was full of cash. He explained to Brett and Terry that he'd even counted the money and there was bang on £47,000 in total. That, added to the £9000 that Tariq had offered them earlier, made a total of £56,000. They were happy enough, easy money for the fearless.

Johnny handcuffed Tariq to the radiator in his kitchen, leaving him with a stern warning.

"If you display any aspirations of retribution then myself or any of our many associates will be at your door!"

Tariq took a deep breath of relief as the three of them left the house, each of them more than a few grand richer, all in a day's work. They didn't fear the police being involved, as big-time heroin dealers tended not to go to the police when their drug proceeds had been robbed.

Brett just didn't care about any comebacks, and Johnny was always prepared for war. Johnny was a different breed for a town like Leicester. Leicester had its hard men and a few half-arsed big-time Charlies and a few nutcases, but the city's underworld was nowhere near ready for a former member of a loyalist paramilitary organisation, and this particular tag carried colossal weight. Terry was fearless, and strangely thought that it was his right to carry out such acts against people like heroin dealers. The three of them were quite a force.

Terry was buzzing and he was talking about the three of them becoming a hit squad as they made their way to drop Brett off. Terry was talking about getting rid of all the scum from the streets of Leicester. Anyone associated with rape, heroin dealing, abuse of kids, beating up women, and bullies in general were all on his radar. He even started coming up with names for them to call themselves. He was inspired by the kind of organisations he'd seen when he served in Belfast that dished out severe punishments to anybody breaking their codes within the community. Brett wasn't really interested in any vigilante-style situation, he just wanted people to know that if they crossed him then they had to be prepared to die.

Brett had a bag full of money tucked away in his jacket and was about to jump out of the van after Johnny had pulled up outside of his flat. Brett then remembered he still had the gun on him. He discreetly pulled it out of his pocket.

"Here you go, Terry, here's your shooter, mate," said Brett.

"That's all right, mate. You can keep that, that's yours," said Terry with a smile.

Brett smiled back.

"That's the nicest gift anyone's ever given to me," said Brett with a sarcastic grin as he went calmly on his way.

31

DEAD AGAIN

It had just gone midnight as Brett looked down at his watch, and then as he glanced around he found himself sitting in his old flat. As he looked around he could see all of Macy's belongings on the floor. He could see her hairbrush next to her overnight bag with bits of her hair still in the brush, and her Disney DVDs that she had brought to watch. His flat was exactly the way it always used to be when Macy came to visit.

He could feel that Macy was in the flat. He could hear her in the bathroom brushing her teeth. He quickly shot up from the settee and opened the bathroom door but she was not there. He then looked in the box room that he'd made into her bedroom but she wasn't there either. Her bed had been slept in and he could see that she had been there. His head was in a spin. Macy was nowhere to be seen but he could feel her there.

The house phone then began to ring loudly and he quickly marched into the living room and answered it.

"Hello!" he said in a state of utter confusion.

"Hello, Daddy!" replied Macy on the other end of the line in her cute little voice.

Brett began to become hysterical. It was his little girl and she was alive.

"Baby, oh my baby, where are you?" said Brett crying uncontrollably.

"I'm at Mummy's, Daddy. Come and get me, I want to come to your house!" said Macy.

"I'm coming now, I'm coming to fetch you now, baby!" said Brett enthusiastically whilst still in floods of tears.

"Daddy, can I have some ice cream?" said Macy.

"Yes, yes, you can have all the ice cream you can eat!" said Brett excitedly.

She's alive! She's alive! he thought to himself.

It was at that point that he could feel himself waking up. It was just a dream. He was still in the dream but now conscious that it was only a dream. Macy's voice was getting fainter and fainter until finally he found himself waking up in bed. Macy wasn't alive and she wasn't on the phone. It was just a dream, a relentlessly cruel dream. Brett was in a complete fit of sobs as he lay in his bed. Crying and crying until there were no more tears left, and it felt as though his soul was dying all over again, and after the sorrow came the hate, and in abundance.

32

TUMBLING DOWN

After the dream about Macy, Brett needed a remedy for the pain, and that remedy was dishing out suffering to somebody. The first person on his mind was Lisa, but he still had no idea of her whereabouts. Kristian was still nowhere to be seen, so the next person on his radar was Glover.

Glover was back to his old self, feeling invincible again after he'd put the word out that he was responsible for Brett's shooting.

Glover had surrounded himself with muscle since the shooting, as he knew that Brett was now a major force. He was mob-handed more than ever before. This didn't bother Brett one bit, he was going to make Glover curse the day that he'd crossed him. Glover wouldn't be hard to find, he still felt that he was a big player and wasn't going to hide.

Brett had other ideas, and he also now had a loaded gun.

It was no secret that Glover liked to party and would usually be playing toy gangster around the bars in the city centre at the weekend. Kieran and Franny had recently been in touch with Brett and were eager to get him out for a drink after the shooting, so Brett decided that he would put himself about until he bumped into Glover.

Brett didn't mention anything of his plans to Kieran and Franny as they were knocking down the shots in the city centre the following Saturday night. The gun was tucked away in Brett's casual mini-bag that was draped over his shoulder and it was loaded. Bouncers on the doors of the bars no longer asked Brett to wait or gave him any hassle. They would try to nod at him or say hello but Brett wouldn't even notice them. Kieran and Franny had asked Brett several times what he was going to do about Glover, but Brett would play it down.

Brett's eyes glanced around every room of every establishment as they hit the city's bars. He looked calm on the outside but inside he was ravaged with monstrous thoughts and hate. He kept hearing Macy's voice on the phone and all he wanted to do was see her. Even if it was just for one minute, he just wanted to hug her and tell her how much he loved her. The fact that this would never happen continued to rip at his heart.

The three of them made their way to the Terrace lounge. Franny was enjoying the fact that a few people had noticed that Brett was standing at the bar, and there were a few women who had gradually started to circle as people began to whisper whilst inconspicuously pointing over at Brett. Brett just stood there, stony-faced. His mind was on one thing, and that was Glover.

It wasn't long before Brett noticed one of Glover's cronies walking down the stairs making his way from the VIP lounge, and this meant one thing, Glover wouldn't be that far away. Brett immediately made his way up the stairs. He bumped into the bar owner as he was walking up the stairs. He was a guy named Darryl Barnes. Darryl was well known for his sneaky backhanders and dodgy dealings. He was quite a shifty-looking character. Darryl tried to say hello to Brett and make a fuss of him. This infuriated Brett as Darryl had never tried to speak to him before. Brett made it clear that he didn't want Darryl to talk to him.

"Don't fuckin' talk to me, I don't know you and you've never tried to talk to me before," said Brett.

"Well, I didn't mean to offend you, mate," replied Darryl, looking shaken.

"I'm not your fuckin' mate! Is Glover up there?" snapped Brett.

Darryl paused for a second looking bemused.

"I said is fuckin' Glover up there?" snapped Brett as he moved up close to Darryl's face.

"Yeah… he's up in the VIP area," said Darryl as he leaned backwards.

"Good! Now listen, Darryl, your CCTV has a technical hitch tonight, do you understand?" said Brett.

Darryl again looked bemused, not knowing what to say.

"If your CCTV catches me then I promise you, your

missus will be getting a call from the police at four in the morning, now do you get me?" snarled Brett.

"Yeah!" nodded Darryl as he backed off before swiftly making his way down the stairs.

Brett unzipped his mini-bag and reached for the gun. It felt cold, but again Brett enjoyed the feel of it in his hand. He cocked it back just like they do in the movies. He'd had a good play around with the gun previously, but had never fired it. Now was the time.

He slowly made his way to the top of the stairs, then glanced at the balcony of the VIP area. He noticed Glover straight away. He was sat comfortably in a chair by a table littered with drinks. There were the usual faces with him plus a few more that Brett had never seen before. There were a few of the usual wannabe glamour-model-type girls there as well, but it wasn't as busy as it was downstairs in the main area.

Brett stood at the top of the stairs and held the gun down by his leg in plain sight for everyone to see. It was brighter in the VIP area than it was in the main part of the club and Brett was certain that the gun would be seen.

After a few seconds, one of Glover's pals looked over and noticed Brett. Brett smiled as he brandished the gun. Glover's pal looked over and a look of total disbelief overcame his face. He then tapped the guy next to him and pointed over at Brett.

Before long the whole of the table were looking at Brett standing there with the gun. The laughter died down to a complete stop as Glover and his pals realised that they were faced with Brett and a loaded gun. Brett then raised his hand

and pointed the gun at them, smiling as he slowly walked forward with murder in his eyes.

Chaos ensued as Glover's party made a run for the fire exit door. Any bravado or gangster personas had crumbled now. This wasn't a gangster film, this was reality, and people's only instincts were to survive and see their loved ones the next day as they felt the uncompromising presence of death.

The sound of glasses smashing and a table overturning filled the air, along with the screams of the wannabe glamour models who were shoved to the floor and bundled aside as Glover's cronies ran for their lives. The fire exit door was locked and there was no way out. People desperately ran around Brett leaving Glover behind, chancing darting past him in the hope that Glover was the main target and the main focus. Glover was the last to try and make a run for it but it was too late. As the room emptied Glover was faced with Brett with his back towards the ledge of the balcony. He stood there totally helpless and at the mercy of Brett. He glanced over at the drop wondering if he would survive should he take a leap rather than a bullet.

"I want you to think of every move you made that night at the Empire. I want you to think of that and every smug comment before you die, and next time you shoot me, get the job done properly, you plastic twat," shouted Brett to Glover with a smile.

Brett was in no hurry. He was enjoying the moment and thriving off the fear that was in Glover's eyes.

Then, before Brett could say another word Glover just leapt from the balcony before hitting the barrier of the DJ station, which painfully broke his fall. There were screams as Glover's body crashed 35ft to the floor. Brett was surprised but chuckled to himself as he looked over the balcony to see Glover's twisted body sprawled out in the middle of the dance floor. Again, sheer chaos ensued as nobody knew what was going on. There were shouts of somebody having a gun and people began to rush out of the doors, apart from the revellers that were too drunk to be aware and still attempting to get another drink from the bar.

Brett quickly made his way down the stairs. Kieran and Franny noticed him amid the chaos and were shouting at him asking him, "What the fuck is going on?" Brett walked over to where Glover lay. He was still conscious but his body looked broken and he was struggling to breathe as his eyes rolled over white. His left arm was bent backwards behind his head pointing in the opposite direction to where it should. Brett began to laugh as he looked down at Glover and was in two minds whether to piss on him again, but instead he just laid a few boots in with a spiteful snarl as he kicked. People couldn't believe what they were seeing.

Brett then made his way outside, shoving past anybody that was in his way. He saw Kieran and Franny near the entrance and they quickly made their way over to him.

"What the fuck happened?" shouted Kieran to Brett in bemused excitement.

"Well, first Glover thought he was invincible, and then he thought he could fly! He was wrong both times," said Brett with a sadistic snigger.

Kieran and Franny were shaking their heads in amazement at what had just happened.

"Come on, let's get the fuck away from here!" said Kieran.

"Fuck that, I'm going for something to eat!" said Brett as he made his way to the high street.

Brett began to make his way to the high street to get something to eat from one of the street's many fast-food outlets. Kieran and Franny wanted to leave the city centre but Brett just continued to walk as if he didn't have a care. Kieran eventually managed to talk Brett into leaving the city centre to continue the night's drinking as far away from the city centre as possible.

33

LEICESTER'S FINEST

In the days that followed the incident with Glover, the news had hit the streets that Glover would never walk again. Glover was paralysed from the waist down and on the left side of his body after a bad break in his back and serious nerve damage from the fall. He would never be the same again.

Gone were the days of largin' it in the clubs and being the bully boy. Gone were the crazy nights out, and the women on his arm, and gone were the flash cars and designer clothes. He would now be spending the rest of his days in a wheelchair needing around-the-clock care.

Brett felt satisfied that he was now even with Glover. He was also satisfied that Glover had got what he deserved.

The wrongly reported story of a man being 'thrown' from a balcony in one of the city's most popular bars had been featured in the local paper and on the local news broadcast. The police were looking for the assailant but nobody had come forward. A girl from the bar had made an initial report an hour or so after the incident but soon retracted this when she found out who Brett Kelso was. People had advised her that it was not a good idea, and Terry Shepard and Johnny Hammill had also made their presence felt.

The police had a good idea of who was responsible and wanted Brett to feel their weight. There was no CCTV footage of the incident as the system was down, and Glover wasn't yet medically fit to give a statement. The following Wednesday, the police paid Brett a visit.

There were two officers standing there as Brett answered his door after the hefty policeman's knock. He smiled at the both of them. He knew what they were doing there. They were two youngish-looking officers, not suited and booted like you'd expect. One of them was a dead-pan Asian chap that to Brett looked more like a doctor than a police officer. The other was a more rugged white chap with a shaved head. He reminded Brett of Jason Statham, as he was unshaven and expressionless. He seemed keen on looking Brett straight in the eye.

"Hello, this is DC Chauhan, and I'm DC Porter. We would very much like to talk to you with regards to an incident in which Aiden Glover was thrown from a balcony in the Terrace bar," said the officer with the shaved head, careful to keep eye contact with Brett.

"Fuckin' hell, that must have been a big lad who threw a fat cunt like him off a balcony!" said Brett as he laughed.

"Would you mind coming down to the station just to answer a few questions?" asked DC Porter.

"Am I under arrest?" said Brett with a sarcastic frown.

"No, you're not under arrest, but it would be a great help to our enquiry," replied DC Porter.

Brett was not threatened by this visit. He knew that the only thing that would connect him to the incident would be a witness statement, and he was confident that nobody would have anything to gain by being a witness against him. Brett was happy to go to the station as he wanted to toy with the police.

"I'm proud to come to the police station to help out Leicester's finest," said Brett sarcastically.

Once at the station DC Porter began to question Brett. It wasn't a recorded interview but Brett knew that they would push him as hard as they could, and try to find something that would indicate his guilt.

"Were you in the Terrace bar at the time of the incident?" asked DC Porter.

"Yes, I was just on my way to the VIP lounge when Glover thought he had wings," said Brett as he cackled.

"The word on the street is that you don't like Glover very much," said DC Chauhan.

"You're right there, I can't stand the cunt. In fact I'm over the moon that the horrible bastard is gonna live out the rest of his life having to have his arse wiped by someone on £7.20p an hour," said Brett as he laughed again.

"Do you blame him for your shooting?" asked DC Chauhan.

"I've not really thought about it," said Brett.

The police had nothing and they knew it. There were no witness statements, and no CCTV footage. DC Chauhan left the room leaving Brett alone with DC Porter. DC Porter began to look a little frustrated.

"This is off the record! We know all about you Brett. And we know what you've been up to. I've seen many like you, and you all fall in the end," said DC Porter confidently.

Brett's face straightened as he looked at DC Porter intently.

"You've never seen anyone like me, DC Porter. I'm a walking ghost, and I don't care if I drop dead this second. I'm no plastic gangster. I may be a monster, but I'm no wannabe!" said Brett.

"You're just somebody that thinks he can live by his own rules, like many before you, but you'll have your day in court, believe me," said DC Porter as he nodded his head.

Brett looked at him as if his eyes were burning holes right through him.

"You've got some fuckin' nerve, let me tell you. For years I've watched the Glovers, and the Kristian Bells of this city, swan around doing what they like, bullying people, including women, and being all-round two-bob cunts, and what have you done about people like them? You've done fuck all. And then someone like me comes along and wants to wipe them from the earth, and spit in the face of a society that allows people like that to thrive, and you want to go out of your way to bring me down.

You'd like me to disappear, wouldn't you, because we can't have monsters running around the city streets now can we?" said Brett coldly.

Brett then swiftly left his seat and made his way out of the police station.

34

HEY YOU

Brett became paranoid about the police visit in the days that followed. He started to believe that they were tracing his phone calls. He didn't care about the prospect of prison but he had a feeling that something big was going to happen to him, and this made him all the more determined to find Lisa. He'd asked around about Lisa, and put the word out that he wanted to find her, but it was as though she had just disappeared from the face of the planet.

Again his frustration was erupting out of his body as he punched the living room wall of his flat. He began to search the flat for a large bag of cocaine that he had but he couldn't find it anywhere. He was also beginning to realise that no matter how much pain he inflicted and how much punishment he dished out his pain would never leave him. He rummaged through his kitchen drawers, adamant that he would find the cocaine, chucking the drawers' contents on the floor in rage. It was then that he noticed the creased piece of paper with Kimberly's number on it on the floor. It was the paper that she had given him when she had visited him in the hospital.

He slowly picked it up from the floor. He had the urge to ring his old friend. The vision of a friendly, caring face infected his thoughts and he was fighting the urge to ring her. He didn't want to feel compassion or fondness or anything that would make him feel human, he just wanted to feel hate, but the urge to ring Kimberly would not leave him. He decided to make the call.

The phone rang as he swiftly made the call. He knew he would have talked himself out of it if he didn't make the call quickly. And then she answered.

"Hello," said Kimberly sounding tired.

"It's me!" said Brett.

"Me who?" replied Kimberly.

"It's Brett!" said Brett enthusiastically.

There was a pause. Neither of them knew what to say.

"Hey you, how are you doing?" asked Kimberly, sounding pleased to hear from him.

"I want to see you!" said Brett.

Kimberly was a little taken aback. She didn't expect to hear from him after her visit at the hospital.

"I've never stopped thinking about you, Brett" said Kimberly softly.

"I wish things could have been different, please let

me see you, I need a friend," replied Brett in complete submission.

Just as he'd submitted to the hate that had infected his soul, he now submitted to the human emotion that was within him. For a second or two there was no more hate, just helplessness. On hearing this, Kimberly couldn't say no. Brett was in need and she would be there for him. She had reservations about becoming involved with him due to what he had become, but how could she turn him away? She knew that deep down he was just crying out for help.

The two of them arranged for Kimberly to meet at Brett's flat later that night.

By the time Kimberly got to his door, she was desperate to see him. She knew Brett, and she wanted to try her best to dispossess him of the monster that had risen within him. As Brett answered the door she could see that the real Brett wasn't completely gone; he looked like Brett, not the empty shell who had been lying in the hospital bed. He quaintly invited her in, noticing how beautiful she was as she walked through the door. He didn't want to wait to see how she felt, he just wanted to kiss her. She attempted to say something as she made her way in, but before she could get her words out, he grabbed her and kissed her. She kissed him back passionately. All of the tension was being released within a kiss.

There was nobody that she had ever wanted more at that moment, and they had passionate sex right there on Brett's living room floor.

35

THE UNINVITED

Kimberly spent the next couple of nights with Brett. It felt right for the both of them to be together. It was as though nothing else existed but the two of them for those short two days. The more time Brett spent in the company of Kimberly, the more parts of the real him seemed to return.

It was time for Kimberly to leave as she had some loose ends to tie up for work and prepare for her return to Bristol within the next few weeks that followed. Brett was sad to see her leave. Kimberly hinted at seeing him again soon, but Brett was now in two minds, he didn't want to bring Kimberly into his world. There was a line of carnage that he'd left behind him and there was still more that he planned. Lisa was never far from his thoughts and he would always blame her for Macy's death. He wanted to see that look of fear in her eyes and make her pay. She was responsible for destroying his life and filling his heart with a world of pain as far as he was concerned.

***

Brett hadn't seen Maria since when he was in the hospital, so after Kimberly left he made his way to her house.

Maria always looked at Brett with such sadness in her eyes since he'd lost Macy. She'd watched him fade more and more as time went on and she longed for her brother's warm smile again.

Maria was again puffing on a cigarette as Brett sat in her living room. They went through the usual chit-chat but any spark was long gone from any of their conversations. Brett put £2000 cash in her hand just before he was about to leave. Maria said that she didn't want to take his money but Brett wouldn't listen. He gave her a kiss on the head as he was about to leave. Just as he was about to walk out of the door, her phone rang. She looked down at the screen with a look of bemusement.

"Hello!" said Maria looking puzzled as she answered the phone

Brett heard a man's voice on the other end of the line. Maria held the phone away from her ear, and looked at Brett with an expression of dread.

"It's Kristian!" said Maria.

Brett marched towards Maria and quickly snatched the phone. Of course Kristian had been off the scene and not seen for months but now the ever-uninvited Kristian Bell was back, and now Brett wanted to tell him that things had changed.

"Oi, cunt, this is Brett, what the fuck do you want?" said Brett loudly down the phone.

Kristian was taken aback. Brett had never spoken to him like that before. Kristian had been in Amsterdam and had not had much contact with anybody associated with Leicester, so he wasn't totally aware of the happenings of the months gone by.

"Who the fuck are you talking to, you little pussy?" spouted Kristian.

"I'm talking to you, you fuckin' oxygen thief, and here's how it's gonna go, you're gonna fuck off back to whatever hole you've been hiding in and stay away from my sister and my nephew! You're a low-down, dirty, horrible two-bob bastard, so stay away or you die!" snapped Brett with utter conviction.

Kristian's anger was at boiling point and his nasty streak rose within him.

"You're getting' fucked up, you little dickhead, trust me, wait until I see you!" said Kristian through gritted teeth.

"Stay the fuck away or die! You have been fuckin' warned!" snapped Brett before hanging up the phone.

Brett was deadly serious. All of the hate had risen back within him at that moment and he couldn't wait to see the terror and fear in Kristian's eyes. Brett was hell-bent on Kristian getting what was coming to him, and paying for the bastard that he'd been over the years. Maria looked concerned and a bit scared. She knew what Kristian could be like and she knew that Brett would take hell to Kristian. She was certain that one of them would end up dead.

Brett stayed at Maria's as he was sure that Kristian would soon make his way to the house. He couldn't wait for the war that would ensue between them. But Kristian never came. Brett kept looking at the clock as the hours went by, but there was no impending knock at the door. Brett was expecting a visit from Terry Shepard later that evening, so after a few hours' waiting for Kristian, he decided to leave.

"Listen, if that prick turns up at your door just ring me straight away, and I'll be here in a flash" said Brett as he bade farewell to Maria.

Maria played the situation down. She didn't want to add any more fuel to the fire.

"It'll be fine, don't worry, I don't think he'll start any trouble with me. I'll ring you straight away if he comes, I'm out all day tomorrow anyhow!" said Maria calmly.

"You just make sure you ring me if the prick turns up," said Brett as he again kissed Maria on the head before leaving.

36

UNFORGIVEN

Terry Shepard had paid Brett a visit later that evening as planned. Terry had some work for Brett with a massive payday. And as Terry explained, this work would be a very high-profile target indeed.

In 1984 a Leicestershire man named Donald Kirk-Patrick had been convicted of the rape and murder of fifteen-year-old Vanessa Coombs. DNA evidence had played a massive part in his conviction.

He'd pounced on the fifteen-year-old as she made her way back from a friend's house at 9pm one summer's evening in Oadby on July 6th 1982. He'd left her naked body dumped in a field and she was found by a jogger early in the morning.

It had been reported on past news broadcasts that Donald Kirk-Patrick was to be released after serving over thirty years of his life sentence and that he'd be released under a completely new identity. This angered the local community, and the parents of Vanessa Coombs had started a campaign to stop the release of their daughter's killer. Their campaign failed. Donald Kirk-Patrick was now living free under a new identity. Throughout his sentence, Donald Kirk-Patrick had shown no remorse for his crime. And he'd received a transfer to an open prison in the last year of his sentence as the prison authorities had stated that he'd "shown tremendous progress" over the years. He'd even received praise for poetry that he'd written whilst serving his sentence.

Terry had explained to Brett that he had been approached by Vanessa's father, and that Vanessa's father knew where Donald Kirk-Patrick was possibly living. Vanessa's father, Jonathan Coombs, had been an accountant for high-profile multi-millionaire businessmen throughout his working life, and he was also a Freemason. He'd made a lot of money and had also received compensation from the government as the immediate family member of a victim of murder. What the authorities didn't know was that Jonathan Coombs had used his money to build ties with the kind of people that had the intelligence to find out where Donald Kirk-Patrick was. He was a clever man. He'd also saved and accumulated an amount of money to pay for somebody to deliver Donald Kirk-Patrick to him. It was his life's obsession to one day to have his daughter's killer at his mercy.

It was a big ask and Jonathan Coombs knew this. The kidnapping of a high-profile offender like Donald Kirk-Patrick might not be easy, but Terry Shepard was the man that he'd approached.

Terry wanted Brett and Johnny Hammill to help him with the kidnapping and killing of Donald Kirk-Patrick. Brett didn't have to be asked twice. Brett had always thought that the system didn't show enough empathy towards the parents of the victims in such cases, and offered no real vengeance for them. The cushy prisons and the waste of resources on child killers were an insult to the families of the victims.

The fact that Donald Kirk-Patrick had shown no remorse or empathy towards Vanessa's family made Brett all the more eager to be involved. This was another aspect of society that Brett was keen to confront, and he was glad that this opportunity had presented itself to him.

The price that Vanessa's father had offered Terry was £500,000, and Jonathan Coombs had made it clear that this was for the delivery of Donald Kirk-Patrick and the participation in making sure that he suffered a slow death. Money was no thought for Jonathan. His life's mission was now in progress.

The money wasn't entirely important to Brett. What was important to Brett was how Vanessa's parents must have felt the day that they were told that their daughter had been brutally murdered. How they must feel when they put their heads on their pillows at night and have visions of their daughter in her final moments fighting for her life. The more Brett thought about it, the more he became enraged to the point of tears. Brett told Terry that he would be more than willing to be involved.

Terry said that he would be in touch with a date and a plan in due course before he left.

***

Brett was sitting snorting coke from his coffee table within minutes of Terry leaving his flat. The thoughts of what he was going to do to Donald Kirk-Patrick were bouncing around his mind. He knew the pain of losing a daughter, so he was determined to hand the parents of Vanessa Coombs the vengeance that they deserved. After all, they had lost their daughter in the worst possible way.

It was then that he noticed that his phone was ringing at the side of him on the settee. He picked up the phone and noticed straight away that it was Maria calling. He answered immediately. He knew that something was wrong.

"What's up?" shouted Brett as he answered the phone.

Maria was in some sort of state and her voice sounded faint.

"Brett, please help me, Kristian has been and he has taken Damian!" said Maria sounding tearful but very weak.

The anger in Brett rose up like a flame that had been sprayed with petrol.

"What, I'm gonna kill the cunt! Took Damian where?" shouted Brett.

There was no reply. Maria was no longer on the line. Brett continued to shout down the phone frantically. He didn't know what had happened to Maria, so he ran out of his flat after frantically fiddling around for his car keys, and jumped in his car to make his way to Maria's. He drove almost non-stop as he shouted abuse to anyone that was in his way. He got to Maria's and jumped out of the car and banged her door like a maniac. Maria didn't answer so he booted the door with all his might, busting it open with one kick. He quickly noticed Maria lying on her back on the kitchen floor.

She was unconscious and he quickly noticed the fresh bruising and swelling on her face. Her hair also looked as though it had been burnt on the left side, and the left side of her shoulder and neck were blackened and had been burned in some way.

He didn't know what to do. He shook her to see if she would respond. He was asking over and over again what had happened. Maria opened her eyes and scrunched her face in pain. She grabbed Brett by the shoulder.

"Kristian has taken Damian, don't call the police, the social services will get involved!" whimpered Maria.

All that she kept repeating was "Don't call the police!" over and over again. Brett couldn't understand why she was saying what she was saying. Maria had woken from her unconsciousness and was trying her hardest to get to her feet, but again she was scrunching her face in pain.

"Kristian won't hurt him, don't call the police!" mumbled Maria again.

Brett did what Maria asked. But he told her to lay back down and not try to move whilst he rang an ambulance. By the time the ambulance arrived, Maria had slipped back into unconsciousness. Brett accompanied her to the hospital. The paramedics were asking him what had happened but all he could say was that she had been assaulted. He had to respect the fact that Maria didn't want the police involved, even though he couldn't understand why.

He quickly made a couple of phone calls, one to Kieran, as he knew that Kieran knew people that moved in the same circles as Kristian, and one to Terry Shepard, as Terry always seemed to be able to find the information he wanted on people. Brett put the word straight out that he was now targeting the life of Kristian in the hope that this would entice Kristian to confront him.

The next morning Brett went straight back to the hospital. He wanted answers. Maria was up and about sitting on her bed but she looked bruised and her head was bandaged. She also had suffered burns to her shoulder and neck. Brett demanded answers.

Maria had explained to him that Kristian had turned up at the door demanding to see Damian. When she told him that it wasn't a good time, and that he shouldn't just turn up out of the blue, he became nasty and forced his way into the house. Kristian then attempted to turn on the charm, to which Maria asked him to leave. Maria had just had her hair cut and styled by a friend and Kristian began to tease her saying she looked like a whore.

For once Maria relentlessly stood up to him and told him to leave and never come back. Kristian wasn't used to this. He began to flick a lighter near her hair, and pretend to set her hair alight. The hairspray that she had used was flammable and her hair caught fire. She picked up a tea towel in panic and managed to dab the flames out with it but the flames had burned her skin.

Kristian, still angered by Maria, stood there cruelly laughing. Maria then slapped him around the face as she was absolutely livid at what he had just done. She'd finally had enough of his control and abuse. He then smashed her to the ground and repeatedly kicked her where she lay whilst shouting obscenities. He couldn't accept that Maria was adamant that she would no longer put up with him in her life. He stamped on her face and body as the anger over took him. He then made his way up the stairs and picked Damian up out of bed. Maria had managed to get to her feet and tried to stop him taking Damian, who by this point was terrified and screaming out, reaching for his mum. Kristian then punched Maria, knocking her unconscious in full view of Damian.

Maria also explained to Brett that Kristian had taken Damian on a few other occasions in the past and that she had called the police. She explained that the last time that she had reported this, the social services went to her house expressing concerns for Damian's welfare, and that's the reason that she didn't want the police involved. She was terrified that the social services would take Damian. The anger in Brett almost crippled him. Maria begged him to get Damian back as she sobbed in Brett's arms. Brett made the promise that he would find Damian.

37

ALL IN HAND

Brett was waiting for Kristian to attempt to confront him. He'd put word out on the street that he was going to end Kristian's life and he was certain that this would coax Kristian into facing him. Kristian's ego alone would make it almost impossible to not retaliate against Brett's threats. Brett was not proved wrong when surprisingly, the next afternoon, Kristian turned up at the hospital at Maria's bedside. He knew Maria wouldn't go to the police and the sheer cheek was typical of him. Taking Damian was just a tactic used to viciously spite Maria and keep her gripped by fear. And it was also to show Brett that he didn't care about any of his threats and that he was still in control.

He handed Damian back to a distraught Maria right

there at the hospital and wasn't concerned about the scenes that he created when Damian cried out aloud and scrambled to his mum.

Kristian coldly warned Maria that if she messed him around, or tried to stop him from ever seeing Damian, then he would throw acid over her face and make sure that no other man would ever want her, and he was deadly serious. He also said that he would take Damian out of the country next time and that she would never see him again. This was something that he'd said many times in the past and Maria didn't doubt him. This was testament to just how nasty Kristian could be. Brett was happy that Maria had Damian back, but the threats that Kristian had issued made Brett more determined than ever to end Kristian for good.

***

The following weekend, Brett received a phone call from Terry. Terry had received information that Donald Kirk-Patrick was possibly living in a supported living complex in Norwich.

Johnny Hamill had followed the lead, and he was satisfied that the man in question was Donald Kirk-Patrick. The plan was for the three of them to go to Norwich to the accommodation and then bundle Kirk-Patrick in the back of a van. They would then take him to an abandoned garage which was situated on an old unused industrial estate on the edge of south Leicester. Brett was more than keen to go along with the plan but his terms had changed. He now wanted Kristian to be taken back to the abandoned garage as well as Donald Kirk-Patrick. All he had to do was talk Terry and Johnny into also throwing Kristian into the mix.

Brett had arranged to meet Terry and Johnny in the car park of the Empire pub on the Sunday morning to go through all of the planning.

Johnny was particularly reluctant for Kristian to be involved in the plans as he felt that it would accumulate more risk. Terry also shared Johnny's views on this. It was only when Brett explained the situation that they both reluctantly agreed, and Brett offered them both an extra ten grand each of his cut of the money. Johnny was as loyal as he was dangerous, and he had empathy towards Brett's situation, as did Terry, so Terry and Johnny agreed that Kristian would be joining them, provided that Brett would come up with a neat and tidy plan. All Brett had to do was find a way to get Kristian in the back of the van.

Kristian was a ladies' man and that was no secret. This was something that Brett was going to take advantage of. Brett had watched Kristian mistreat and abuse Maria for years, and he was known for his ill treatment of any woman associated with him, so in the concept of cruel irony, Brett was determined to make sure a woman would play a big part in Kristian's downfall.

Kristian was big pals with a guy named Leon Walton. They were a close duo. It was very rare to see one without the other. Leon Walton had attained the lease for a bar in the Syston area of the city. He had given the place a full refurbishment and had renamed it 'The Esco-bar'.

The big opening night for the bar was a fortnight away, and with Leon being such a good friend of Kristian's, it was almost certain that Kristian would be there playing the big man on the opening night. This is where Brett's plan would unfold.

Brett knew a girl called Cassie Reynolds who had lived around the corner from him when he was growing up. Cassie was a tough cookie, streetwise and common. A guy didn't have to wait until the second or third date before he got the green light for a shag so to speak. But Cassie was also very likeable. She was a sweet girl and could be very giving, and had always had a bit of a soft spot for Brett.

Brett went to Cassie's house. She was very welcoming and pleased to see him as always. She quickly made an effort to neatly tie back her blonde hair as she welcomed Brett into the door, and the pupils of her blue eyes dilated as she said hello.

After they exchanged pleasantries and had some brief chit-chat, Brett then explained to her that he needed a big favour. Cassie was intrigued, but she was all ears as she listened expectantly with her cute smile.

Brett asked her to go to Leon Walton's bar in Syston on the opening night. He knew that Cassie knew who Kristian was. Everybody knew who Kristian Bell was. Brett asked Cassie to dress herself up to the nines, and then go to the bar and look out for Kristian.

If she saw Kristian, she was to then approach him and offer him some casual sex in a very forward manner. Kristian being Kristian would almost certainly take Cassie up on her offer. Cassie was to then take him back to her house where Brett would be hiding. Brett's plan was for Cassie to then get Kristian naked, making him totally vulnerable, and then Brett would make his presence known.

Cassie was reluctant and didn't want to be involved in anybody getting seriously hurt. She asked Brett what he planned to do with Kristian. Brett played the whole situation down and told Cassie that Kristian owed him money and that he just wanted to punish him a little and humiliate him, not causing him any real harm. Brett was very convincing. Cassie wasn't too sure, and she let out a sigh as she pondered on the offer, but she was soon persuaded when Brett told her that he would give her £5000 for her trouble.

This would all take place the following Saturday night during the grand opening of Leon's bar.

In an earlier phone call, Terry had explained that the kidnapping of Donald Kirk-Patrick could take place in the early hours of the Sunday morning, so if everything went according to plan it would all tie in nicely. Kristian would be bundled into the van from Cassie's house and then taken to the abandoned garage. He would be left there bound and gagged with no possibility of escape. They would then go and kidnap Donald Kirk-Patrick and take him back to the garage.

The only issue that Terry had was how Jonathan Coombs would get to the abandoned garage. This gave Brett the opportunity to offer Kieran and Franny a role in the mission. Brett arranged for Kieran and Franny to pick up Jonathan Coombs and drop him at the unused industrial estate. Terry was to pass the details onto Jonathan. It would be a testing mission with a lot that could possibly go wrong, but with £500,000 as the prize and Brett's uncompromising thirst for vengeance, the risks were worth it.

38

BAIT

Everything was in hand on the night of the planned kidnappings. Brett, Terry and Johnny were sitting in the Empire awaiting confirmation from Cassie that Kristian was in the Esco-bar. It was 9:40pm. Brett was looking down at his phone every few seconds and Terry and Johnny were sitting there looking tense without much conversation flowing at all.

Brett had no nerves at all. He actually wanted to cause havoc. He was determined to erase Kristian out of Maria's life once and for all, and the fact that he was going to get his hands on a notorious child killer like Donald Kirk-Patrick was making his heart pound. Images of torture and screams filled his mind.

Brett had also had another dream about Macy that morning. This time he dreamed that he could see Macy in the distance at the bottom of his street, and he was running towards her, but as he got closer she would disappear. He cursed God for the cruel taunts of these dreams and his heart filled with more and more hate.

Brett's phone vibrated on the table, and as he quickly looked down at the screen he was pleased to see that it was a message from Cassie confirming that Kristian was there at the bar. *He is here*, the message read. He didn't have to say anything to Terry and Johnny, he just gave them a nod of the head.

The three of them then made their way to Cassie's house in the Ford Transit van. The next phase of the plan was for them to wait outside Cassie's house and enter the house with Cassie's spare key as soon as she confirmed that she was on her way.

Almost an hour went by and there was no other word from Cassie. Brett noticed that Terry had become fidgety as he waited. Brett was about to text Cassie when his phone then vibrated. It was Cassie confirming that she was on her way. *In taxi, on way, all going to plan*, read the message. Again Brett didn't have to say anything to Terry and Johnny, he just gave them a nod and the three of them made their way out of the van and walked to Cassie's front door with Brett letting them in. They then sat in the back room in the dark waiting for their victim. There was no talking. All that could be heard was the faint sound of their breathing.

Cassie had been clever and had carried out her plan with extra assurance. She had taken a friend with her to the bar, a girl by the name of Hayley Pateman. Hayley was a local girl from the estate where Cassie lived, and she liked her kitchen parties, bad boys and free coke. Cassie wanted to make sure that Kristian was coaxed back to her house, so she figured that the offer of a threesome would favour the odds, and as expected Kristian didn't need much in the way of persuasion. Cassie and Hayley wasted no time in working on him as they had spotted him in the bar, and he was in a taxi with them in no time at all.

Brett could hear the taxi pull up outside as he lay in wait. The adrenaline was pumping by now and he couldn't wait to see the look in Kristian's eyes. The sound of the front door opening and the giggling of the girls broke the silence. Everything was going according to plan. He could hear Kristian's voice, which made him scowl, but he knew it wouldn't be long before his retribution. The sound of cocaine snorts became apparent and then the clumping sound of Kristian and the two girls frolicking on the stairs as they made their way to the bedroom.

The giggling became fainter as they reached the bedroom. Another couple of minutes and then Brett, Terry and Johnny would make their move. Time was up for Kristian. Brett eventually led the way as he slowly crept out of the back room. The three of them made their way up the stairs as quietly as they could. Brett got to the top of the stairs and all that was between him and his retribution was a bedroom door. He paused for a second or two, savouring the moment as he heard the sound of sloppy kisses from the bedroom. He then slowly opened the door.

"HELLO KRISTIAN!" he shouted with a callous grin loudly as he entered the room.

Cassie and Hayley, who were down to just their knickers, immediately jumped up from the bed and made their way past Brett, squeezing past Terry and Johnny in the doorway as they hurried out of the room. There was a look of sheer bemusement on the face of Kristian as he raised his head to see Brett standing there with the look of the devil on his face. There were no words, and the look of bemusement turned to terror as Terry and Johnny entered the room with Johnny casually loading bullets into the magazine of his 9mm automatic pistol.

Kristian was on the bed totally naked and he knew he was in a life-and-death situation. The big bad Kristian Bell could do nothing but turn to jelly as he glanced at Johnny, who was now clutching the gun that was fully loaded. He tried to talk his way out of the situation he was in, as any bravado whatsoever had abandoned him.

"All right, Brett, you have the right to be pissed, but please, just listen to me for two minutes!" said Kristian as he raised his hands in defence, feeling unbelievably vulnerable in his naked and submissive state.

Terry raised his index finger to his lips. "Shhhhhhh," he said with a soulless look in his eyes. Brett began to laugh quietly as he looked down at Kristian in his sorry state.

Kristian was helpless and he didn't know what to do. He began to breathe heavily as he wondered whether he was actually going to be alive the next day. He was staring into the eyes of death and he knew it. Everything he'd ever known looked like it was going to end, and playing the big man in the fancy motorcars and the big-money drug deals meant absolutely nothing now.

In a fit of sheer desperation and pure survival mode, Kristian quickly jumped off the bed and ran for the door whilst shouting "Help!" as loud as he could. He tried with all his might to run through Brett, Terry and Johnny as he screamed in desperation for his life. Johnny and Terry grabbed him and swiftly slammed him to the floor, with Johnny smashing his face repeatedly with the handle of the gun. Brett immediately began to smash his heel down on Kristian in utter rage, completely smashing his jaw. Kristian was now out cold and his face running with blood.

On hearing the commotion, Cassie made her way from the living room to the bottom of the stairs asking what was going on. Brett told her to "chill" and not to worry.

"Just go into the living room."

Brett looked at Johnny wondering how they would get Kristian from the house into the back of the van.

Johnny was calm. He walked over to the window and looked out onto the street. He then walked back to where Kristian lay unconscious.

"Right, let's get him down the stairs," said Johnny in a commanding tone. "Terry, you take him by the arms, Brett you take his legs."

Brett and Terry did as Johnny instructed. They struggled with the weight of Kristian as they awkwardly carried him down the stairs. Cassie and Hayley by this time were at the bottom of the stairs wondering what was happening. Cassie was horrified when she saw the unconscious and bloodied Kristian with his head feebly dangling close to the ground.

"I thought you were just gonna slap him about a bit and scare him?" said a shaken Cassie.

"Well, he looked pretty scared to me!" laughed Brett.

Cassie and Hayley were in disbelief.

"What are you gonna do to him?" asked Cassie.

"Don't worry, Cas, you won't have to worry about anything!" replied Brett.

It was then that Cassie realised the situation. At best, Kristian was going to be seriously damaged and she had played her part in it. She held her head in her hands as it dawned on her that there was nothing that she could do.

"Don't worry. I promise you, Cassie, nothing will come back to you. Go to bed and don't worry about it, just forget about everything. Kristian had it coming to him either way!" said Brett.

Hayley was speechless and was also shaken. She was looking at Cassie in shock, not knowing what to make of it all.

"Right, you two ladies get yourselves off to bed!" said Terry with a deadpan look on his face.

The two of them did as they were told. They made their way up the stairs and into bed. They hugged each other intently as the horror of the reality of their actions penetrated their minds.

"Right, Brett, go to the bathroom and see if there is a dressing gown or something. We'll put it on this piece of shit, then carry him out of here and into the van. If anybody sees us, we've two choices, we can either tell them that he has had too much to drink and we're getting him home, or we can stick a gun in their face!"

Brett wasn't keen on sticking a gun in the face of a random stranger going about their business, so he was happy to take his chances. He went to the downstairs bathroom and by a stroke of luck there was a towelling dressing gown hanging on a peg at the back of the door. They held Kristian's arms aloft and dragged the dressing gown on his body. He began to groan and roll his head forward, and for a second it looked like he was coming around. That was until Terry gave him an almighty couple of whacks, which subdued him again.

Johnny grabbed a tea towel from the kitchen and rinsed it under the tap. He then wiped all of the blood from Kristian's face as the blood would only draw more attention to anyone who could be walking the streets.

Johnny and Terry held the dead weight of an unconscious Kristian aloft and placed his arms over their shoulders. Brett had a quick look out of the window to see if there was anybody on the street. The street was empty. He then signalled Johnny and Terry forward and quickly opened the door.

Terry and Johnny were huffing and puffing as they struggled with Kristian as his feet dragged along the floor. They finally got to the back of the van and threw him in as if he was a sack of old rags. Johnny had some duct tape stashed in the back of the van and he quickly taped Kristian's hands tightly and securely behind his back before taping his feet together.

Terry then drove the van to the squalid industrial estate.

All that remained of the estate was the sight of broken

fences and worn-out parking signs. Old and tattered clocking-in tickets scattered the bleak concrete floors, and silence filled the air as Terry parked the van. Johnny had been to the site previously and had made the necessary preparations.

39

THE KILLING MOON

Brett noticed that the moon shone brightly as he made his way out of the van. He hadn't noticed it until now, but it was as if it was shining down on the three of them as though it knew what they were doing. This haunted Brett's mind.

All that could be heard was the sound of an echoing drip as the three of them carried Kristian into the garage. The electricity was still working and there was a buzzing sound as the lights flickered as Johnny hit the switch.

The remnants of the daily workings of the garage were in sight as Brett looked around. There was an old kettle that was now thick with dirt and dust on the draining board of a sink, with a couple of broken teacups.

The tiny office of the garage still had an old dust-covered

calendar on the wall, a calendar of scantily clad women with their tits out on every page. Brett noticed the calendar was displaying the month of December and there was a stunning brunette pictured, smiling and wearing a Santa hat.

Brett imagined the buzz of the working day, and the banter between the grease-monkey lads that had once worked there. Once this place would have been full of working life, but now it was to be a lair of pain and death. Nobody had been here for years, but the ghosts of normal day-to-day life were all around.

There were two tatty wooden chairs in the centre of the room, the kind of chairs that looked like they belonged to some sort of an old-fashioned dining set. At the foot of the chairs was an large old toolbox, and two cans of petrol.

Johnny and Terry placed the unconscious Kristian on the chair where he slumped to the side. Terry began to slap his face. Kristian began to murmur and breathe heavily. His eyes began to roll as he came to. Johnny began to wrap duct tape around him, taping him to the chair to stop his body from sliding off. He was totally helpless. His eyes widened as he looked around, and he pleaded with Brett to show mercy as he realised that his life was surely going to end. Brett shook his head.

"Why have you made me do this?" said Brett as he looked deep into Kristian's eyes.

Kristian's eyes were now full of tears. The big, bad Kristian Bell was now just a quivering, shaking mess who was pleading for his life.

"Why couldn't you just leave my sister alone?" said Brett with frustration and regret now etched on his face.

"Sorry to interrupt you two, but we'll be going now, Brett," said Johnny again in a matter-of-fact tone.

Brett just looked into space.

The pleading and whining from Kristian was beginning to piss Johnny off, so in a state of agitation he swiftly wrapped the duct tape around Kristian's mouth.

"Do what you've got to do, mate, and don't forget to keep your eyes peeled whilst we're gone. If you see anything you don't like, let us know straight away," said Terry sternly as he and Johnny made their way out of the garage and onward to pick up Donald Kirk-Patrick.

Brett nodded his head. He was now alone with Kristian. Kristian couldn't say anything. He was hyperventilating through his nose. He was shaking his head, trying to talk. Half of Brett remembered the vile, nasty creature that Kristian was, the violent bully that had abused his sister for years. The arrogant, cocky, spiteful swine that was so sure of himself and wouldn't think twice before threatening someone's life should they compromise his interests. But another part of Brett just saw a helpless human being who was begging for his life. It was as though the real Brett Kelso was trying to break through.

Brett began to talk to Kristian and continuously ask why he couldn't have just left his sister alone. The pain of Brett's life and the regret that his life couldn't have been a better one was starting to pour out of him in the form of pure frustration. Finding himself in an abandoned garage that was being used as a chamber for brutal retribution wasn't the way it was supposed to be. This wasn't who Brett was, but he was too far over the line to turn back now.

Brett took a massive sigh and sat down on the floor with his back leaned up against a wall. He was staring into space with a complete look of despair on his face.

Kristian was starting to feel that Brett was now wavering. As he looked over at Brett he didn't see a killer. Instead he saw a guy full of despair. Maybe this was his chance to try and find a way out of the situation. True to his manipulative nature, Kristian was already thinking way ahead. He was thinking about what he would do to Brett should he be let free. Already he was thinking how he was going to make Brett suffer and pay, but first he had to get out of the spot he was in.

Kristian began to mumble through the tape as if he wanted to say something. He was nodding over at Brett. Brett was still staring into space with the look of despair still etched on his face. He looked up at Kristian. He slowly leaned up from the floor and slowly walked over. Kristian was animated and Brett was intrigued at what he wanted to say. Brett began to pull the tape from his mouth. Kristian let out a massive gasp of air as the last of the tape was finally off.

"Brett, I promise you, I'll get out of Leicester for good. I'm already due to move out of Leicester, I'll never bother Maria again. I'm wanted by the police! If you ring the police I'm looking at a stretch inside. Don't be a killer. Just ring the police and you'll have your payback, but don't be a killer! That shit will stay with you for life!" said Kristian desperately as he looked up at Brett.

Brett was lost at that moment. He didn't want to look at Kristian. A strange feeling overcame him. He was almost emotionless. The only emotion he could feel was sadness.

Even after all Kristian had done. Brett began to think back about what Brett Kelso used to be, a happy-go-lucky lad who just wanted to live a good life and do good things. He sat back down against the wall and feebly rested his head against it. He felt totally and utterly drained and exhausted. He closed his eyes. He could hear Kristian in the background.

"Don't be a killer, Brett!" said Kristian repeatedly.

It was then that Brett began to drift off out of sheer mental exhaustion. He felt as though he could just give up and drift off into death. But death didn't come, and he had to make do with sleep.

***

Brett could feel the phone vibrating in his hand. It was the only thing that had woken him up. He'd been in and out of sleep for over an hour as he looked down at his phone he noticed that it was Kieran ringing. Brett quickly answered.

"Listen, we've just picked up this Jonathan Coombs guy. You told me to call you once we had him in the car!" said Kieran frantically.

This woke Brett out of his state of despair. He realised that there was work to be done and he had to get himself in order sharpish. He looked over at Kristian who had been making as much noise as he could whilst Brett was asleep in the hope that someone would find him, but his cries had fallen on deaf ears.

"Yeah, bring him to the spot. Everything is in hand," replied Brett before ending the call.

Brett rose to his feet and swiftly lifted up the garage door before closing it behind him. He then walked to the end of the block and gazed around to see if there was any sight of anyone nearby; again, the light of the bright full moon shone hauntingly.

Brett was confident that nobody would have any business all the way out in the unused industrial estate at this hour, but Terry had told him to look keep his eyes peeled.

He made his way back to the garage. Kristian, who had now been taped up in the chair for nearly two hours, began to plead again.

"I'm sorry, Kristian, you've brought this all on yourself!" said Brett as he shook his head.

Brett wanted to put Kristian out of his misery. He didn't want torture, but there was a massive need for Kristian Bell to be no more. It was time now, Brett couldn't let Kristian live and that was that. A bullet to the head and it would be all over. It was then that Brett realised he didn't have his gun on him. As Brett began to think of another way to end Kristian's life quickly, he noticed the sound of a car outside the garage. This had to be Kieran and Franny with Jonathan Coombs. Brett made his way out of the garage once again.

He could see a car that he didn't recognise slowly creeping the block of the estate. It was, as he thought, Kieran and Franny with Jonathan Coombs. Kieran drove to where Brett was standing.

"Right guys, this is gonna have to be quick. Leave Jonathan here and then get on your way," explained Brett as he leaned down at the driver's side of the car where Kieran had lowered the window.

With that an old man stepped out of the back passenger seat, struggling as he shifted himself out of the car. He was dressed in plain blue denim jeans and a plain black anorak. He looked frail and gaunt and there was an empty look in his eyes, which were filled with tears. Brett was speechless as he glanced at the frail-looking Jonathan Coombs. Franny and Kieran looked on. It was a very strange moment. Nobody knew quite how to feel but Brett felt proud that he was playing his part in making sure that the killer of an innocent fifteen-year-old girl was going to face a true and deserved punishment.

Jonathan Coombs made a grab for Brett's hands and grasped them whilst shaking them. He looked at Brett with a look of sheer sincerity in his drained, blue eyes.

"Thank you! Thank you so much. I've dreamed about this day for thirty years!" said Jonathan, his voice fragile and croaky.

Brett looked at Jonathan. All that Brett could feel was his pain. This was a man who had had to live with the fact that his own flesh and blood had died a horrible death. Jonathan and his daughter had been let down. Let down by a system that sees fit to release someone like Donald Kirk-Patrick back into society, a system that didn't seem to think about how Vanessa's parents must be feeling, a system that used tax-payers' money to give Donald Kirk-Patrick a second chance of life. Something that Vanessa Coombs could never have. Something that Jonathan Coombs could never have.

Brett had no words for Jonathan. Jonathan began to speak again.

"Do you know what kills me every day? The fact that the bastard has never shown any remorse, he's never once shown any sorrow for what he has done. He even appealed against his sentence, what about the sentence that we've had! Every night when I lay my head down on my pillow I hear my darling daughter's screams in my mind. I wonder if she screamed out for me, and I think about how scared she was. My heart dies every single day, and all that has kept me alive is the thought of getting my hands on the bastard!" said Jonathan as his body drooped as he broke into tears.

Brett placed his hand on Jonathan's shoulder.

"Today belongs to you! Today belongs to you and your daughter!" said Brett as his heart filled with anger.

Franny and Kieran also felt the anger rising within them. After seeing Jonathan in this state, Franny wanted to witness the payback that Jonathan was going to dish out. Kieran knew that the best thing for him to do was to leave as soon as possible. This wasn't about right or wrong, this was about the thought of the amount of prison time that he could possibly receive for being in the thick of all this, and that was enough for him to want to get out of there, and in quick time.

"Right guys, I'm out of here, are you coming with me?" said Kieran as he looked over at Franny.

Franny looked at Brett. The beast in him wanted to stay. The situation with Donald Kirk-Patrick's release had been front-page news. The kidnapping and killing of him would go down in underworld folklore. This was the kind of thing that made Franny tick. And the fact that he was going to witness Donald Kirk-Patrick pay for his crime was the icing on the cake. He was now walking close to the razor's edge and he was too close to walk away.

"I'm staying, mate. Fuck it!" said Franny.

Brett looked over at Franny. It didn't matter to Brett whether Franny stayed or not, but if he wanted to hang around, it was no problem.

Kieran didn't hang around long enough for Franny to change his mind. He shook Brett's hand and swiftly sped off on his way.

Brett led the way into the garage with a stony-faced Jonathan Coombs and Franny. The sight of Kristian taped to the chair didn't faze Jonathan but even someone like Franny felt the coldness of an eerie shiver down his spine.

40

IN THE HEART OF DARKNESS

The sound of a van pulling up outside of the garage could be heard loud and clear and Brett knew for sure that this was Terry and Johnny with Donald Kirk-Patrick. Brett's heart began to beat and there was an intense look in the eyes of Jonathan Coombs.

As the van came to a halt, the sound of the back door of the van being swiftly pulled open could be heard. The sound of Terry swearing and abusing someone could also be heard in the still of the night. Brett leaned down and pulled up the garage shutter quickly.

The sight of Donald Kirk-Patrick filled the air with silence, a silence that wasn't broken for a few seconds. Donald Kirk-Patrick looked like an old man. He was shaking, and his hands were tightly taped together. He was a podgy-looking bloke with thinning hair and a few weeks' growth of scruffy facial hair. He had soulless eyes that appeared to have no life in them apart from total fear and terror. He looked resigned to his fate and he wasn't trying to talk his way out of anything.

Johnny who had been making himself busy taping Kristian's mouth was now standing behind Donald Kirk-Patrick. He callously kicked him in the back hard, making him crash to the ground. Brett went to walk forward towards him.

Jonathan Coombs held his hand out in the way of Brett, halting him from walking forward.

"Leave it to me!" said Jonathan in a croaky tone.

Brett was more than happy to oblige. Jonathan walked forward as the rest of them looked on in silence. Jonathan's eyes never left Donald Kirk-Patrick from the moment he was revealed. It was as though nothing else on earth existed to him. As he reached Kirk-Patrick he sternly told him to get up.

Kirk-Patrick struggled to rise but eventually got himself up from the floor. As he slowly stood up Jonathan walked forward and looked him in the eyes. Johnny Hammill told Kirk-Patrick that if he looked away from Jonathan he would take his eyes out with the claw of a hammer. The silence grew as Jonathan stood there face to face with the killer of his daughter.

"I'm Vanessa's dad!" said Jonathan as the stone-cold look on his face turned to a grimace.

Donald Kirk-Patrick didn't speak. He just had the kind

of look on his face like that of an animal that was on its way to the slaughterhouse. He began to urinate uncontrollably but made no move to stop himself.

"Did my daughter scream for me?" asked Jonathan as he looked Donald Kirk-Patrick dead in the face.

"Right, that's enough!" snapped Johnny Hammill as he was overcome by anger.

He walked forward and grabbed Kirk-Patrick by the scruff of the neck and dragged him as he walked, grabbing one of the wooden chairs with his other hand.

"Terry, bring the box," said Johnny Hammill as he walked to the back of the garage. Jonathan Coombs followed, along with Terry also. They walked to the small corridor at the back of the garage where the toilets were located. Brett looked on. Franny looked at Brett wondering if he should behold the slow and painful death of Donald Kirk-Patrick.

For once in his life, Franny didn't know what to do, he'd imagined many times what he would do with a person such as Donald Kirk-Patrick, but now the opportunity was here staring him dead in the face. This was real, a real death and a real killing. Franny had no pity or remorse for Donald Kirk-Patrick, and was glad he was going to get what he deserved, but he found himself stuck to the spot.

A few minutes of near silence passed, and then came the screaming, the high-pitched screams of a man on the verge of a slow and painful death. Jonathan Coombs was finally taking his vengeance. Brett and Franny both felt a sense of satisfaction as the screams of Donald Kirk-Patrick echoed throughout the garage.

Brett turned to Kristian. Kristian was by now almost

motionless with his head hanging. He oddly looked as though he had submitted to whatever his fate would be. His adrenaline had faded and exhaustion had kicked in.

Franny screwed his face as he looked over at Kristian. A better man may have had some pity for Kristian, but Franny had none.

Terry then suddenly appeared, swiftly marching over to where Brett stood. As Terry got closer Brett could see the blood of Donald Kirk-Patrick on Terry's face. It looked as though Terry's face had been sprayed with blood. His pupils were dilated and there was no sight of any humanity within his eyes.

"Right then, let's do away with this one!" said Terry referring to Kristian.

"Have you got a gun?" asked Brett.

Terry paused for a couple of seconds.

"They're in the van. I'm not going back out there now! We need to wrap all this up and be gone!" said Terry.

Kristian began to breathe fast, faster than ever before. Brett was now wondering if there was any other way. Did he have to kill Kristian? He again realised that he'd passed the point of no return.

The real Brett was no killer of a helpless human being, and in the worst moment possible his true essence was beginning to emerge. The words "A person never loses their true essence", which Kimberly had spoken when she visited him at the hospital, were ringing in his mind. Terry could sense this.

"Killing a man is never the way you imagine it. It's never as straightforward as you think it's gonna be. When you think about killing somebody, you feel justified, but when you are actually faced with being a killer, no matter the circumstances, it feels as though you are handing your soul to the Devil, and closing the door on God, because you know you'll never be the same again!" said Terry as he looked intensely at Brett.

Brett looked back at Terry.

"But believe me, Brett, this piece of shit deserves to die, and you have to do it!" said Terry.

Brett didn't respond, he just looked back at Terry. Terry, in an attempt to encourage Brett, reached down and grabbed the can of petrol. He swiftly unscrewed the lid and handed the petrol over to Brett. Brett grabbed the can of petrol and looked down at Kristian. Kristian was crying and now breathing uncontrollably. Brett paused and this frustrated Terry.

"OK, if you're thinking of giving this piece of shit a second thought why don't you check the messages on his phone?" snapped Terry as he frantically fidgeted around in his pocket pulling out an iPhone.

It was Kristian's iPhone, and Terry had pocketed it from the bedroom in Cassie's house. He prodded away at the home button and fiddled with the phone. He then handed the phone to Brett.

"Go through his messages, Brett," said Terry with a scowl.

Brett had no idea how Terry had got into Kristian's phone and he didn't give it much thought, but it didn't take long before he could see the foul and abusive messages that Kristian had recently sent to Maria.

I'LL FUCKIN' KILL YOU AND YOUR BROTHER!!!
read one of the messages.

I'LL POUR ACID OVER YOUR FACE SO NO MAN WILL EVER WANT YOU! read another.

I'M TAKING DAMIAN, AND YOU'LL NEVER SEE HIM AGAIN TRUST ME YOU FUCKIN DIRTY WHORE, read another.

The messages went on and on. Now the monster was back. The dark shadows that had engulfed Brett's soul had taken over his entire being once again as if they had never faded. He began to pour the petrol over Kristian slowly whilst looking him in the eyes and smiling. Kristian was desperately trying to shout through the tape on his mouth whilst rocking on the chair frantically, and the tears were almost squirting out of his eyes as he was now certain of a brutally painful death. Brett continued to smile as he poured the last of the petrol out of the can.

Franny, who was looking on, didn't really feel anything, but he couldn't help but feel strange about the fact that he was about to watch someone die.

Terry pulled a lighter out of his pocket and handed it to Brett.

"I want you to think about all the misery that you have caused my sister before you die!" growled Brett as he leaned forward with the lighter.

Kristian's eyes widened in utter terror before Brett pushed down on the lighter, releasing the flame and igniting the petrol.

There was a roar of the blaze as the flames engulfed Kristian. Kristian squealed as he was overcome by fire. The flames took the shape of his body, and his features couldn't be made out as fire was all that could be seen. His body was violently jolting to and fro, and the pitch of his squeals got higher and higher. Franny had to turn and look away after a short while whilst retching up the contents of his stomach, but Brett just looked on.

The squeals continued for what seemed like an eternity, but gradually the movement of Kristian began to slow down. The violent jolts became laboured twitches and the smell of burning flesh overcame the atmosphere.

The fire continued to roar with great momentum as the squeals eventually died and the movement of Kristian's body came to a stop.

Kristian Bell was dead. Dead and not coming back... ever!

He would never be back to bother Maria again. He would never be around to burden her or Damian's life, and he would never again be a threat or a nuisance to anyone. Kristian was dead, and at that moment, the monster within Brett felt nothing but delight.

41

BETWEEN HEAVEN AND HELL

In the days that followed the killings of Kristian Bell and Donald Kirk-Patrick, even more of the true essence of Brett Kelso was buried deep beneath the hate and carnage that had ensued since the death of Macy. There was hardly any of the real Brett Kelso left.

Terry Shepard had made sure that the word had gone around about how Donald Kirk-Patrick had met his end. Kirk-Patrick had been tortured by Jonathan Coombs and then set alight. The disappearance of Kirk-Patrick was national news and there was a massive investigation. The disappearance of Kristian Bell had hit the local headlines but word had circulated that it was Brett who was responsible.

Terry and Johnny Hammill were not concerned about the police as there were no bodies. Without the bodies there was no evidence. Terry and Johnny had disposed of the bodies and were quite confident that they would never be found.

It was never mentioned by Terry or Johnny how they had disposed of the bodies. This didn't seem a major concern to either of them but they both seemed to be enjoying the fact that they had dished out their brand of capital punishment.

***

Kimberly had been trying to get in touch with Brett over the past couple of days but every time Brett looked down at his phone and saw that it was her ringing, he couldn't answer. He knew he wouldn't be able to look into her innocent eyes knowing what he had done. Kimberly was not the kind of person to give up on someone, so she turned up at his door.

Kimberly smiled at Brett as he opened the door. He didn't feel worthy of her smile or any of her affection.

"Have you forgotten about me again already?" said Kimberly with her radiant smile, unaware of the events that had taken place a few days before.

Brett couldn't help but force a half-smile. Even though he'd killed a man in cold blood, Kimberly still managed to make a piece of the real Brett Kelso shine through again. He wanted so much to tell her to leave. He couldn't face the possibility of her being dragged into his world, but he couldn't. She made him feel like Brett again and in a strange kind of way, made him feel close to Macy.

Brett and Kimberly spent the next couple of days together. They spent most of the time talking and passionately making love. It felt like the two of them were just meant to be together. Every moment they spent with one another, more of the real Brett seemed to emerge. It was surprising to Brett how much one person could bring out the true spirit of somebody's soul. Just days before, he felt like the angel of death, totally unworthy of any affection, but now with Kimberly by his side he felt nothing but love.

42

MALAKI

Kimberly and Brett were dining in the city centre on a particularly warm Thursday night. Brett didn't feel like dining out but Kimberly had talked him into it earlier that day. They were having a chat and Kimberly was hinting at the idea of him moving to Bristol with her. She wanted him to get away from Leicester and all of the things that connected him to the brutality that he'd been involved in.

There was every reason for Brett to now leave, but a massive part of him still didn't feel worthy of Kimberly's presence.

As the two of them sat eating, Brett noticed somebody over at another table staring at him from the corner of his eye. It was a young black guy and Brett immediately grimaced thinking that it may be someone out for trouble.

"Hey, is that you, Brett?" said the guy as he stepped up out of his seat.

The guy seemed excited to see him.

"It's me, it's Malaki!" said the guy.

Kimberly looked at Brett somewhat bemused but Brett knew exactly who the guy was and Brett's face changed from a frown to a smile. The guy was a young chap named Malaki Davis. Brett had supported Malaki when he was working in mental health a few years ago. Malaki was suffering from severe depression at the time and had a massive crack-cocaine addiction. Malaki was nineteen years old at this time and was a lost soul. He'd been allocated a flat within the supported accommodation service and Brett was his key-worker.

Brett was pleasantly surprised how clean and fresh Malaki looked and Brett noticed that he'd put on some weight. Brett's face seemed to glow as Malaki made his way over from his table.

Malaki grabbed Brett as Brett stepped up from his chair and gave him two massive pats on the shoulder followed by a big, boisterous hug.

"This guy saved my life!" said Malaki looking at Kimberly as he grabbed Brett.

"If it wasn't for this man, I'd be dead by now!" said Malaki again, giving Brett another big pat on the shoulders.

Brett played it down.

"Nah, I'm sure you'd still be here, mate, you did all the hard work, it was you who made the changes," said Brett.

It was then that Malaki's facial expressions changed and his face straightened. He again placed his hands on Brett's shoulders and looked him dead in the eye.

"Listen, you saved my life! You were one of the only people that gave a shit about me when I didn't give a shit about myself. You told me once that I could be anything that I wanted to be if I just used my imagination, well, I listened to you, mate, and now I've turned things around!"

It meant a lot to Brett that Malaki remembered him so fondly and Brett was happy to see that he had managed to make some positive changes in his life.

Malaki was keen to take Brett over to his table and introduce him to his girlfriend, Tori. Malaki introduced Brett to her as "the man who saved my life".

Tori gave Brett a very warm smile. Tori seemed like a bubbly girl. She had midnight-black hair and golden-brown skin and the glow of youth was uncompromising and unmistakeable. It didn't take Brett long to notice that she was pregnant.

Brett congratulated Malaki and Malaki was keen to tell Brett how much he was looking forward to being a dad and how he was going to make sure his kid never wanted for anything.

During this exchange of conversation, Brett then took notice of the other couple who were sat at Malaki's table. Brett realised that the lad who was sat there was the young cousin of Kristian Bell, a lad named Ruben Carter. Ruben gazed hard at Brett. Brett was about to ask Ruben what he was looking at when Malaki realised the situation. Malaki cleared the tension by taking Brett's attention away from Ruben by talking about his unborn child. Brett smiled along with Malaki, but was now a little concerned that Malaki was hanging around with somebody like Ruben Carter, and Brett was also thinking that maybe Malaki hadn't completely turned away from the bad-boy lifestyle.

Ruben Carter was a chip off the old block. He was very similar to Kristian Bell but with all the added ignorance of youth. He'd already spent time in prison and he was only twenty-two years of age. He thought he was every bit the little bad boy and this was apparent from the way he gazed at Brett as he sat at the restaurant table. Again, the monster in Brett began to surface. *If he thinks he's the little bad man then he can have it the way that Kristian had it*, he thought to himself.

Ruben of course knew that his cousin Kristian was missing and he, like a lot of other people, thought that Brett might be responsible. But he only thought he knew, nothing had been proven, it was all speculation, but Ruben was also ready for confrontation with Brett.

Brett offered Malaki a drink and took him over to the bar. This was really just a ploy to get Malaki alone for a minute or two. Ruben Carter was looking at Brett's every step as he walked with Malaki over to the bar.

"Malaki, what are you doing hanging about with that Ruben? That lad will get you into massive trouble, you need to stay away from people like that now you have a kid on the way," said Brett directly as he and Malaki reached the bar.

Malaki was quick to play it down.

"Don't worry about me, Ruben's cool, I don't get up to

any bullshit with him, don't worry," replied Malaki with a smile.

Brett looked at Malaki and took a deep sigh.

"Be careful, Malaki, you're only as good as the people around you!" said Brett looking at Malaki poignantly.

Malaki assured Brett that he would be fine and that he wasn't stupid enough to become involved in anything dangerous with Ruben. Brett then said his goodbyes to Malaki and wished him all the best for the future.

Brett had guessed right about Malaki. Maliki had made some big changes but he still hadn't put complete closure to the bad-boy lifestyle. He was clean and off the crack and chances were that if it wasn't for Brett's involvement in his life he would surely be in jail or dead, but he was very much under Ruben Carter's wing and was involved in some pretty nasty stuff. He was involved in robbing rich City-type guys that had big coke habits. Former public-school boys who had become entangled with people like Ruben Carter who was supplying their coke were easy pickings after false trust had been built. Ruben and Malaki would rob them of things like their Rolex watches and demand money with the threat of beatings and blackmail. Even Malaki's girlfriend Tori was involved. She would swipe jewellery from victim's houses and intimidate their girlfriends. Tori looked innocent but under the influence of the rough Highfield district streets and the tutelage of Ruben Carter, the worst had been brought out in her and Malaki.

***

A little later on that evening as Brett and Kimberly were walking to the taxi rank, Kimberly was eager to tell Brett just how big a thing it was that had just happened with Malaki in the restaurant.

"Remember when you were lying in the hospital bed, Brett, when I came to see you?" said Kimberly as she warmly held onto Brett's arm.

"Yeah, course I do," replied Brett.

"Well, you said that you being a good person was bullshit and it basically meant nothing, but do you realise now that you have managed to save somebody's life! All the good things that are now happening to Malaki, you have played a massive part in. That work you did when you were working in mental health was priceless to somebody like Malaki!" said Kimberly with a smile.

Brett didn't say anything, but Kimberly's words made him wonder how many more people out there had benefitted positively from the work that he had done. How many more Maliki's had managed to avoid imminent destruction because of something that he'd said or done. These thoughts were Brett's thoughts and Brett's alone. But none of that mattered now, Brett had been on a one-way mission to his own destruction and he couldn't help but feel that it was all going to come to a climax soon.

43

DISNEYLAND

Brett was walking through Abbey Park alone on a particularly bright Saturday morning. Kieran had earlier asked him for a massive favour: the loan of eight grand to help him start his own business.

Kieran had drummed up enough money to start his own plush gym and fitness suite but needed a further eight grand for some extra equipment. Brett was more than happy to help a friend and it wasn't like he didn't have the money spare, so he grabbed eight grand in cash and wrapped it in a carrier bag. He'd made the journey through Abbey Park on the way to meet Kieran as the sunshine was too welcoming to be missed.

Brett had left Kimberly asleep in the flat. She soon had

to be heading back to Bristol to start her new job. She'd been talking to Brett about him moving to Bristol and although he hadn't said much, the idea was growing on him.

Brett's status on the street had now become legendary, all the regulars of the pubs and clubs and the characters within the backdrop of Leicester's underworld now knew that Brett was a killer, and they knew that he'd played a massive hand in the murder of Donald Kirk-Patrick which, in the eyes of a lot of people, made him a hero. Even a quiet stroll through the park drew whispers and glances from passers-by.

As Brett was walking along the canal he glanced upon a rather frail-looking chap in a wheelchair. He eventually realised that the chap in the wheelchair was in fact Glover. It was a very different Glover, a shadow of the big-framed, confident-looking Glover that had stood out in many a packed pub. This Glover was painfully thin and pale and sort of hunched sideways as he sat uncomfortably in the wheelchair. A young child was with him, a young lad of no more than five years of age who was helping an almost helpless-looking Glover to throw bread in the canal to feed the ducks. Brett then realised that the young lad was in fact Glover's son.

Brett immediately thought of Macy at the sight of Glover's son. Brett was then overcome with sorrow. He felt overwhelming compassion for Glover at the sight of his son giving him a hand to throw bread to the ducks.

A slender, grey-haired woman in around her sixties who was a short distance away then shouted at the lad.

"Come on then, let's go and get the ice cream!"

The young lad then went running over to the lady,

who was Glover's mum. Glover was left alone sitting there looking into the water. Brett began to make his way over.

"Hello, Glover!" said Brett poignantly as he reached Glover.

Glover awkwardly turned to see who was there, obviously in pain at just the turn of his head. His eyes widened as he saw that it was Brett and he began to try to shout over at his mum and young son. Brett noticed the strain on his face and he noticed that his features looked crooked and had shifted to one side, similar to that of a stroke victim.

"Don't upset your son and your mother, I'm not here to do you any harm," said Brett with a whisper.

Glover ceased shouting but his face looked as though he was boiling with anger.

"I just want to know why you went out of your way to bully and humiliate me that night in the Empire?" said Brett softly.

Glover realised there was no malice in Brett and the look on Glover's face changed from anger to almost nothing, an emotionless look overcame his face as he paused for a while.

"I don't know!" said Glover as he solemnly closed his eyes for a second or two, his words sounding a little slurry and laboured. He then began to speak again.

"I suppose I thought I was the big man. Having the big-man reputation, bouncing around the pubs and the clubs meant so much to me! All the boys, with their pats on my back, who would buy me drinks, and the slags that would circle me wanting some attention and some cash spent on them, was what I used to live for! Well, it was all bullshit!

Since I've been in this wheelchair, the boys and the slags have found other people to stand at the bar with, hanging around with me doesn't carry the same appeal, what a load of bollocks my life was… I should have been looking after my son instead of living for that shit… well, you putting me in this wheelchair has at least taught me one thing, it's taught me that what little life and money I have is better spent with my son," said Glover as he looked over the water with tears filling his tired eyes.

Brett didn't say anything. Just the silence filled the air and the sound of a few ducks splashing about in the water could be heard. He took one last glimpse of Glover before walking away. What Glover said about people not bothering with him since he was in the wheelchair stuck in Brett's mind. The truth was that when Glover first sustained his injuries people were still around for a while, but one by one they faded. A few of them promised to give Glover thousands of pounds to pay for him and his son to go to Disneyland, but of course it never happened. A piece of the real Brett then began to break through as Brett could now feel nothing but sorrow for Glover.

As he walked on for a while he noticed Glover's son sitting at a table near the café. Glover's mum was standing ordering the ice cream from the ice-cream parlour so she had her back turned. Brett then made his way over and sat on the table close to Glover's son. Brett could see that the young lad felt awkward.

"Have you ever been to Disneyland?" said Brett to Glover's young son.

Glover's son just shook his head, looking a little scared.

Brett then reached into his pocket pulling out the eight grand in cash that he had wrapped in the carrier bag. He quickly grabbed Glover's son's tiny hand and placed the carrier bag full of cash in it.

"Tell your dad to take you to Disneyland!" said Brett.

Brett then walked away.

44

COLLATERAL DAMAGE

Brett had surprised Steve and Bez by turning up out of the blue one night at the Empire. It was now a rare occurrence, the three of them being together. Brett had felt like they had been avoiding him, but he didn't say anything about it to them. For a while it was just like old times, knocking the beers back and having a laugh in the Empire, but for Brett there were too many uncomfortable silences until Brett couldn't stand it any longer.

"Right, come on, what is it with you two?" said Brett as he placed down his pint.

"Nothing, mate," said Bez almost immediately.

"Look, lads, I know a lot's changed and a lot has happened, but I'm here now, let's just have a laugh like we used to," said Brett with a frown.

"You should move to Bristol with Kimberly, mate," said Steve with a nod.

"Maybe I will!" replied Brett.

***

Later on the three of them decided to head into the west end. Steve and Bez did their best to ignore the atmosphere that Brett's presence created when he walked into a pub. Being with probably the most feared man that ever walked the city streets was intense at times, but the three of them managed to get drunk and take the piss out of each other like they always did.

By the time they decided it was time to get a taxi home it was once again Steve who was in the worst state, Bez and Brett weren't much better off but Steve had managed to out-do them as usual.

They were walking up towards the taxi rank when they noticed around eight black lads standing outside the taxi office. The atmosphere had begun to change and the three of them noticed a few of the black lads start to stare and mumble to one another. It was then that Brett noticed Ruben Carter.

Ruben Carter scowled as he looked at Brett and he immediately began to charge at him. Brett in his drunken state struggled to respond proactively. Bez, who was standing just in front of Brett, stood in the way of Ruben and made a grab for him as it was obvious that Ruben was intent on causing some damage. Ruben swiped at Bez who immediately dropped to the floor holding his stomach.

Ruben then threw furious swipes at Brett, and Brett could now see that he had a knife.

Brett's rage overtook him and he steamed into Ruben with absolutely no regard for the fact that he had a knife. Ruben dropped the knife as Brett grabbed him and flung him to the floor. It was then that the lads who were with Ruben jumped in.

Brett and Steve had no chance in their drunken state as they were overcome by punches and kicks. Steve was knocked unconscious but Brett's attention was now on Bez, as he could see the puddle of blood that surrounded him. As the sight of the blood became apparent to passers-by and the people that worked in the taxi office, a crowd had gathered and there were shouts of "I'm calling the police!" from the staff in the taxi office. Ruben could see the state that Bez was now in and knew that the police would soon be on their way. Ruben and his boys quickly scarpered from the scene leaving Brett cradling Bez and Steve unconscious.

"That's for my cousin, and it's not done yet" shouted Ruben as he quickly disappeared into the night.

"For fuck's sake, call an ambulance," shouted Brett as the blood poured from Bez's stomach.

45

JUSTIFIED

Bez was very lucky to be alive. That was the news from the doctors as Brett sat in the hospital corridor. But Bez was not totally in the clear yet. The dirty blade that he'd been stabbed with had caused some infection and he was in a medically induced coma with a drip pumping him full of antibiotics. It was expected that he would make a full recovery but the next twenty-four hours were crucial. Now the monster had again fully resurfaced and Brett was determined to hand out the same punishment to Ruben Carter as that he'd handed to Kristian Bell. Steve, who had regained consciousness shortly before the ambulance had reached the scene, was also sat in the corridor.

"This little cunt's dead!" said Brett as he sat with Steve alongside him.

Steve's face screwed in frustration.

"It's all your bullshit that's landed Bez where he is!" snapped Steve

"What! How can you say that to me?" replied Brett.

"Well, it was all this bullshit in the first place, you becoming this big madman and going on a rampage, that's what's caused all this, that's why we tried to avoid you, we couldn't be doing with it all! Can't you see that you have become what you most despised, Brett?" said Steve, his eyes all puffy and his face reddened.

Brett looked at Steve intently.

"Do you think I became this big madman? I never became this, I was turned into this, and I have no remorse! Kristian Bell would still be slapping my sister around and making her life a misery if I hadn't have taken his life, and all the others that I made examples of made it their business to fuck with me and I wasn't taking it anymore!" said Brett.

"Why couldn't you just have stayed as Brett? Brett Kelso, the lad we knew and loved?" said Steve as he sat down with his head in his hands.

"Hey! All I ever wanted to be was that person. That's all I wanted until this world chewed me up and spat me out. Macy didn't have to die! The system allowed her to die, and you expect me to be Mr Happy-go-lucky, Mr Happy-to-help Brett Kelso, going through life being shat on with a smile on my face? Well, I'm sorry for you and I'm sorry for Bez, but that Brett Kelso died a long time ago!" growled Brett.

"I just hope Kimberly doesn't get dragged into anything. Let her go back to Bristol, Brett and make sure she doesn't get hurt" said Steve quietly with his head still in his hands.

46

LOVE HER MADLY

Kimberly felt like she had lost Brett all over again by the time he had told her the news about Bez. She knew that he would have to put things right in his own way and that would mean getting even with Ruben Carter. She loved Brett dearly, but she realised that maybe there wasn't enough of Brett left to love. The Devil was back in his eyes and she could feel it. All her bags were more or less packed for leaving for Bristol within a few days but Brett's thoughts were on organising the downfall of Ruben Carter with Terry Shepard and Johnny Hammill.

Brett was not trying to talk Kimberly out of heading on the next train to Bristol. He didn't want to drag her into anything. He loved the bones of her, but the intensity of his love was now stifled by the thirst for inflicting pain on Ruben Carter.

Kimberly wiped away the tears from her cheeks as she left Brett's flat. She was going to stay at her sister's for the last few days before heading to Bristol, knowing that she would probably never see Brett again. Brett looked at her and loved her madly as she walked out of the door.

47

SOULLESS

Brett was driving back from the hospital after stopping by to see Bez. Bez had been given the all-clear but he was still in a bad way and the doctors were not yet sure if they would have to operate.

Brett had been smoking crack as he drove along the city streets. He'd never smoked crack before but quickly developed a taste. He couldn't get hold of any coke that night as his usual dealers were not answering the phone, but he soon come across an old friend's number and it was an old friend that sold crack.

He was using the crack to bury the pain of losing Kimberly. No matter how much he was hell-bent on getting even with Ruben Carter, he couldn't get Kimberly out of his mind, but he didn't contact her.

He'd also had another dream about Macy. It was another dream in which Macy was talking to him on the phone and it again left him in excruciating pain.

It was a Saturday night and there was plenty of life on the streets as he drove along the west end on his way back to his flat. He was static at the red traffic lights and was just facing a night club called The Urban Music Café. It was lively as there was an old-school house and garage night taking place. Just outside the entrance of the club was a group of people who were gathered outside smoking.

Brett could then not believe his eyes, within the crowd that was gathered he could see Ruben Carter, and not just Ruben carter, there was also a handful of his cronies with him, the same cronies that were present on the night that Bez was stabbed.

Brett thought of Bez lying in the hospital bed before putting his foot down on the accelerator and heading straight for Ruben. Ruben and his handful of his cronies didn't stand a chance. By the time they realised that the car was heading straight for them, it was too late. Ruben took the full force as Brett's car crashed into him crushing him against a wall, Brett reversed and spun the car wildly, smashing bodies out of the way as he spun away.

There were people lying broken on the floor as Brett drove from the scene. He looked back in his mirror and managed to glimpse the broken body of Ruben Carter.

Brett grimaced as he looked back at Ruben, feeling absolutely no remorse. He drove back to his flat not concerned that it wouldn't be long before the police would catch up with him. He got back to his flat. The first thing he did was text message Terry Shepard.

Just introduced Ruben Carter to the bonnet of my car lol, read the message.

Within forty minutes there was a loud knock at the door. Brett expected the police but to his surprise it was Terry Shepard with his eyes bulging looking unhinged.

"Where's your car?" snapped Terry.

"Fuck it, Terry, it's all over, if the police get me, they get me!" said Brett, still a bit worse for wear from the effects of the crack.

"Give me the keys!" said Terry firmly as he held his hand out.

The car wasn't in Brett's name, it was a ringer that had been given to Brett a few months before as payment for a debt, there was nothing connecting Brett to the car apart from his DNA that would be on the steering wheel and in the carriage. Terry quickly took the keys and drove the car to a nearby nature reserve and burnt it out completely.

The next day the news of the hit-and-run was everywhere. The CCTV footage of the incident was unreliable and the incident happened so fast the few witnesses that were there to see it were busy running for cover. It had also circulated on the street that Brett Kelso was likely the responsible party so any would-be witness accounts were not likely to be written. The news reports had also stated that two other people were killed in the incident.

48

THE END

The following night Brett couldn't help but wonder who the two other people were that had died in the hit-and-run. He thought that he had just smashed into Ruben and a couple of his cronies but he couldn't be absolutely sure. He hadn't totally intended to kill Ruben or anyone else that night, he just thought he'd break a few bones and make an example as payback for what had happened to Bez, but a car doesn't have to be at top speed to cause fatal damage.

The police were doing their best to close in on Brett and by now wanted him off the street. Brett could feel in his heart that in one way or another he was close to an end. Franny and Kieran had tried to contact him but he hadn't answered their calls. Franny wasn't quite the same since the night that Brett killed Kristian. The last time Brett saw Franny he kept drifting off into little daydreams. When Brett asked Franny what was wrong he just said, "I keep hearing them high-pitched screams." It was also the day before Kimberly would be leaving for Bristol.

Brett was sat there in his flat sipping on Jack Daniels. He felt empty, he didn't really feel anything.

His phone began to vibrate again and as he looked down he could see that it was Kieran calling. Again he didn't answer. After a few minutes a text message came through from Kieran. The message read:-

Brett Lisa is in Leicester, I've just been to a flat and she is there!!

Brett almost leapt up from his chair. He then rang Kieran's number frantically. Kieran quickly answered.

"Brett, I swear to you, mate, she's at a flat in Beaumont Leys, mate, I've dropped some green off to a girl there and she is sat there, mate!" said Kieran directly.

Brett ran to the kitchen drawer and quickly pulled out a pen, he then ripped off some kitchen towel from a roll on the kitchen side.

"Gimme the address, Kieran!" shouted Brett.

Kieran gave Brett the address. It was 25 Oronsay Walk. Brett knew the area well. He quickly wrote down the address on the piece of kitchen towel and said the address over and over aloud. The address was now locked in his brain. Lisa was finally gonna pay for Macy's death and everything else she had ever done, and Brett hadn't forgotten about the threats she had left him with when she had disappeared out of town.

Brett ordered a taxi for 25 Oronsay Walk and then sat and waited. It had been such a long time since Brett had looked Lisa in the eye and this time he wasn't going to hold back. There was no way Lisa was walking away unscathed. The pain he had felt since losing Macy was going to be unleashed and this made Brett's heart pump almost out of his chest.

***

The taxi beeped as it waited outside and Brett leaped to his feet. He opened his front door but to his total shock there was a tall figure standing there dressed in black cycle leathers and a black-tinted motorcycle helmet pointing a gun directly at him. The assailant was silent as the gun was now pointed directly at Brett's face. He stood still. All that was on his mind was the fact that if he died here on this spot he wouldn't get his hands on Lisa. Brett was overcome with anger.

"What's up? Haven't you got the bollocks to look someone in the eye when you kill them?" snapped Brett.

The assailant was shocked that something like that had come out of the mouth of someone who was about to die and he hesitated, much the same scenario as the last time Brett had had a gun pointed at him. Brett then lunged forward and shoved the assailant down the first-floor flight of stairs sending him crashing to the floor.

Brett ran to the bottom of the stairs and laid a few heavy boots in. He tried to snatch the gun but the assailant wouldn't let go. It was then that Brett noticed that the taxi was beginning to pull away as he glimpsed through the entrance doors. Brett gave the assailant one more big boot before running out of the doors.

"Wait!" shouted Brett as he ran for the taxi.

The taxi's brake light appeared and Brett swiftly opened the door to the back passenger seat.

"25 Oronsay Walk!" said Brett as the taxi driver pulled away.

Brett in his frantic state had shouted the address at the taxi driver. The assailant heard the words 'Oronsay Walk' so he now knew where Brett was headed.

Brett's heart was still pumping as the taxi made the way to Oronsay Walk. Unbeknown to Brett the assailant would soon be on his motorbike and also on his way to Oronsay Walk.

As Brett sat in the back of the taxi he began to text Kieran.

So the slag's brave enough to set foot back in Leicester! On the way to her as we speak! Time for comeuppance, waited too long for this! read the text.

Brett sent the message, but what he didn't realise was that he'd accidentally sent the text to Kimberly.

Kimberly was at her sister's getting the last of her things ready for the journey to Bristol when she received the text. Kimberly was horrified, she was certain that Brett was going to do something stupid, she knew very well that the text was referring to Lisa.

She tried to ring Brett but he wouldn't answer the phone. She knew in her heart that Brett was ready to give up on everything and this could spell the end for him. She had to try and talk him out of it but how could she if he wouldn't answer his phone?

Kimberly decided to get in her car and drive to Brett's flat; she couldn't think of anything else to do. She continued to try and ring him but he would not answer. As she reached the entrance doors to Brett's flat she quickly ran up the stairs. She still had a key to the flat that Brett had given her and she hastily let herself in struggling to get the key in the door in a panic. Just as she thought, Brett was not present. She couldn't think of anything else to do. She sighed to herself but as she glimpsed down to the floor she saw the piece of kitchen towel with the address '25 Oronsay Walk' scribbled on it. She knew in her gut that this is where Brett was heading. She then googled the address on her iPhone before racing back to her car.

***

The taxi pulled up to the Oronsay Walk flats and as Brett left the taxi he could see '25 Oronsay Walk' clearly labelled on the wall with an arrow signalling diagonally upwards. He hurried over to the concrete staircase that led upwards to the flat.

What Brett was unaware of was that his would-be assassin was not far behind him, turning the corner to Oronsay Walk on a motorbike.

Brett reached the door to 25 Oronsay Walk. Time seemed to pass in slow motion. This was it; after all this time Brett was now going to be face to face with Lisa again. His senses heightened as he felt the dull thud of his heart throughout his body. Brett knocked on the door and waited.

After a few seconds Brett could hear the turning of the door handle, and as the door opened a pale, ponytailed woman answered the door. Brett wasted no time in shoving straight past her, marching down the hallway with the shouts of protest of the woman as he marched. Brett shoved the living room door open and there she was. Lisa was kneeling on the floor next to an ashtray and a can of lager as she puffed on a cigarette.

"Hello again!" shouted Brett as he looked down in disgust at Lisa.

Lisa screamed as she beheld Brett standing above her. She tried her best to scramble away but Brett pounced on her. The other woman in the flat tried to slap at Brett whilst screaming obscenities at him. Brett leaned up and swiftly punched her, knocking her unconscious, as his eyes bulged with intensity and hate. Brett made a grab for Lisa as she screamed. He lifted her by the throat. He pulled her head towards his and looked her in the eyes. He then gave her an almighty slap and she landed on a coffee table which went crashing across the living room. Lisa held her head and groaned in pain as she hit the floor. Brett snarled as he slowly walked over to her.

He looked down at Lisa and as he did so he noticed a set of keys on the floor next to her. What caught his eye was a photo that was placed inside a key ring on the set of keys. It was an old photo of Macy. It was one of Brett's favourite photographs of Macy. Brett had asked Lisa for a copy of it a year or so before Macy died but Lisa never got round to sorting him out a copy. Brett leaned down and picked up the key ring and looked at Macy's smiling face. Her little button nose and her dimples made him smile and her eyes looked right into his. It was at that very moment that all of the hate left him.

No more, no more blood, no more death. Enough! he thought to himself, just like that.

He looked down at Lisa cowering as she waited for more punishment. She looked up at Brett and it then dawned on him what she had become. She was tremendously pale, scrawny and totally unkempt. She looked beaten out, and her teeth were brown and yellow and broken as she cried. It was obvious that she had succumbed to drug abuse. Lisa was ravaged by heroin.

"I let Macy down and I have to live with that everyday!" said Lisa as she sobbed where she lay.

"Yeah, you live with it!" said Brett calmly.

Brett took the key ring from the keys and held it tightly in his fist. He looked down at Lisa once more watching her sob before throwing the keys down to the floor and turning around, walking out of the flat.

Brett got to the bottom of the concrete stairs and stepped out into the driveway. He immediately saw his assailant stood by his motorbike waiting for him, his face still hidden underneath the motorcycle helmet. Brett was now ready to die! He was tired, exhausted. The pain and the hate had drained the life out of his soul and he was now ready for death in the hope that he would be joining Macy. The assailant reached out with the gun and pointed it at Brett as Brett walked towards him.

"Do me a favour! Take off that helmet and look me in the eye before you kill me," said Brett.

The assailant then slowly began to lift the helmet from his head. The lifting of the helmet slowly revealed the features of the assailant and to Brett's surprise it was Malaki Davis. Brett didn't understand.

"Why you, Malaki?" asked Brett poignantly.

Malaki looked at Brett with utter sadness as Brett got even closer.

"The night you drove into Ruben and killed him, well you also hit Tori, my girlfriend. You killed her and our unborn baby!" said Malaki with his voice croaking in pain.

Brett couldn't believe what he was hearing. He felt as though his soul had been broken all over again.

Malaki again pointed the gun in Brett's face.

"You once saved my life but now you've destroyed it!" said Malaki as the tears rolled down his cheek. "But it wasn't just your fault. You told me to stay away from Ruben. You told me he was trouble. What was I doing having my five-months-pregnant girlfriend in a club amongst people like Ruben Carter?" said Malaki as he cried. "We wanted one more night out before the baby, but I should have looked after her and kept her safe. She only stepped out of the club for some fresh air but she shouldn't have even been there!" said Malaki.

At that moment a car could be heard pulling up. Brett looked over. It was then he heard Kimberly's voice.

"Brett!" shouted Kimberly as she scrambled out of the car and ran toward him.

"Kimberly, get the fuck out of here!" snapped Brett.

Kimberly noticed the gun pointed at Brett's face. Malaki then pointed the gun at Kimberly.

Kimberly froze.

"Shall I destroy your life now?" said Malaki.

"Don't do that, that's not what you want, Malaki. I'm here, don't take it out on an innocent life," said Brett now overtaken with anger.

Malaki then pointed the gun back at Brett but there was no conviction in his eyes.

"I wouldn't hurt her, Brett!" said Malaki.

Kimberly began to cry but she noticed that Malaki was starting to lose his conviction. He didn't have the look of a killer in his eyes. He was starting to lower the gun. Kimberly then knew that Brett had a chance.

"Just kill me, Malaki, I'm ready to die!" said Brett as he looked into Malaki's eyes.

The gun was now down by Malaki's side. Kimberly didn't want Brett to talk himself into being killed.

"Brett... I'm pregnant!" said Kimberly painfully as she scrunched her eyes closed.

Kimberly had known for a few days that she was pregnant but she hadn't had a real chance to tell Brett; this was not the ideal time but this was life and death. Anything that would stop Brett's death would surely have to be said.

Tears filled Brett's eyes. He didn't want to live anymore, he couldn't live with himself knowing he was responsible for the death of Malaki's girlfriend and their unborn baby, and he was so tired of all the pain. He looked at Malaki and he knew that Malaki was starting to waver. But he also knew that if he made a lunge for Malaki there was every chance that Malaki's reflex reaction would be to pull the trigger. Brett tried to summon the monster but every time he looked at Kimberly, the monster faded.

"Kimberly there's over a seventy grand in my sister's loft. Make sure you go and get it!" said Brett as he sullenly blew her a kiss as the tears rolled down his face.

He then snarled and made a lunge for Malaki. Malaki quickly reached up the gun and let out a shot.

As the bullet hit Brett's head all of his pain was finally over. Kimberly screamed and dropped to her knees.

Malaki looked down at Brett, he was shaking as he looked at the gun in his hand and looked at Kimberly as she was crying over Brett. Malaki then pointed the gun to his own head and slowly walked away. Kimberly saw him disappear into the night with the gun firmly held to his head, she looked down at Brett in a fit of painful sobs before hearing another gunshot in the distance.

The wind swept over Kimberly and Brett as the silence then fell, and that was the end of Brett Kelso's tale.